THE TIME WALKERS

Also by this author

Maggie Magee and the Last Magician
Village Life
The Jethart House
A Most Peculiar Hotel
Fields Of Stone
Tiggie
The Pineapple King Of Jarrow
Uncle Freddie & The Prince Of Wales
Putting Out The Lights

THE TIME WALKERS

*A tangled tale of Time Walking for any reader
adventurous enough to dip a toe into Time...
Beware, Time Walking is not for the timid!*

Alex Ferguson

Copyright © 2018 Alex Ferguson

All rights reserved, including the right to reproduce this book, or portions thereof in any form. No part of this text may be reproduced, transmitted, downloaded, decompiled, reverse engineered, or stored, in any form or introduced into any information storage and retrieval system, in any form or by any means, whether electronic or mechanical without the express written permission of the author.

This is a work of fiction. The persons and events in this book may have representations in history, but this work is entirely the author's creation and should not be construed as historical fact.

The views expressed in this work are solely those of the author and do not necessarily reflect the views of the publisher, and the publisher hereby disclaims any responsibility for them.

ISBN: 978-0-244-73183-0

PublishNation
www.publishnation.co.uk

ALEX FERGUSON is a national award-winning writer with Silver and Gold Awards from the Writers' Guild. He worked with Corin and Vanessa Redgrave to write three successful plays for Moving Theatre. THE FLAG was performed at Battersea and CASEMENT at the Riverside. He has contributed to a number of television series and built a successful reputation in radio and theatre drama. His comic radio series ran for six years on Radio Four. He created and ran the youth theatre company, Bold As Brass, on Tyneside for ten years which climaxed in a wonderful run at the Jermyn Street Theatre with DO YOU SEE WHAT I SEE? In 2016 he wrote the feature film, BLISS! which has been chosen for screening by four International Film Festivals in the United Kingdom, Europe and the United States. Tiring of chasing actors to perform, he sat down to write books and filled a shelf on Kindle.

In March 2018, Alex Ferguson was admitted to Trusteeship of the Customs House Theatre Trust for his services to the Arts.

CHAPTER ONE

Joan Jennifer Anne Flete d'Urquart hated her name since she first struggled to pronounce it, dragging the title behind her as a ball and chain to a convict. Military families tend to acquire names, generation by generation. Other girls had names as ridiculous as her own. More importantly in her fourteen years she had never once met a time walker nor taken any interest in time travel until she met Christopher Marlowe, the Elizabethan playwright and his adopted daughter Hannah.

She was content at her boarding school, the Brooke Randall Boarding School for Girls of Military Parentage; so named in honour of the heroic Major General Vernon Brooke Randall. The school was referred to by girls and staff as the Randall.

Joan's father, Captain Toby Ralph Flete d'Urquart, could trace his ancestry back to the Norman knight, Esmond Flete d'Urquart. While invading England, this unfortunate warrior fell face down in the shallow surf of Pevensey Bay. He was unable to rise because of the weight of his mail shirt. His noble line would have ended there and then if his disappearance had gone unnoticed. Gasping for breath, he was hauled to his feet by his men-at-arms, struggling to hide their amusement.

Where Joan's father went in the world or what he did was never discussed by the Flete d'Urquarts. It would've been considered 'bad form'. All Joan knew was that her father had died a hero in a firefight in Helmund, Afghanistan, a tragedy that entitled her to a place at the Randall.

On this particular Sunday morning, as the chaplain droned on, competing with the stray bumblebee that droned on, banging its head against the chapel window, Melanie whispered to her friend, "Lecture tonight, Jo. Time Travel! Would you believe it?"

Joan frowned behind her prayer book.

"So?"

"Old Granny Meadows is on."

"Can't be worse than Knots I Have Known."

Every Sunday evening at the Randall there was arranged a lecture for the older girls by a visiting speaker; a cultural event to broaden the students' horizons. The Randall girls had less leisure time than a domestic skivvy in a nineteenth century household. They knew this because they had endured the lecture, The Victorian Household: Girls in Service.

At the Sunday evening lecture it was not unusual for older girls to vanish for a smoke when the slide show began. Particularly when Miss Meadows was supervising. She didn't seem to care what they did. She sat in the front row with her favourites to whom she gave peppermint creams. She wasn't liked or respected. Only good manners restrained girls from firing projectiles at her grey hair.

Joan hated smoking, but suffered it for friendship's sake. Melanie was a member of the exclusive clique, the Angels. Joan was tolerated as Melanie's friend. The trick was to time one's return to the hall as the slide show ended, stinking of tobacco, giggling and nauseous, to applaud the lecturer, eyelashes fluttering to signal eternal devotion.

"My friends and I really did enjoy your talk, sir. Knots and all that. Absolutely wizard! Perhaps you could come again soon? And bring more slides, sir? They were wicked, weren't they, miss?"

What else could Miss Meadows do but agree?

Which left the lecturer, an elderly Merchant Navy captain, bewildered as to what was so captivating to adolescent girls about a series of slides illustrating knot making. His wife was similarly baffled. His granddaughters anticipating a good giggle were sadly disappointed. However, the captain accepted the advice given. The next school he lectured to was stunned into such boredom that seventeen of the younger children wept under a barrage of one hundred and thirty-five band slides of knots, made and unmade.

Joan and Melanie had already borrowed the most comfortable armchair from the Senior Common room for Miss Meadows and were industriously laying out chairs in preparation for the lecture when Laura arrived in a panting rush to announce, "He's here.

Head's quite taken with him, Norma says. They're having sherry. He's got a girl with him. Come on a motorbike. Imagine that!"

Joan sat down on the nearest chair to consider this breathless bulletin.

"It's a man. You're sure? Older or younger than Captain Birdseye?"

"I haven't seen him, actually."

Melanie asked, "So, how d'y'know?"

"The housekeeper, Norma, she answered the door. She said it was a gentleman."

"Don't like the sound of that word. Gentleman," mused Joan, "Why's he having sherry with Ma Savage?"

"Norma said she was quite taken with him."

"And he's got this girl with him? What's she like?"

"Didn't say. Oh! And Norma got your ciggies."

Laura moved to hand the cigarettes to Joan, but was intercepted by Melanie. Joan made no protest.

"Well?" Melanie demanded of Laura, "What're you hanging about for? You can buzz off now."

A disappointed Laura said, "Yes, Mel. If there's anything else."

Laura dawdled her way to the door and stopped.

"The slide projector's here. Should I bring it in?"

"You might as well."

Laura dragged in the projector on its stand. It wobbled precariously.

"And the screen?"

Laura carried in the screen.

"Shall I set up the screen, Mel?"

"Don't call me Mel."

"No, Mel."

Melanie sighed with exasperation and Joan laughed.

"Should I set up the screen?"

Laura set up the screen and stood awaiting Melanie's approval. Or otherwise. Melanie tugged a corner, stepped back and nodded.

"Right! That'll do. You can buzz off now."

Laura vanished reluctantly.

Joan said, "She only wants to help."

"She's always hanging round."
"She's a nice kid."
"Not one of us, Jo."
Joan shrugged, "What's so special about us?"
"Do you know what her father is?"
"No idea."
"R.A.S.C. Can you imagine it? Run Away Someone's Coming? I ask you!"
"What's wrong with Service Corps?"
"D'y'know what Natalie is?"
"A girl with a weight problem, a very loud voice and a lot of spots?"
"Blues and Royals. Jill? Her father's a Coldstreamer. Tina's grandfather's H.A.C."
"Which is what? Hacking Awful Cough?"
Melanie glared.
"The Honourable Artillery Company."
"You don't really go for all that snob stuff, Mel, do you?"
Melanie hesitated.
"One has to have standards."
"What about me?"
"You're Rifles. You're okay."
"But Laura isn't?"
"Laura isn't one of us. Definitely not."
Joan sighed and gave up.

She was aware Melanie's position among the Angels was insecure and how important it was to her to be a member of the clique. But Joan's head was flooded with the image of finding the new girl, Laura, weeping behind the vaulting horse in the empty gym; of the girl begging her not to tell anyone.

Randall girls don't cry. Randall girls don't get homesick. Randall girls don't cry for dead fathers. I could tell Melanie Laura's father isn't anything anymore. Dead, trying to defuse a roadside bomb. He didn't run away, someone's coming. He ran towards it. But such talk is taboo at the Randall.

"Don't you like Natalie?"

"Love her to bits," Joan lied, "Just don't get stuck beside her at lacrosse. She'll blow your ears off."

* * * *

Melanie went to borrow a footstool to enhance Miss Meadows' comfort. Joan decided to investigate the notion of a lecturer on a motorcycle. She imagined a blond muscular six-footer astride a great beast of a Harley-Davidson; a glamorous sylph-like girl, her arms clamped about his waist, her head at his shoulder, a blonde pennant of hair flowing in the slipstream. She was sadly disappointed. Parked in the Great Quadrangle, outside the Headmistress's Lodging, was a solitary vehicle.

It was a motorcycle and sidecar of a venerable age. It was shabby and paintworn. It was just what one might expect to find mouldering under an old tarpaulin in a farmer's barn. The horn with its rubber bulb seemed dispirited. The sidecar might've been carved from a tree trunk by a Neanderthal. The leopard skin plastic covering was tatty and worn. Leaking oil was beginning to form a pool under the engine. What was lurking in the sidecar Joan struggled not to imagine.

Joan walked around the vehicle twice. The tyre on the sidecar was quite worn. A stained flat cap and goggles hung on the handlebars. The saddle bags were fat as pillows. One thing for sure, he wasn't making a fortune with his lectures on time travel.

Then she became aware someone was watching her. A girl of her own age was sitting on the steps leading up to the Lodging, listening to her I-pod.

"Nice bike!" Joan offered.

The girl removed one earpiece.

Joan repeated, "Nice bike!"

"Yeah! If you like rust buckets," the girl returned.

Joan nodded judiciously, not knowing what to say. The girl was thin, dark hair, dark eyes, worn jeans and imitation leather jacket. What looked like Doc Martins were on her sockless feet. Joan had always ached for Doc Martins.

"You know nothing about bikes, do you?" the girl enquired, removing both earpieces.

Joan confessed, "No."

"We call it This Thing, Or That Thing."

"Nice name. Has a ring to it."

"What's yours?"

"Joan."

"What is this dump? An orphanage?"

"Boarding school for Army brats."

"Same thing. Parents dump unwanted kids in boarding schools."

"So you say."

"You ever noticed boarding school is not an anagram for orphanage?"

"No," Joan said, feeling confused.

"That's so as to fool you."

"I don't understand."

"So what're Kit and me doing here?"

The question struck Joan momentarily dumb.

"Isn't your Dad? Supposed to be giving a lecture on time travel?"

"Our audience is usually crackpots. So what're we doing at the Orphanage?"

Joan explained, "Well, every Sunday we get a visiting lecturer."

"Lucky you!"

"It's to broaden our minds."

The stranger considered the explanation.

"Well, you're not going to believe Kit. You'll try to be polite 'cause that's the way you've been dragged up. Fearfully polite. But you'll be struggling not to laugh. If you laugh, he'll just try harder. That's the way he is. But it hurts and I'll hate you."

Joan was silent.

"So why are you here?"

"You might pay us?"

"We will pay you," Joan asserted, "We always pay the lecturer," and then, "You mean sometimes they don't? When they've booked you?"

"When they've had a good laugh, they'll say we're not paying for that rubbish."

"Is it rubbish?"
"Do you believe travelling through time is possible?"
Joan considered the question.
"Don't know. Never thought about it. I'd like to believe."
There are moments. When I long to go back. To say sorry. To say, I love you. To listen to what you said. Not to do what I did. To do things differently. To beg forgiveness.

She was surprised at the intensity of her feelings; startled at the sudden uprush. One thing the Randall taught successfully was to suppress emotion. She saw in the stranger's eyes that her face betrayed her.

"Perhaps you won't laugh."
"What's your name?"
"Hannah. My Dad is Kit. Kit Marlowe."
"Kit? Christopher? Christopher Marlowe?"

* * * *

Joan was returned to Miss Sheridan's class reading Christopher Marlowe's masterpiece Doctor Faustus. She was overcome by the sheer power of Marlowe's words; his description of the matchless Helen of Troy. *Is this the face that launched a thousand ships and burnt the topless towers of Ilium?* She felt the constriction of the desk upon her knees. Miss Sheridan stood in silhouette, black against bright sunlight; an ebony image of the wayward Helen.

"Joan, continue, please."
But she was lost among the groundlings, captivated by the Admiral's Men and was slow to return to the classroom.
"Attend me after class."
"But, miss, I was."
"Deirdre, continue, please!"

* * * *

Hannah was saying, "I'm his keeper."
"Why would you say that?"
"Everyone thinks he's mad."

Joan didn't know whether she was expected to laugh.

"Really?"

"He's looking for someone who can help him travel through time. When it doesn't happen, he becomes depressed."

"He must be depressed a lot."

Hannah's phone began to play Handel's Music for Fireworks. Joan walked away. When she looked back the girl was gone.

* * * *

"Billy Brakspar wants another tuppence, Kit."

"For playing Second Devil atrociously? By right, he should be paying me," suggested Christopher Marlowe.

"He complains he has no words."

"Because he cannot learn words! It is enough he cackles and gloats to fright the groundlings."

"He says he is not seen enough."

"As he comes on stage when not cued, I'd suggest he is seen too often."

Christopher and his friend, the actor Edward Alleyn, were sitting in the stageside box seeking a little privacy in a place where there is no privacy, the Playhouse at Shoreham. Above, the grey London sky threatened rain.

Alleyn rebuked him mildly, "Dear friend, to give him his due, when Billy is dressed and painted up, he frights the groundlings to fits. And myself, if I speak truly. What if he were in reality Beelzebub come visiting? Is tuppence too much? Should we not pay the Devil his dues?"

"So all rascals, and indeed children, may take on the Devil's dress and go from door to door demanding payment and sweetmeats? And the good householder give up his money and goods lest it be the Devil himself behind the paper and paint?"

"It might be wiser, old friend."

Edward continued his list of problems.

"The good wife Dorrie will deliver no more hot pies. Until we pay for what we have already gobbled."

"We can do without hot pies."

"Alas, not, Kit! Actors will do anything for a hot pie."
"Except act, it would seem."
Around the two men swirled the noise of a playhouse in preparation. Behind the stage, hammers beat briskly on metal and saws on wood. Men shouted one to another. On stage, a group of dispirited actors stood, lay, muttered, squatted, strutted and slept, awaiting judgement on hot pies and pay.

"Regard our fellows," Christopher gestured, "If they had been paid, they would have vanished without trace. Never to be seen again, until every penny had been deposited safely in Dorrie's pie shop or the alehouse."

"That they haven't been paid might suggest a reason why they appear so mutinous?"

"I am not paying good coin for old cheese."
"Persons of quality do and esteem it highly."
"Don't humbug me, Edward. You understand me well enough."
Edward regarded the shamble of actors on stage.
"Then someone must humbug these gentlemen yet again. Or we shall have no play."
"And there is no argument among us who is the greater humbug," Edward decided.

* * * *

The first words the audience of Randall girls heard from the speaker of the evening were, "No, thank you. I have no use for a slide projector," and, "No, no! Please leave it where it is," as prefects moved to dismantle projector and stand. The projector remained as an abandoned robot, its blind gaze focussed on the speaker.

When the last murmur died away, Christopher Marlowe said, "Good evening, students and staff! My name is Christopher Marlowe. I am known as Kit to my friends. I bear an illustrious name that you may believe confounds me as a thieving rogue. I can only hope the evening concludes without suffering the same fate as my famous, infamous name's sake."

In that instant, Melanie Mackenzie fell in love with Christopher Marlowe; her whole being consumed by raw emotion. She saw only how beautiful the man was; not tall, not short, of a dark beauty, midnight hair, dark bright eyes, moustache and beard; too young in every respect to be Hannah's father. She recognised a spirit, not of sunlight, but moonlight. Her heart ached

"I am here tonight to attempt what I have never succeeded in doing before."

It was a long pause, perhaps seven, eight seconds, before he continued, "And that, dear friends, is to convince you of the validity of travelling through time. Hasn't that a wonderful resonance? To travel through time! As if you took your old tin alarum clock and turned the pointers back? And tomorrow would be yesterday! Or last week or ten years ago or a hundred! And in that regained time, you would put right that which pained you yesterday and today."

He paused, smiling, looking over his audience, and then, as speedily, seemed to fix his eye upon Joan, saying, "To be able to return to where you have longed to go. To say sorry for the hurts you never intended and be forgiven. To say to that person from whom you hid your heart, I love you. Forgive me that I turned away from your love. To be able again to listen to the loving voice you ignored. To listen to wise counsel you disregarded. Not to do what I did, but to do things differently. To find forgiveness."

The audience was transfixed. Joan found herself unable to move, scarcely able to breathe, close to tears. It was a voice that spoke to the grieving heart. There was a silence in the hall that was full of voices.

"Normally," said Christopher Marlowe, "I speak to audiences of crackpots, the sadly, mentally deluded, chairs tenanted by scoffers, rude and illiterate. It may surprise you to know I am normally hired as a figure of fun. Because they have paid for my presence, they feel free to insult me, even throw things at me. For more than one reason I am grateful that smoking is no longer permitted in public buildings. To be struck by an ashtray is a painful experience."

The laughter was warm and sympathetic.

"Therefore, tonight I am delighted to be speaking to an audience of intelligent young people. I do not say so to flatter you, but I know you will judge what I say by intellect and not ignorant ridicule. If you do not believe me, if I do not convince you, so be it. But perhaps tonight, I will find. . ."

He looked around upon his audience as if expecting a response.

A voice from behind Joan asked, "Have you got a time machine, sir? One that actually works?"

The hall was silent. Everyone suppressed breath in expectation of his answer.

"No," confessed Christopher Marlowe, "I do not have a time machine."

The disappointment was audible.

The same voice asked, "Are you building one, sir?"

The speaker shook his head to say, "No, I am not building one."

He stopped and smiled at Hannah who stood up to say, "My father won't be offended if you leave as he hopes you will not be offended by his honesty. Please feel free to go. He wouldn't want to waste your evening."

A considerable minority of the audience rose and left. Joan felt Laura's breath in her ear from the row behind.

"Isn't he absolutely gorgeous?"

CHAPTER TWO

The Chairman of Governors of Clatherthwaite Primary School, West Yorks, was a Dickensian character; complete with twinkling eyes behind gold-framed spectacles, head set upon an indeterminable series of wobbling chins and a globular body straining the arms of the cushioned chair in which he was encased.

He smiled upon the young teacher and said, "Do you understand, Miss Meadows, that this is not a legal proceeding?"

The young woman's nod was so indeterminate that the Chairman tried again, "This is not a courtroom. We are not judges or magistrates. We are Governors of the school, the Education Officer and his Deputy. Miss Wilson is the clerk who will take notes as we proceed."

Miss Wilson, complete with notebook and pen, smiled apologetically. The Chairman too, apologised.

"As we grow older, so do our memories fail us. Miss Wilson will make sure you have a copy of her notes."

The Education Officer at his elbow, a skeletal figure in contrast to the Chairman, murmured in his ear.

"Quite so," agreed the Chairman, twinkling ever, "Would you be so kind, Miss Meadows, as to affirm you understand this proceeding is not a trial."

The young teacher was very nervous. In a subdued tone, she asked, "What would you like me to say?"

The Chairman turned to the Education Officer who responded, asking, "Miss Meadows, do you understand this is not a court of law and you are not on trial?"

"Yes. You asked me to come in for a talk."

"You don't have a Union representative with you?"

In the faintest of voices the young woman replied, "I didn't think it necessary. I haven't done anything wrong."

The Education Officer consulted his Deputy as the Chairman consoled the young teacher.

"My dear, I'm sure you haven't done anything amiss. The report on your first year is satisfactory."

"Thank you, sir."

The Education Officer said, "I'm advised we may continue. Miss Wilson must note the teacher is without Union support."

Miss Meadows raised a hand.

"Yes, Miss Meadows?"

"May I be excused?"

The Chairman faltered.

"You mean?"

"I need to use the lavatory."

The Deputy Education Officer suggested, "Miss Wilson, would you?"

The two women left the committee room.

"Nerves," commented the Education Officer.

"Quite understandable," agreed the Chairman.

They sat in silence until Governors began to talk among themselves. The Chairman consulted the timepiece wallowing in the folds of fat upon his wrist.

"I say, fifteen minutes?"

He looked to the Education Officer who shrugged.

"Toujours la femme!"

The room door opened as if on cue.

"Ah!" the Chairman cried, "For this relief much thanks!"

Miss Wilson entered alone.

"Miss Meadows won't leave the lavatory. She says she's being picked on. And it's not fair."

Everyone looked to the Education Officer who sighed and said, "Miss Wilson, would you be so kind as to ring the Union chappie? Pinner, I believe?"

The Chairman announced, "Capital! Pinner's the man to winkle her out."

One of the Governors laughed.

"This is no laughing matter," rebuked the Education Officer, "A very serious matter. If charges are laid and proven against Miss Meadows, she will go to prison for a very long time."

* * * *

Christopher Marlowe surveyed his mutinous cast and sighed with exasperation.

"Hot pies are of more consequence than the play to you?"

The rumble of agreement corroborated his assertion.

Angrily, the author cried, "If this were a vessel at sea, I would drown the whole scurvy pack of you! How can you pretend to be Lord Pembroke's men? He would be shamed to acknowledge you!"

Turning to Edward Alleyn, he suggested,, "Best would it be to be shot of all?"

To his surprise, Alleyn ignored the remark and spoke instead to the cast.

"We are actors, therefore, let us make pretence that we have all swallowed one of Dorrie's hot meat pies. That Billy Brakspar has withdrawn his extortionate demand for tuppence extra per performance. And instead, given his attention to the play and less to frighting foolish lasses in the pit."

The cast laughed. Billy Brakspar didn't.

"Pies eaten. Billy behaving himself. What then divides us?"

There was a muddy silence disturbed by muttering among the cast. When Christopher would have spoken, his friend gestured him to silence.

"Let them take counsel among themselves. We shall withdraw. Then, we shall have our answer."

The friends dropped down from the stage and in the pit, found a barrel and a carpenter's bench to wait out the answer.

The cast trooped down from the stage to join Christopher and Edward who said, "We should not be divided. Pembroke's men are a worthy company. Whatever you say, we shall not take offence, shall we, Kit?"

Christopher gritted his teeth and shook his head.

"John Prentice will speak for us."

"Speak up, John!"

"We are concerned," said John Prentice, hesitantly, "We are concerned this play smacks of heresy."

"How so?"

"It glorifies the Devil."

Edward Alleyn laughed and shook his head.

A surprised Christopher Marlowe demanded, "How can this be so? Doctor Faustus, in his wickedness, calls up the Devil, Mephistopheles, and makes a pact with him. He sells his soul for twenty-four years in which he may savour every earthly pleasure. In due time, the Devil comes to take his soul and carry him off to eternal punishment in the furnaces of Hell. What message could be clearer? The wicked shall be punished beyond measure. Where is the heresy in that?"

The cast were impressed and somewhat reassured.

"In truth, you are doing God's work in bringing His message to the sinners of London. And, by God, there are enough of them!"

Nothing could have been better said. The cast saw themselves in a different light. They were God's messengers.

"Does God dole out hot pies!" inquired Billy Brakspar.

"Tomorrow there will be hot pies!" Christopher announced.

Edward Alleyn suffered a fit of coughing.

"After rehearsal, every man shall eat of my purse!"

John Prentice asked, "And when shall we be paid?"

"When the pit is crowded and the boxes are applauding. When there is money in the house."

On this optimistic note the cast dispersed happily.

* * * *

When the hall door closed upon the last departing schoolgirl, there was an echoing silence broken only when Christopher Marlowe said, "Seventeen. Splendid! Seventeen inquisitive spirits!"

He smiled and the sun shone. It was a smile that mesmerised seventeen inquisitive spirits. If he had invited her to climb Everest or dive the Mariana trench, Melanie knew she would have followed him willingly.

"I have no time machine. I am not building one... Then why are you still here when so many of your schoolfellows have left?"

He looked to Melanie.

"I suppose. Curiosity, sir?"

The speaker nodded and moved away.

Addressing his meagre audience, he asked, "Would you say that is true? You have remained out of curiosity? You want to know what happens next."

There was a murmur of agreement. He turned his smile upon Miss Meadows.

"Your mistress stays, of course, out of duty."

Turning to his audience, he said, "Thank you for your trust. Hopefully, I won't bore you. Perhaps I may stir your mind? May be, I shall convince you that travelling through time is a reality?"

He stood in thought for a moment and then declared, "There is no such thing as Time with a capital letter. It is a device we humans use to record the order of events."

Melanie said hesitantly, "The sun rises, sir. The sun sets."

"Of course, but that is not a measure of time. There is no past, present or future. There is only Now."

He waited for a response that did not come and encouraged, continued, "We are living in the echoes of the explosion, the Big Bang, that created our universe. Time has no reality."

He paused at the murmur of disagreement.

"With the aid of radio telescopes, we can view the birth of our universe; the moment of the explosion that created this universe. It still exists. We can look into what you call the Past and we see our beginning. Now!"

He appealed to his audience, saying, "Borrow a flying machine. Ascend to the greatest height. You are looking down on a great plain. The dinosaurs, the first men, the Norman invasion, John at Runnymede, bloody battles, the rise and fall of kings are all visible to you. From the first explosion to the last moment of extinction is Now. Is that so difficult a concept to grasp?"

Joan struggled to understand. Melanie noted that her love-rival, Hannah's lips had moved in syncopation with the speaker as if it were a script, Kit Marlowe had learned under direction.

"Think of it in terms of an explosion. From that first spark to the ultimate darkness is one event."

The voice that Joan recognised as Tina asked, "What is that to do with time travel, sir?"

"Everything is within reach. It's as simple and difficult as that."

"And time travel is real?" questioned the prefect Chalmers.

"In nineteen hundred and one, two English ladies met ladies of the court of Versailles in the palace gardens. Look it up on your magic machine. In nineteen fifty-three, Harry Martingale met a patrol of Roman soldiers in a cellar in York. In both nineteenth and twentieth centuries, hikers have met and walked with travellers in Northumberland whose sudden disappearance cannot be accounted for."

The girls were silent.

"Then how does it happen?" asked Miss Meadows, "This time travel?"

"If I understood the how and why," said Christopher, "I wouldn't be here."

Joan grasped the irony and laughed.

"Sometimes, the mind has an reasonable expectation. In the gardens of Versailles, it wouldn't seem unreasonable to meet persons in historic dress. The young man in the cellar in York had already been teased about ghosts. It is not unreasonable that one family will fall in with another to walk together sharing a summer's afternoon."

Joan experienced such a sudden longing as brought her close to weeping openly. The loss she had fought so hard to suppress overwhelmed her. She hid her tears from Melanie.

"There is sometimes a longing, an act of will, an extreme cerebral impulse. There are numerous examples of dying persons appearing to their beloved. Hundreds of miles away. The extreme cerebral impulse."

"But you haven't been time travelling, have you, sir?" asked Melanie. The spontaneous murmur showed the question had formed in every head.

Christopher Marlowe stood in silence, shook his head, saying, "I have seen time travel by others."

The gasp of incredulity was audible.

"On three occasions. At three separate events. And each was condemned as trickery. Conjuring. Cheating."

"Events for which you were being paid, sir," a voice questioned. Joan recognised Tina.

"I understand your doubting. Perhaps Hannah, may answer you?"

Joan was surprised to find she had forgotten the presence of Hannah sitting aside as quiet as a faithful hound.

"There have been occasions when we weren't paid. They refused to believe their own eyes. It had to be a trick."

A voice asked, "Was it a trick, sir?"

"I do not engage in trickery."

Joan couldn't restrain herself.

"What happened, sir?"

"On each occasion, I invited audience members to come forward. To try to find that cerebral impulse that would transport them to another space and time."

Joan, though mesmerised by voice and presence, looked about her. Melanie had eyes for no one but the speaker. All the girls were similarly transfixed. Miss Meadows, old as she was, appeared involved, which was unusual.

"Three different occasions. A teenage girl. A young man. An old man. We watched in silence. The girl disappeared and reappeared in the winking of an eye. This happened twice. In the silence of a village hall, we saw the young man rise to walk, vanish and then fall into the room. He fell into the room from mid-air. He fell, perhaps, four feet."

Joan found she had held her breath too long.

Miss Meadows suggested, "In truth, they went nowhere?"

Joan thought, *Always negative! No wonder she's a rotten teacher.*

"The speed of their return is no indicator as to how long they were elsewhere."

"Ask where they'd been," Laura breathed in Joan's ear.

"They wouldn't say. The girl was obviously shocked. The young man refused to speak."

"The old man?" asked Miss Meadows.

"We should never have accepted the booking," confessed the speaker, "The upstairs room of a public house in North London. An old man came forward."

He paused and Hannah said, "He wasn't unwilling. We sat in silence for some minutes. The pub goers were getting bored. Then the old man stood up, cried, 'Mary?' and vanished. He didn't return."

Silence.

Joan ventured, "Maybe he found his Mary, sir? Maybe he didn't want to come back?"

"I believe there are men, women, children who have the ability to manipulate time. There is the adult or child who is the energy source. The power house. He or she may not travel in time, but radiates a frequency that facilitates time travel. He or she is the marker point for return. But that energy is finite. When the energy is dissipated, the time travelling ceases. Second, the explorer, the guide who marks the path. Third, the time travellers. Here, in this school there may be energy source, guide and time travellers."

Miss Meadows demanded, "Are you going to ask these children to attempt to travel through time?"

"Yes."

Miss Meadows' grey hair bristled in denial.

"Then I forbid it!"

* * * *

The Chairman smiled at the young teacher and said, in his kindliest tone, "I'd like you to tell us, Miss Meadows, what happened in the gymnasium of Clatherthwaite Primary School on the morning of Friday, the twenty-third of April."

The young teacher turned to Mr. Pinner, her Union representative, who nodded encouragingly to her.

"I can only tell you what I remember."

"That's precisely what we want to hear," the Chairman smiled benignly, "Just what you remember."

"It was my last gym class of the week."

She hesitated and added, as if in explanation, "I also teach Biology."

The Chairman nodded encouragingly. Miss Wilson looked up expectantly.

"Half eleven. Form 4A."

"May I ask a question?" said the Deputy Education Officer.

Miss Meadows looked to Mr. Pinner who nodded to the Deputy.

"How were you feeling? Tired at the end of a long week? Looking forward to the weekend?"

"That's three questions," responded Mr. Pinner.

"How were you feeling, Miss Meadows?"

The young teacher hesitated before saying, "Normal. Yes, normal."

"Tell us about the class, please" suggested the Chairman.

"A decent lot. A few who need pressing to engage with the activity."

"Angela Jacobs? A reluctant gymnast?"

"She needed chivvying sometimes."

"Not your favourite pupil."

"I can't just let a girl stand idle. Some do need encouraging to take part."

"What was the activity?"

"A game. Four teams. Four ropes to climb. A race. Most of the girls enjoy climbing."

"But Angela didn't," asked the Deputy, "So, what did you do?"

"I slapped her leg lightly. To encourage her."

"You slapped her leg to encourage her to climb the rope. How high is the rope?"

"Twenty, twenty-five feet. But I would accept any decent attempt."

"Did Angela climb the rope?"

"Despite grumbling she didn't want to, she was climbing slowly."

"Go on."

"Her team complained she was climbing too slowly."

"So what did you do?"

"I shook the rope."

"Shook it hard?"

"No. I shook the rope and said, 'Do buck up, Angela! You're letting your team down.' Something like that."

Miss Meadows turned to Mr. Pinner and murmured in his ear.

"My member would like to request a break," said Mr. Pinner.

"We're almost done," smiled the Chairman, "I'm sure Miss Meadows can bear a few minutes more of our company."

"What happened after you shook the rope?"

The Education Officer's voice held no warmth.

The young teacher crumpled a tissue in her hand and said, "It wasn't my fault."

The Chairman said, more gently, "We must know what happened, my dear."

"What happened after you shook the rope?"

"Angela fell."

From the street, only the faintest rumble of traffic disturbed the silence.

"She had pretended to faint in other lessons. So I picked up her and laid her in the corner on the gym mats. If she were going to sulk, at least she wouldn't spoil the game for others. I did everything as I should."

"A classmate says you dropped her on the mats."

"That's not true!"

"You didn't notice she was bleeding from both ears?"

Miss Meadows shook her head.

"Then what did you do?"

Miss Meadows seemed surprised.

"I continued with the lesson."

One of the Governors gave a gasp of disbelief.

"Did you know it was almost one o'clock before Mister Palmer found Angela? Dead. On the gym mats."

"So I was told. All I can say is I did everything I should."

Miss Wilson was struggling to complete her notes through her tears.

"So this poor child lay unattended, dead or dying, for more than an hour in the gymnasium?"

"Angela had pretended to be hurt and faint on other occasions."

"So, Angela called wolf once too often, did she?"

"I wouldn't say called wolf, but she was something of a nuisance."

When the meeting was adjourned and the last Governors had departed, the Deputy returned to where his superior sat alone in the Committee room. He sat beside him and waited as the Chief read from a file. When he closed the file, his Deputy said, "I've been involved in accidents before, but I've never met such cold indifference as our Miss Meadows has shown."

The Chief didn't respond.

"I would suggest she has as little to do with Angela's parents as possible. Perhaps we can indicate the teacher is in shock? Which might excuse the lack of concern."

"She killed the girl," the Education Officer stated, "Coldly and calculatedly, this young teacher murdered Angela Jacobs."

His Deputy was shocked.

"You're saying she...."

Interrupted by, "Angela Jacobs was a bright girl. Perhaps being Jewish was a factor. But she made an enemy of our Miss Meadows and paid the price. Miss Meadows knew exactly what she was doing when she shook that rope. There was no need to do anything. The nervous child was climbing slowly. I would suggest when Angela had one hand free of the rope, Miss Meadows shook the rope violently. The very gym mats she laid her victim on should've been at the foot of the ropes."

"What do we do?"

"We can't prove murder. We can't prove intent. We can't pursue negligence. We can't even blacklist her. I suggest if you wish to be a successful murderer, train as a teacher."

"You're joking, surely?"

The Chief handed his Deputy the file he had been reading.

"The child at Danefield who drowned? Nine years ago? Page twenty seven."

The Deputy thumbed through the file.

"Check the staff who were present at the time of the tragedy."

The Deputy conned the page carefully, but his face displayed disappointment.

"No Miss Meadows."

"Look again. Page twenty-seven."

The Deputy recited slowly, "Summer term. Students on teaching practice from Saint Peter and Paul's."
His gasp was audible.
"Gillian Meadows! On teaching practice!"
"A remarkable coincidence, don't you think?"
"Perhaps our Miss Meadows should find another profession?"

CHAPTER THREE

Miss Meadows demanded, "Are you going to ask these children to attempt to travel through time?"

"Yes."

"Then I suggest this is the ideal moment to end your lecture."

A storm of protest exploded over Miss Meadows's head.

"Please," implored the prefect Chalmers, "Please, miss, don't stop it now!"

"Madam, do you believe it possible to travel through time?" asked Christopher Marlowe.

"No."

"Then let us prove you right."

Miss Meadows hesitated and then nodded.

* * * *

As his audience had all begged to be chosen, Hannah picked at random.

"The skinny girl, " she announced, pointing at Joan.

Skinny? Was that a compliment or what?

"The prefect? And the dark girl. At the end of the row?"

They came to sit on chairs before the group.

"There is somewhere, someone you long to return to," urged Christopher Marlowe, "Perhaps you are strong enough to break the bonds of time?"

There were no giggles, no chatter; silence fell.

For an eternity no one breathed. Chalmers coughed. The dark girl fidgeted on her chair. Joan opened her eyes, stood up and fell, striking her head on the slide projector stand. It fell over with a startling clatter. Melanie suffered a blinding headache that faded almost as fast as it exploded. Laura saw something no one else seemed to see. Melanie, as her sight returned, saw two men standing behind the chairs. As a soldier's daughter, she knew exactly who they were. Two Riflemen of Wellington's army, dark uniforms for camouflage, rifle and bayonet at the port, battered shakos on their heads, looked about them in astonishment. The younger said something to the older man who shook his head. They vanished. Someone screamed, which a Randall girl shouldn't do. Chalmers took Joan in her arms, mopping the blood from her forehead and called for the First Aid box. Miss Meadows seemed more concerned over the wreckage of the slide projector. A prefect ran to inform Miss Savage.

No one paid any attention to Christopher Marlowe or Hannah. The audience decided discretion was the better part of avoiding blame and melted away. Laura returned with the First Aid box from the kitchen. When Miss Savage arrived with the porter, Chalmers was bandaging Joan's forehead, supervised anxiously by Melanie and Laura. Christopher Marlowe and Hannah were seated awaiting the arrival of authority.

When the Headmistress entered, Christopher Marlowe rose to apologise.

"I'm so sorry, Headmistress. The child stood up, fell and struck her head on the contraption. An unfortunate accident. Yet, I feel in some measure responsible."

"As indeed, you are! I would be grateful if you and your daughter would leave the premises without causing any further disruption."

Hannah said, "There is a question of the fee."

The Headmistress turned an arctic gaze upon the girl, but Hannah did not flinch.

She began, "My father has," but was brusquely interrupted.

"Be thankful the Randall is not suing you for the injury to this child."

Father and daughter left the hall without another word.

* * * *

The porter unfolded the stretcher and lifted Joan gently onto the canvas. Prefects carried the unconscious child to the sanatorium.

Laura burst out, "That wasn't fair, miss!"

The Headmistress's icy gaze fell upon her.

"What do you consider unfair, MaCallaman?"

"It wasn't Mister Marlowe's fault, miss. Like he said. It was an accident."

"Do you agree, Mackenzie?"

Melanie wriggled, hesitated, but admitted, "Not his fault, miss. Laura's right!"

"I shall speak to you both tomorrow," decided the Headmistress and marched away.

"I bet she won't pay them," complained Laura.

Unfortunately, the good lady's hearing was more acute than Laura had assumed. The Headmistress turned to say, "You doubt my integrity? I shall weigh the issue in due course."

Laura stood uncomprehending, not knowing whether to nod or shake her head.

"One thing you may bet on, MaCallaman, is there will be no more time travelling at the Randall! I shall take charge of the extramural lecture programme!"

The Headmistress quit the hall as stately as a galleon upon a summer sea.

Laura looked to Melanie.

"What was that about her teggitry?"

"She may pay them. Or again she may not."

"Why didn't she say that?"

"Because she's the Headmistress."

Which left Laura further confused.

From a window of the hall, Melanie and Laura watched a man kick a motorcycle into reluctant life. The girl in the sidecar wrapped a scarf about her head. The man settled himself astride the machine and drove away. The erratic cacophony of the old engine echoed about the Great Quadrangle.

"That is the best lecture we've ever had ever," Laura declared.

"Know what?" Melanie gloomed.

"What, Mel?"

"She'll have that old zombie back with his knots to punish us!"

* * * *

Robert Simpson, formerly Sergeant Simpson R. 235419, Anglian Rifles, didn't fall asleep in the train. If he had slept on past his destination, he may have escaped the unseen net that was beginning to draw together the most unlikely people in a confusing series of events... However, he had chatted with the guard who recognised in this quiet, middle-aged man a fellow former soldier.

"Not so easy in Civvy Street," the guard had commented.

"Totally different world."

The guard regarded the neat haircut and shaven cheeks, shined shoes, pressed suit, clean shirt and regimental tie.

"I'd guess you were on your way to an interview. If I'm not poking me nose in where it's not wanted."

"Nothing special, but better than On the Doors. Shifting drunks."

"That what you been doing?"

"To my regret. Thought it would give me the days to find something better."

That morning Robert Simpson, looking himself over in the landing mirror, had questioned why he was attending this interview. Obviously the question of free accommodation was attractive, but he had never considered working in a school. He knew he had overstayed his welcome in his sister's house. Her husband, Joe, had made that clear. Time to be moving on before causing friction in the household.

"I'd hire you on the spot, Bob," Shirley said, as he came downstairs, "You look honest, responsible, competent, trustworthy! And the spitting image of Colin Firth!"

"Whoever he is. Thanks, sis! I'll try to remember I'm honest. Responsible. And whatever else you said."

She kissed him, saying, "Competent. Trustworthy. And my very own Colin Firth. Don't forget to ring."

Robert Simpson didn't sleep past his station, but alighted with the guard's good wishes in his ears. Ignoring the taxis, he consulted his map and set out to walk to the Brooke Randall Boarding School for Girls of Military Parentage.

In the familiar surroundings of the Bull's Head alehouse at Deptford, Christopher Marlowe and his friend, Edward Alleyn, had enjoyed an excellent meal of spiced mutton. The chamber was private. The fire burned briskly. The chairs were comfortable and the ale not too watered.

"Kit," declared his friend, "you and Faustus are the rage of London! You have a grasp on the capital tighter than the Plague."

"From which, God be praised, we are spared this year!"

"I am grateful to you for the finest role of my career."

Christopher was about to say there would be greater roles yet to perform, but Edward silenced him with a gesture.

"You are a success! No one has ever written a play of such power."

"May I press you to record those sentiments with pen and ink?"

"You may jest, but I swear the groundlings were weeping when Faustus is taken to Hell. For the Doctor? For themselves? They would not know. You have moved a city to tears. Did you mark the silence when Helen appears? Veritable worship!"

Christopher interrupted again to complain, "I would we were rid of that rascal, Brakspar! Yet again he was in the pit giving alarm to young maidens! And ruins Mephistopheles' entry to the play."

"Of no account, Kit! Billy is a pimple! You give him the honour of a painful boil! You have all you ever wanted, my friend. Success, money, hot pies, half the women in London perspiring after you."

Edward Alleyn stopped and sat silent, staring into the fire.

"Why stop, dear Edward, when you flatter me so? I fear there is a but to follow."

Christopher tapped his friend's knee with his ale pot.

"Have I offended a lady? But no! Have I stolen another's words? But no! Am I not the handsomest playwright in England? But no!"

"There are worse playwrights of worse appearance. Some that change shirt more often and smell better."

"Well, dear heart, thank you for such generous words, but, but me your but. I have all I desire, but."

Edward Alleyn hesitated, "I speak only in your best interest."

"As always! But!"

A burning brand tumbled from the fire and Alleyn cast it back into the hearth, turning to say, "Is it not risky to continue parading Catholic sympathies?"

The maelstrom of voice and music from below sounded loudly in the quiet chamber.

Christopher said, "'Tis said one can see the future in the fire's heart?"

His friend pressed on.

"Why risk all that we have struggled to achieve? Why risk the pleasure of Dorrie's hot pies?"

His friend didn't laugh or smile.

"You may be sure," persisted Edward, "that the papists are bent on our destruction."

"A fortress set in a silver sea for a moat?"

"Has the Armada taught you nothing? How close we came to disaster? How much we owe to that gallant few, Drake and his captains?"

"We are not so few!"

"Believe me, Kit, their Catholic Majesties are bent on destroying our blessed Queen and the Kingdom to restore the Bishop of Rome to supremacy!"

Christopher laughed out loud, irritating Alleyn.

"How come I am the writer and you the actor? Here, dear heart, take my pen. I will fetch you ink, black as doom."

"I speak seriously, Kit. You have enemies. I don't want to see you taken for a heretic and put to the rack."

Christopher sat so long silent his friend feared he was offended. When he finished his ale it would seem he was about to leave.

Discarding the pot, he asked of Edward, "You are my true friend? The friend I may count on to the death? Do not say me false."

"I swear by all that is holy," answered a Edward answered, "I am your true friend to the death."

"What I am about to tell you may be the death of us both."

Edward answered, "Speak on!"

"I have been for some years a servant in secret service to her Majesty"

Edward was surprised, even astonished, but did not doubt the truth of what his friend spoke.

"I have undertaken certain missions that must remain secret even if I be disowned."

"Is that true politic? Not to stand by the truth?"

"I have disclosed Her Majesty's enemies conspiring at Douai in France. A nest of vipers!"

"But that is admirable, Kit! Deserving of gratitude from the highest to the lowest!"

"By pretence of being Catholic, I have brought to Her Majesty's attention those in London who bear one face and hide another."

"But such deserves the highest reward!"

Christopher Marlowe smiled at his friend.

"In this shadow world the irony is, I am suspect both to the papist traitors and the forces of the Crown."

In a disbelieving silence, Edward Alleyn digested these disturbing words.

"Is this true? You fear both?"

"Truly, I stand between the hounds and the boar."

"Then you must fly, Kit! You must save yourself!"

Christopher laughed, "Then tell me, friend, where in this world I may hide?"

CHAPTER FOUR

When the Deputy Education Officer retired to his native county of Cornwall, he developed an interest in local history. Researching a Cornish family, he came upon a familiar name in the yellowed files of the Kernow Chronicle.

It was a story of a school trip tragedy. The school was not local, but from Nottinghamshire. A local school would have been more aware of the danger. At Lands End, the Headmaster and his wife had gone off for a cup of tea, leaving the children in the care of a senior teacher and a probationer. The children were allowed to clamber down onto the rocks. Four boys and three girls were washed away to their deaths by the Atlantic swell.

What made the story remarkable was that the older teacher attempted to rescue the children. She was saved by the local inshore rescue boat. The heroine of this incident was a Miss Gillian Meadows. What the retired Education Officer wondered was whether it was a genuine rescue attempt. Seven children drowned. On what the former Deputy Education Officer knew, Miss Meadows' total of suspicious deaths had reached nine. Nine dead children.

It troubled the old man so much that after a sleepless night he remembered a former colleague and telephoned Nottingham. He was relieved to learn that Miss Meadows was no longer teaching in a state school.

* * * *

Robert Simpson stood on the brow of the hill and gazed down at his destination. He had not known what to expect, but the size of the school buildings surprised him; centred about a large quadrangle. The establishment resembled a figure of eight by the presence of a smaller quadrangle. Beyond the school were sports fields, formal gardens, greenhouses, a farm with farmhouse and working buildings. There were stock in the fields and a lake bounded by trees. The tower at one corner indicated a chapel.

Robert Simpson realised the school was the creation of a military mind. The quadrangles were easily secured against Sudanese tribesmen, Napoleon's Imperial Guard and the Household Cavalry. Under Russian cannonade, each building would be yielded yard by yard, the enemy paying a heavy price for every broken window; buying time for the relief column to arrive and scatter the assailants. At the centre of the larger quadrangle flew the Union flag.

"And this is a school?" he said aloud, "It's a barracks. A palace of a barracks."

He laughed at his own feeble joke and wondered what it was like to be part of this Boarding School for Girls of Military Parentage. Whether it would win the loyalty he felt for the Regiment that had been his home. His family. His boarding school. He set off down the hill with a growing sense of anticipation, surprised at how excited he felt. A large van entered the gates and later exited as he walked.

At the left-hand side of the ornamental gates, topped by iron lions, stood a porter's lodge. Simpson rang the bell on the gate pillar and while he waited, deciphered the BR in the centre of each gate as Brooke Randall, the Victorian hero who had set up this Boarding School for Girls of Military Parentage.

The gate began to open as a young woman came from the lodge.

She smiled to say, "Mister Simpson? We are expecting you."

Why Robert Simpson was surprised to be met by a woman at a girls' school he couldn't explain, but he managed to say, "Thank you," without falling over his feet.

The gate closed behind him. The young woman led him towards the school and through the arch into the large quadrangle. He was aware she was reciting facts and figures about the school, but little filtered through to his consciousness. They crossed the courtyard and up the steps into an oak lined hallway redolent of floor polish. He followed the young woman into a doorway to an office and at her request, took a chair.

"Miss Savage will be with you shortly," she smiled and sat down at a desk. She began to type on a keyboard. Robert Simpson studied the names of students who had brought credit, if not glory, to the school. He noted the names of young women who had served in Air Transport Command, ferrying aircraft of all types to squadrons wherever needed and whatever the weather. There were a surprising number of names of those who had served in the ATS, WAAF and WRNS. He found his respect for these gallant young women rising. His reading was disturbed when a young man came out of an inner door and left the office without a word. The young woman's cry, "Your expenses, Mister Morris!" was wasted on the empty air.

* * * *

"I shan't be seeing you for some time, Bonny, Becky," said the girl to the old terriers through the iron gate of Number Thirty Two, "But I don't want you to think I've forgotten you."

She held Digestive biscuits through the gate and each dog accepted the gift without snatching. The girl watched them eat the biscuits.

"They're Digestives so I guess they'll be good for your digestion. And less sugar."

She offered her hands through the gate and the terriers licked them.

"I expect they will let me come home sometimes. I'll come to take you walks. It's all been very confusing. And so quick! But Mum says, it's a Great Opportunity, not to be missed. So, I can't. I'm not sorry to be leaving Hadley Street School. Missis Wade never liked me."

She stood up. There was a woman in the window and the child waved to her. The woman waved back.

"Goodbye, my loves," the girl said, struggling to control her tears, "Take care of yourselves. I'll be back."

She ran down the street and pretended interest in the newsagent's window to wipe away her tears. When she was composed, she went into the shop. The Asian shopkeeper sat on a stool at the end of his counter. The shop was empty. The newspapers had been delivered and work-going customers had purchased their crisps, snacks, chocolate, soft drinks and lamentably, cigarettes.

"Good morning, Mister Patel."
"Good morning, Laura. No school today?"
"I'm not going to Hadley Street any more."
"They have burnt it down?"
Laura and Mr. Patel laughed.
"No! I'm going to a different school. You don't come home at teatime from this one. You live there."
"Is that a good thing? Taking you away from your mother?"
"My mother says it's a Great Opportunity. It's because of my Dad."
"If your Mother says so, then it is a Great Opportunity."
"I'm going today. I thought I would come and say goodbye."
"How kind! Then I will not be worrying where my worst customer has vanished to."

Laura laughed because it wasn't true. She knew there were boys who stole from the shop. She was ashamed of them. When she told Mrs. Wade she knew the teacher wasn't listening.

"Then I must give you a present so you will come back."
"Oh! Really? Thank you, Mister Patel!"
"What would you like? Remember, I am not a rich man!"
"I would like," said Laura, "A pencil and a biro, please. So I won't forget you."

Mister Patel rose and brought to the child a set of pencils and a packet of biros.

"Oh, this is too much! Far too much!"
Mr. Patel answered, "Nothing is too much for the child who does not ask for sweets."
"Thank you, thank you very much!"

She held out her hand to the old man and they shook hands gravely. Then Laura cried, "Goodbye, Mister Patel," snatched her hand away and ran from the shop. The old man stood looking after her, thinking his own thoughts.

Laura ran into the back lane and hid beside the telegraph post to weep until she could cry no more. Then she wiped her face and went home to help her mother pack for the Great Opportunity.

* * * *

The signboard that creaked in the wind outside the Deptford tavern depicted a bull's head. In the darkness, the torch that flared by the door illuminated the signboard only by chance. Yet the stranger who approached the door was satisfied he had found the right house. He stepped into a maelstrom of noise. No one took notice of the tall man as he made his way through the throng to the bar. He ordered a drink, paid for it, and stood sipping from the tankard, watching the tidal flow of customers. A thin man appeared at his elbow, apologised for pushing through and ordered a drink. They took as little notice of one another as moored craft in a restless tideway, bumping and being bumped as others pushed through to be served.

Regarding the noisome mob, the thin man commented, "Why, this is hell."

To which the tall man replied, "Nor am I out of it."

The thin man emptied his tankard and returned it to the bar. He made his way through the crowd to the stairs in the corner and vanished. The tall man took time to finish his drink and then followed the thin man up the stairs.

He climbed cautiously to a landing where an older woman sat on a chair.

"Should you be here, sir? When we have sickness in the house?"

She indicated the fouled chamber pot by her chair.

"Rosie, it's me! Do you not recognise me?"

The woman relaxed and smiled, showing a mouth lacking teeth.

"'Deed I do, sir! Forgive me! Good to see you again, sir!"

"Likewise! And I give thanks for the care you are taking of him."

The woman, embarrassed, shook her head. The tall man rapped on the door behind her three times and then again, once.

The door opened and he passed in.

Christopher Marlowe embraced his good friend Edward Alleyn.

"You are well, Kit?"

"Fatter than a cockroach! Not an hour goes by without a tray being brought in. And if I don't clear the platter, Rosie looks so sorrowful I am shamed."

"You are well in spirit. And safe. That is what matters."

"What matters all this tomfoolery? Secret knocks. Sentries on the landing. The house barred for sickness where there is none. Passwords as if we were embattled in les Pays Bas. How can I take it seriously?"

"You must, Kit. When you were arrested on the twentieth..." Christopher interrupted, "They were forced to let me go."

Alleyn commented, "Only by Walsingham's grace. He knows what service you had given to her Majesty. But Cecil is the man behind the arras now."

"He knows me well!"

"It might not serve his purpose to acknowledge you."

Christopher was sobered by these words.

"I warn you, Kit, they are determined. Today, a list of charges has been laid against you to the Privy Council. The charges include treason, heresy and blasphemy. They are all capital charges."

Christopher was visibly shaken.

"I am innocent of all."

"Tonight all London looks for you, Kit. It's only a matter of time before they arrive here. We have to smuggle you out of the city."

"When can we do this?"

"Tonight is the only opportunity. When the drinkers have all gone home, I will return to set you free of London."

* * * *

Christopher Marlowe had fallen asleep despite his fears when Edward Alleyn, Billy Brakspar and two other members of Pembroke's Company came to lead him, sleepy and confused, down the stairs. He was alarmed when they continued down the cellar steps.

"Whoa! Where are we going?"

"Dear Heart," soothed Alleyn, "The only way to smuggle you past the Watch and out of the city is if you are dead."

Christopher stared at the grinning faces.

"I take it you are jesting or relishing the prospect of my death?"

Billy Brakspar pulled aside the canvas to reveal a coffin. Christopher walked around the box.

"You should be ashamed to have provided such a whited sepulchre! I can only assume you have bought shipwreck timbers!"
When the lid was lifted the stench appalled them all.
Alleyn explained, "No one will challenge such a stench. Two dead dogs. You will not be disturbed."
"I shall need more than a nosegay."
"That smell," Alleyn explained, "is the scent of freedom."
"And where are we going?"
"Stratford," said Alleyn.
"But you said out of London?"
"Stratford upon Avon," said Billy Brakspar, "I have family there."

* * * *

A voice crackled from a box on the desk.
"Is Mister Simpson there?"
The young woman replied, "I'll send him in."
She smiled at Robert Simpson, "You can go in now."
As he rose, she added, "Good luck!"
"Thanks. I'll need it."
He opened the door into the inner room that was lined with bookcases. An angular woman in her late fifties, browbeating spectacles and greying hair stood behind the desk.
"Come in, Mister Simpson."
He entered warily. The woman did not invite him to sit down. For one terrifying moment, Robert stood before Miss Berrisford, the Headmistress of Priory Road School. He had endured many firefights in Iraq and Afghanistan with murderous fanatics trying to kill him and sharp metal flying past his ears. He had been less afraid than in the Headmistress's study at Priory Road. Reality returned.
"Have you come to waste my time, Mister Simpson?"
Flustered, he said, "Why would I do that, miss? I've come a long way."
This answer seemed to satisfy her and she nodded at him.
"Sit down!"

He took the chair before the desk. It was little difference from standing before Miss Berrisford, legs trembling. The Headmistress sat down.

"I am Miss Savage and I have the honour of being the Headmistress of this school."

She opened the file on the desk and continued, "I know something of you. The Criminal Record check is clear. If this file tells me the truth, you are competent, trustworthy, honest and hardworking?"

Robert Simpson almost smiled.

"I am waiting for an answer."

He hesitated and then suggested, "I would like to be all that."

"Well, are you or are you not?"

"My sister thinks so. She added 'responsible' and something about some actor I can't remember his name."

"You're not married?"

A shadow crossed Simpson's face.

"I lost my wife and son. An accident."

"Your service record is exemplary. Sergeant Rifleman."

She said Rifleman as if it had a particular significance? Surely a tanker, an electronics dork, an S.A.S veteran has a shade more fizz than a grunting, plodding, grumbling, muddy Rifleman?

"What do you think you could do for the Randall?"

"Whatever you asked me to do. No particular talent, but I can learn."

"What brought you here?"

"Looking for somewhere that makes sense. Somewhere I can be useful."

"Go on."

"Leaving the Army, I felt. Useless. Not a mechanic, a chef, nothing useful. My job was to shoot people. Next stop a security man? No thanks. Maybe I can be useful here."

"So whatever the task? Whatever the hour? Boilerman? Porter? Minibus driver?"

"Yes. I'm accustomed to odd hours."

Miss Savage was silent, pondering. Robert Simpson waited.

"We have a sacred trust here. We have the care of almost six hundred girls from ten to eighteen. I emphasise the words sacred trust. You think this an old-fashioned notion?"

"No."

"We are their guardians. We stand in loco parentis. We must ensure no harm comes to these children. They are very vulnerable. Many of them have already suffered severe trauma losing their fathers in combat. Their fathers were your comrades. This is something I know you understand."

Robert Simpson nodded because he did understand.

"The young man who preceded you seemed to think this was Saint Trinian's. I disillusioned him very quickly."

He couldn't think of anything to say, so wisely, he said nothing.

"I want you to consider the security of the school as your particular responsibility. Do you think you could do that?"

"I can do my best."

Miss Savage said, "I think we shall suit each other very well, Mister Simpson."

To his astonishment, the Headmistress stood up and shook his hand across the desk as he leapt to his feet. The Headmistress of Priory Road had never treated his hand so kindly.

"Miss Wallace will sort out everything with you. Salary, holidays, accommodation. Do you think you'd be happy in the Lodge?"

A bewildered but happy man was bustled out of the office to where the secretary, Miss Wallace, awaited him with forms and congratulations.

From the sitting room of the Lodge he rang Shirley. Joe answered.

"Hang on!"

Robert Simpson hung on. He waited an eternity before his sister answered.

"Well?"

"Got the job!"

"Well done! I knew you could do it. What's it like?"

"Bit like Hogwarts. But the boss has the right attitude. Think I'm going to like it. Would you believe I have a whole house to myself?"

"Lucky you! Joe didn't tell me you were on the phone. So I won't tell him you got the job. That'll crease him."

Before he turned in, Robert Simpson took a walk around the school as if on fire piquet. He smiled when he realised he had created his first routine. To patrol the premises in the late evening.

CHAPTER FIVE

The first time walker was Harry Milward. An old man of ninety who had been an excellent carpenter. Old Harry, in his loneliness, spent every Saturday evening in the Old Grey Hen. The pub was only five minutes from home. The old man was well known in the area and well liked; a man who wouldn't talk your ears off, but was a good listener. He was often in his corner seat five, six nights a week, but his presence could be guaranteed on a Saturday night. There was often entertainment of one sort or another at the Hen.

On this particular Saturday night when Harry came in and took his drink to his corner there was a lively debate in progress. A young man, bearded, dressed in black, was leading the case for time travel. He argued well and gave numerous examples of unexplained time travelling. The longer he talked the more he held Harry Milward's attention. Harry had never got over his wife's death. He couldn't accept that life would never ever be alright again. He was told the pain of her loss would diminish in time, but it never did. From childhood they had shared a lifetime together. Harry felt as if he had been torn limb from limb, but was, unfortunately, still alive. From this pain there was no healing and no respite.

There were those who had come to enjoy a good laugh at the speaker's expense. They wanted a time machine. They wanted the fun of seeing it fail to work. Instead, they were faced by a man who said the brain directed time travel. He cited many cases where men and women were seen hundreds of miles away from the place where their physical body was dying. It was the urgency of the cerebral impulse that drove them to travel in time for these last words. It was a robust debate and the landlord called for order a number of times, but the mood was good-tempered and the barmaids were busy. Harry sat quietly, sipping from his glass, listening to believers and sceptics alike.

It was when the speaker, dark and bearded, called for three volunteers to come forward and sit silent for five minutes. To try to reach that place, time or person dearest to their heart. To reach outward with their mind fuelled by love, loneliness or loss. Which he described as three of the best motivations. The saloon bar became very quiet.

"No Doubting Thomases, please," the young man demanded, "A genuine attempt to reach out across time, ladies and gentlemen, please!"

Laughter stirred reluctance. Then Harry stood up to modest applause. His heart pounded. He felt ridiculous. But no one mocked the old man. Harry Milward came forward to sit in a chair. His sense of loss, never absent, was overwhelming.

Perhaps it is true? Perhaps it is a matter of the power of the mind. What have I to lose?

A tall girl of uncertain age, fifteen, sixteen, laid aside her Pepsi and crisps to join Harry. They were joined by a middle-aged woman.

"Splendid!" agreed the speaker, "A fair selection!"

There was a rumble of amused agreement from the assembly.

The speaker declared, "We're not going to sit silent for an hour. I ask you only to be silent for five minutes. Which I would judge is time enough to focus the mind."

The landlord suggested all drinks be ordered now and pumps closed for five minutes. When everyone was settled and peace reigned, the speaker said, "Focus on one place, one person, one time. You won't be able to maintain it for five minutes. Perhaps you may make two efforts."

The guinea pigs nodded agreement. Harry's longing for his wife overwhelmed the silence. Mary's presence, the sweetness of her body, the echo of her singing filled Harry Milward's mind and being.

When the old man vanished, it took measurable time for the assembly to realise Harry Milward was no longer present in the saloon bar of The Old Grey Hen. When they did become aware they sought him among themselves. No one noticed the girl too had vanished from her chair. For the briefest of moments, she vanished as a light bulb flickering and returning to brightness. She sat ignored, amazed, speechless at what had occurred while all around hunted for old Harry. She almost spoke out, but changed her mind. Hannah Cato was the second time walker.

What was astonishing was that no one considered what had happened as anything, but a wonderful conjuring trick. They congratulated the landlord and the speaker on the free entertainment.

The voice of the saloon bar cried, "Well, I don't know how you did it, Kit. But congratulations! Absolutely brilliant! You should be on the goggle box! You're gona find it hard to top that next Saturday, Micky!"

The speaker refused to say a word except thank you when accepting a congratulatory drink and cash from the landlord.

Almost as unobtrusively as Harry Milward, the speaker too vanished from the saloon bar. He exited by the front door of the Old Grey Hen into the crisp night air of Port Carlisle. Nobody saw him leave except the girl called Hannah who was the second time walker. She followed him out and watched him try to kick-start an old dilapidated motorcycle with sidecar. When he finally kicked the engine into grudging life the girl slipped into the sidecar. He regarded her with astonishment.

"I have no interest in little girls."

"Don't flatter yourself. I have no interest in old men."

"Please get off my machine."

"I'm not going back to that hell. Anywhere's better than that. I'd top myself first."

"What have you done?"

"It's what's been done to me."

"You're not my problem. Off, please!"

"Your problem is you're unbelievably naïve. No street smarts. Are you just out of a coma? Or the sixteenth century?"

The engine faltered and died.

"You didn't recognise when they were making fun of you. You just went on being patient and charming while they made a fool of you."

He pretended to adjust the carburettor because what she said was true.

"Do you think so?"

"Even when the old man vanished you just stood there. As if that proved you right."
"But it did! Didn't it?"
"They all knew it was a trick. A very clever trick. But a trick."
"But it wasn't a trick!"
"Trick or not that was the moment for me to take the hat round!"
"What hat?"
"To collect their money. They enjoyed the show. They'd've coughed up happily."
"I wasn't there for their money."
"More fool you!"
"I'm looking for the person who can..." but he was interrupted by the girl.
"How much did Micky give you?"
"Not your concern."
"How much?"
"Twenty pounds. Is that not good?"
"Doodly squat! We'd've made loads more if I'd taken the hat round!"
"We? There is no we!!"
The girl questioned, "Do you know where the old man went?"
"He went to find his wife."
The girl asked, "How do you know?"
"That's what the old men do. I have asked them."
"I went with him, but no one noticed."
His interest quickened.
"Tell me what you saw."
"We stood on the corner of a street of terraced houses."
He nodded acceptance.
"I knew why we were there."
"To see his wife again."
"I shared an overwhelming sense of excitement. To see his wife again. Just one last time."
"He loved her. Without her, life had no meaning."
"He stood there holding a bunch of flowers. Waiting for Mary. Then I was back in the pub and everybody was searching for the old man. I could've told them where he was, but no one asked me."

He was silent for an eternity and then said, "All I can say is, you are safe with me. I would not harm you. If my word is good enough for you, then if you wish, come with me. I suspect we will do well enough."

He kicked unsuccessfully to start the engine.

Hannah said, "They must've seen you coming when they sold you this heap of junk. How much did they give you to take it away?"

"It is a fine machine. The gentleman said it is a classic."

"Really? Prove it."

He kicked the antique engine into life as the girl shouted, "Name's Hannah. Hannah Cato."

He shouted, "Kit," but the rest was lost in the protesting clatter of the old engine that echoed and re-echoed through the cold streets of Port Carlisle.

* * * *

Harry Milward was discovered sleeping beyond waking in his own bed. He lay at peace in his best pyjamas. The coroner judged Harry had passed away on the Wednesday before the Saturday when the stranger came to talk about time travel in the Old Grey Hen. Time travel is a capricious beast, creating more paradoxes than it solves.

* * * *

Captain Vernon Brooke Randall said, "Why should I believe you, sir?"

He was addressing a young Ensign of the Rifles who looked twelve years old, but was actually sixteen.

"Why should you not, sir?" queried the Ensign.

The Captain of Cavalry, a regular dandy, complete with waxed moustache and shining accoutrements, was seated at a campaign desk outside his tent. The small encampment was impeccable, the horse lines as geometrical as would satisfy any Ancient Greek mathematician. It was a cavalry troop, the eyes and ears of the Army. The Ensign, standing before the table, was as dirty, dusty, and as tired as his Corporal Rifleman sitting yards away. The Rifleman was kept erect by his rifle from falling into sleep. They had covered fifteen miles at Rifle pace to reach the cavalry troop.

"How long have you been in Portugal, sir?"

The Ensign admitted reluctantly, "Three months, sir."

"And Wellington is doing his best to have you out of here as soon as possible."

"Sir?" said the young officer, surprised.

"We are in retreat towards Lisbon. Where we hope to evacuate the Army without too much fuss. To do so we need to delay the Froggies to gain time for the evacuation."

The Ensign sat bewildered.

"We are quitting Portugal, sir?"

"Your river has been thoroughly surveyed. Every bridge has been blown and every ford holds some very nasty surprises for Monsewer. And you come to tell me you have found a ford."

He smiled indulgently.

"Yes, sir."

The Captain like many of his breed disliked change. The common infantry, described by Wellington himself, as 'the scum of the earth', stood foursquare and exchanged musket volleys at fifty metres distance until one or the other would break. If the British redcoats won the day the gentlemen of the Cavalry would chase the enemy from the field, slaughtering them with the sword and lance.

But now there were the Rifle regiments with a superior weapon who didn't exchange murderous volleys. They wore dark jackets for camouflage and they would fire from cover. They killed officers and sergeants at a superior distance. They were regarded by such as Captain Vernon Brooke Randall as not being real soldiers. Like Americans they would run away to fight another day, which was beneath contempt.

"And how did you find this ford the Army couldn't find?"

"We saw a stag and three hinds cross the river."

"They were swimming, sir."

"I fear to contradict you, sir, but they were not. They trotted across, stopping once to drink."

"How wide is the river at this point?"

"A hundred yards, sir."
"There is no ford. You are mistaken, sir."
"Sir, we saw."
"There is no ford, sir."
When the young man opened his mouth to reply he was silenced.
"That is my last word, sir. There is no ford."
The young Ensign moved to leave. His Corporal stood up; from apparent dozing to instant alert.
"May I be excused, sir?"
"To do what?"
"To return to my duty."
"Your orders are?"
"Firstly, to trail my coat."
The Captain interrupted to say, "I do not accept slang, sir."
"By my presence to make it appear the Army holds the river. And, secondly, to delay the enemy at any ford or river crossing."
"And you will do this on foot?"
"We are less visible than cavalry, sir."
"Of course, I forget, you skulk in the bushes."
The Ensign bit his lip at the insult.
"If pressed we can march twenty, thirty miles a day, sir."
The Captain was silent for a moment.
"And should the occasion arise, how long do you think to hold a ford, sir?"
The Ensign stood his ground, taking time to form his answer...
"If we are evacuating from Lisbon, the enemy must cross the river. Their cavalry will seize a ford. The occasion, as you phrase it, will arise, sir."
The Captain did not try too hard to hide his irritation.
"I asked you, sir, how long do you think to hold a ford?"
A pretty boy like you should be leading the choir or serving in some drapery.
"If the ford is well staked, we will delay the enemy two, three days."
When the Captain hesitated to answer, he said, "Once engaged I would request your assistance, sir."
"What would I do, sir?"

"Request the General Commanding for an infantry battalion to deny the enemy the crossing."

The Captain laughed and the young officer felt his temper rising.

"My boy," said the Captain, paternally, "when Monsewer's horses cross the river, you will last, perhaps, two minutes. Or perhaps you will run away?"

In the silence the cavalry bugle blew for Stables.

"May I be excused, sir?"

"You are excused, sir."

The Ensign and his Corporal saluted the Captain. The two Riflemen walked away. Once clear of the encampment they began to trot at rifle pace.

As they ran, his Corporal said, "'Scuse me speaking out of turn, sir, but we ain't the Captain's favourites, is we, sir!"

* * * *

The buzzer on the desk barked. Miss Wallace and notebook went to join the Headmistress.

"One candidate stood out. When children from her school were swept into the sea this lady jumped in. Alas, a vain rescue attempt! She nearly perished herself. Her name is Meadows. Gillian. Single. Fifty-five. And I promised to look again at the Biology budget?"

"I'll find you a copy, Headmistress."

"Do you think I may have coffee now, please? And a biscuit?"

Miss Wallace smiled, "A long afternoon. I'm sure you deserve both, Headmistress!"

Miss Savage, flushed with the satisfaction of a sound decision, sat back to await her coffee and biscuit. The Atlantic breakers continued to pound the rocks of Land's End, but no children died today.

CHAPTER SIX

It was late evening when the Ensign and his Corporal entered the encampment in the dead ground above the river. Tired as he was, he noted the prompt whistle from the Rifleman on observation to their rear and the Corporal's reply.

Sergeant Springer and four Riflemen stood to attention.

"All present or correct, sir. Riflemen Simpson and Robertson on observation, sir."

"Thank you, sergeant."

The Sergeant dismissed the parade and the Riflemen drifted away with the Corporal who had been briefed on what he might or might not say. The Sergeant brought his officer a mug of tea where he sat on the big stone by the dead fire.

"Sorry it's stewed, sir."

"It's wet. Went the day well?"

"All quiet, sir. We've cut and sharpened the stakes to spike the ford. We'll start first light tomorrow."

"Thank you. Tell them well done!"

"What did Captain Dandy say, sir?"

"I'm sorry, sergeant. I didn't hear that."

"What did the Captain say, sir?"

"He expressed his opinion of Riflemen."

"A rifle can kill a man on a horse at two hundred yards, sir."

"Thank you, sergeant. I have fired a rifle."

"I had Flanagan cross the ford. Water is at mid-thigh. I decided to see how wide this ford is, sir."

"Good thinking!"

"Ten yards broad more or less."

"Narrow enough, but ideal for Monsewer's cavalry."

"Then it drops away quite savage. Paddy got an unexpected bath he much needed. As the Irish don't float he had to be dragged out. So he wasn't laughing. Same upstream. If you don't know exactly where this ford is, yous likely to drown."

The Ensign sipped his sour tea, but indicated for the Sergeant to continue.

"Don't want to sound foolish, sir, but d'y'think somebody's built this ford?"

The Ensign took a last sip and swilled round the mug.

"I'm trying to remember when you last said something foolish, sergeant, but I fail miserably. Let's say, ten minutes and we'll take a look at this ford. They can keep their drawers on if they like."

Seven pale-skinned soldiers clinging to skinned and sharp ash staffs stood on the river shingle.

"Is there any man here who can swim?" the Ensign asked.

No hand moved. Soldiers don't swim.

"Then I must warn you it is contrary to Standing Orders to drown yourself! You will be denied pay and privileges!"

The Ensign decided the laughter was a positive sign.

With the aid of rope and six Riflemen, the young officer surveyed the ford. From a selection of points they ducked under water to bring up stones. It was as Sergeant Springer had surmised; the ford was not a natural phenomenon. Horses and carts had brought the rubble and stone. Human hands had built this trackway under water.

Leaving five overgrown boys to play in the water, splashing each other, wrestling each other, happy as lambs' tails in the evening sunshine, the Ensign and his Sergeant walked back to the camp. They walked in a thoughtful silence until the Sergeant asked, "What did the Captain say, sir?"

"There is no ford."

"But we," protested Sergeant Springer.

To be interrupted by his officer who declared, "And that's my last word, said the gallant Captain."

"He won't change his mind?"

"Monsewer with the aid of traitorous Portugees has prepared this ford. They know exactly where they will cross unopposed. His cavalry will catch and slaughter our rearguard. They will then surprise the Army strung out on the road to Lisbon. As the poet writes, 'The Assyrian came down like a wolf on the fold.'"

"So what do we do, sir?"

"We will oppose any attempt by the enemy to cross the river."

"Then the quicker we spike the river the better, sir. And dig new rifle pits."

Both men were silent as they walked into the encampment: five shabby tents and one tarpaulined small supplies cart. The Ensign retired to his tent to write up his journal. From the river he could hear the echoing shouts and laughter of his Riflemen.

* * * *

Wrapped in a shroud, dagger to his hand, the foulest stench in his nostrils, Christopher Marlowe endured the nailing down of the coffin lid. He was assailed by claustrophobia; struggling not to scream and hammer fruitlessly on the lid of his prison. With a sudden bone-jolting wrench he recognised he was being carried from the cellar to the cart. In the street there was a murmur of voices as the coffin was lifted onto the cart. He fought against the temptation to shout. With further jolting he realised the cart was in motion. His endless journey began.

The stench was so appalling he vomited until his stomach was empty and depression overcame him. In the blackest of moods he raged against Alleyn for encouraging this flight. By attempting to escape the law he knew he confirmed his guilt. If he were taken he would be tortured and executed. Yet he was innocent of all charges. He raged against Walsingham the spymaster who did not lift a hand to help. To have written such a masterpiece of theatre and to have all stolen from him, he wept in despair.

As he left London and began the bone-rattling journey on rutted country roads he composed the words that later would be stolen, as indeed, were his reputation and achievement.

Lying in his own vomit, ceaselessly buffeted by the motion of the cart, a suicidal Christopher Marlowe, in the dark night of his soul, declared, "To be or not to be, Kit? That's the question, my sweeting! Whether 'tis nobler in the mind to suffer the slings and arrows of outrageous fortune? Or to take up arms against a sea of troubles? And by opposing, end them? To die, to sleep no more? One sweet kiss of the blade to the wrist? And end your heartache, Kit?"

He lay in the stinking darkness and fondled the bare dagger at his side.

"What say you, dear heart? Shall Kit Marlowe give them one last surprise when they wrench the nails from this box? Shall I confound them that yet being nailed down I have escaped?"

* * * *

"So what's buzzin', cousin?" Joan mumbled through a mouthful of Bounty bar.

The sanatorium was a haven of peace. Joan was the only patient. Melanie bit back a cry of surprise to see two of Wellington's Riflemen sitting on the empty bed next to Joan. The two men were diligently cleaning their brasses.

They don't see us. Where are they really sitting? What 're they doing here?

She managed, "Sheridan sent you this."

Melanie dropped a shabby copy of Doctor Faustus on the bed.

She realised neither Joan nor Laura could see the Riflemen.

"You're to finish reading it. And write an essay of your first impressions of the play, plot and characters. Then lend me your essay to copy."

"Oh, yeah? Sure she did."

Joan gathered up the play script and thumbed through the pages until she found the quotation she wanted.

"Why this is hell nor am I out of it!"

"Spot on! Ma Savage's been going mad all week," Melanie complained.

Laura added, "Every time you turn round she's there."

Melanie threatened, "Sunday lectures are gona be a nightmare with Ma Savage sitting in."

One of the Riflemen stood up and vanished.

"No more Granny Muddles snoring like a chain saw. Happy days!"

Joan was secretly relieved she need never pretend to smoke again, but contrived to look sympathetic. She broke in two the second chocolate bar in the packet and fed the girls.

"'Bout time," said Melanie, "Was wondering if you'd notice."

She exchanged shares with Laura because her piece was slightly larger.

"When d'y'get out of here?" Laura asked.

"She's only keeping me here case I throw a fit and my mother sues the Randall."

"I bet she didn't pay Mister Marlowe," Laura offered.

A young Rifleman appeared and sat down beside the seated soldier. There must be a connection between something here and where they are.

"He wouldn't be surprised. Hannah said it happened before."

"Where did you go?" asked Laura of Joan, the third time walker. The sudden change of direction rocked Joan.

"Wha'd'y'mean?"

Laura said, "Didn't you notice, Mel?"

"Notice what? And don't call me Mel!"

"For a moment she wasn't there."

Melanie was slow to comprehend.

"You mean Joan went?"

"When she stood up she vanished. For maybe one, two secs, she wasn't there. Blink of an eye. Then she reappeared, fell and hit her head."

Melanie and Laura regarded Joan accusingly.

"Is she right?" Melanie asked.

Laura said, incredulous, "Was I the only one to see her vanish?"

"There was nothing to see," Joan responded, "Laura's making it up."

Melanie wasn't satisfied. Laura looked hurt. One of the Riflemen looked up, but he wasn't responding to the girls.

"Why would Laura say that if it wasn't true?"

Joan hated herself even as she replied, "To get attention?"

"That's beastly!" Laura cried, "And it's not true."

"There was nothing to see."

"No?" Melanie queried, "Somehow you don't sound right to me."

"I got pins and needles. I stood up, lost my balance and fell into the slide projector. That's what happened."

"You vanished," Laura declared, "I know you did. I saw you. Where did you go?"

"I didn't go anywhere. 'Cept the San."

Melanie challenged, "We're your friends. You're not going to tell us?"

"There's nothing to tell."

"I believe Laura. She may be dumb, but she's not blind."

Christopher Marlowe or whatever his name is really has started something totally weird here.

The bell for afternoon school sounded insistently. The two girls rose to depart.

Melanie said, "Anyone else been in to see you?"

Joan shook her head.

"No."

Laura grasped the implication to add, "Nobody else brought you a Bounty?"

Joan shook her head.

"Think on that," suggested Melanie.

"Yeah!" Laura cried, "Think on that!"

The girls departed in a flurry of righteousness.

When the sanatorium door flapped shut, Joan questioned the ceiling above her bed, "Why didn't I tell them?"

She opened her play script and began to read the biography of Christopher Marlowe, born 1564, murdered 1593, lectured at the Randall 2015. Playwright and Time Walker.

* * * *

The Ensign dropped into the rifle pit beside Sergeant Springer.

"Sergeant!" he said, in lieu of a salute.

"Sir!" the sergeant returned.

The young officer was sixteen years old and Sergeant Springer was forty-two. If anyone had suggested he swaddled his officer, Springer would've been deeply offended. It was good practice, the sergeant would've said, to keep your officer alive. They lay side by side looking down on the artificial ford. At this point the river was perhaps a hundred yards from shore to shore.

"How did the Army come to miss this'un, sir?"

The Ensign pondered the question.

"What do engineers look for? Usage? Wheel ruts? No ruts here. Cattle drinking? No sign of cattle. Monsewer cleaned up after himself very particularly. Therefore, no ford visible to our surveyors. It's an underwater bridge."

The sergeant said nothing, his eyes on the river. The Ensign struggled for further justification.

"With the army in retreat, it's understandable."

The Sergeant snorted disbelief.

"Then how was us so clever to find the ford, sir?"

Adjusting the focus of his telescope the Ensign said, "Because we're Riflemen, sergeant."

"You're making fun of us, sir!"

"By no means. The redcoat has his eyes on the man in front's neck. The Rifleman takes note of a shifting wind. Cloud changes. He wonders why those pheasants have suddenly taken flight. Why did that hare bolt from his sett? He hears a voice, sniffs tobacco where no voice or tobacco should be."

The Sergeant agreed reluctantly.

"True enough, sir."

"When others might've ignored what they saw," the Ensign said, "We watched the deer trot across the river. Because we're Riflemen."

"River's falling," the Ensign decided.

He handed the telescope to his Sergeant.

"Willow stump."

The Sergeant surveyed the water level at the mark and nodded.

He closed the precious telescope and returned it to his officer.

"Them two riders that come to look at the ford, sir?"

"Dragoons."

"They put their horses to the water. Could've picked 'em off, sir."

"Then the French would know we're here."

"How far is Monsewer behind us, sir?"

"Three days? Remember they have artillery to transport?"

"Us is lucky, sir. We has naught. Only rifles. How far ahead is the rearguard, sir?"

"Two days."

"Frogs'll catch the rearguard before Lisbon. Evacuation'll be a massacre."

"Do you talk to the men like this, Sergeant?"

"You'd shoot iss if I did, wouldn't you, sir?"

The Ensign laughed a boyish laugh, innocent and whole-hearted.

"So all bridges blown, all known fords spiked and mined, there's naught between Army and the Frogs bar us. Nine Riflemen?"

"Did you see the Captain's face when he saw us wade across the ford, sir?"

"At least he had the good sense to come and view this 'impossible' ford."

"We scared the living daylights out of him, sir. He couldn't get out of here fast enough. If I were allowed to say so, I would say the Captain is a yellow belly, sir. But as I'm not allowed to say, I won't, sir. Out of respect."

The Ensign laughed out loud.

"The captain has ridden for instructions."

The Sergeant snorted.

"The sharpest road to Lisbon, I'll be bound, sir."

"Sergeant, you can't slander an officer and get away by sprinkling your words with 'sir'!"

"No, sir? Thank you, sir."

"Trust to Old Nosey!" the Ensign cried, slandering his Commander-in-Chief, Lord Wellington, "He'll not have us kicked out of Portugal. Nor will the captain abandon us."

The Sergeant prepared to crawl from the rifle pit, surrendering the precious telescope to his officer.

"I'll send Simpson to you, sir."

The Ensign answered, "Sergeant!" in acknowledgement. The sergeant continued, "You hasn't been with us long, has you, sir?"

"I hope to be longer."

"Know why Riflemen believe us'll never die, sir?"

"No notion, sergeant. Why do we?"

"Us does not wear red coats, sir. And us is Riflemen."

The Ensign laughed and the Sergeant smiled.
"Then we'll live to be old men together, Sergeant!"

* * * *

Miss Meadows saw the d'Urquart child rise from the chair and fall. Then everything stopped and she stood in darkness. When she heard the voices she knew exactly where she was. She was standing at the top of a long flight of steps in the Jubilee Park to watch the Municipal Firework Display. She was standing behind the family; Mother, Father with his arm about her shoulders, elder sister Rosemary, elder brothers Bernard and Simon.

Directly in front of Miss Meadows was the wheelchair wherein sat her fragile sister, Eleanor. Her younger self had one hand on the back of the wheelchair. This, she saw very clearly. A terrible dread consumed Miss Meadows as the rockets burst with an unearthly glare to see her infant hand steal down to release the brake pedal. She shouted as rockets burst in an even more spectacular display, but her voice was drowned by the applause. Her infant self, jumping up and down with delight, gave just the slightest nudge to the wheelchair.

Even as Miss Meadows moved to intervene, the wheelchair tumbled down the steps, gathering speed as it fell. Her mother screamed as father and brothers ran down the steps in a fruitless effort to catch the wheelchair. Her father stumbled, tumbled and fell, crying out in pain. Her brothers ran on to where their little sister lay motionless. Miss Meadows stood frozen.

Her mother, screaming unheeded, sat down clumsily on the steps, supported by bewildered Rosemary. Her infant self turned smiling, to look directly at Miss Meadows who ran out of the hall leaving the prefect, Chalmers, to attend a bleeding Joan d'Urquart. She saw the astonished faces of other students as she ran. All this she saw very clearly. Miss Meadows was the fourth time walker.

CHAPTER SEVEN

Robert Simpson was shovelling coke into the boiler when it happened. He stopped shovelling, raked the burn and closed the furnace door. He wiped away sweat and addressed the shabby teddy bear hanging on the temperature dial.

"Right. Ted, me old oppo! I leave the ship in your capable hands. Full speed ahead! And damn the torpedoes! I'll be back at ten.?"

The teddy bear surprised him, calling clearly, in the voice of authority.

"Simpson! Where is you hiding your ugly face?"

* * * *

Robert Simpson found himself lying on a blanket under a dirty canvas roof: a makeshift tent. He smelt drying grass and dirty humans. He had no idea where he was. Robert Simpson was the fifth time walker. The voice called again.

"Simpson! Where you hiding yours mangy hide?"

Astonished, he croaked, "I's here!"

A hard bearded face thrust itself into the crude tent.

"Simma, you deaf? Sergeant'll have your guts for garters! Shift your idle sel!"

Bewildered, he struggled to his feet almost bringing down the tent and falling to his knees. The voice called again angrily. The bearded man held the tent open for him. As he crawled towards the exit, the bearded man spoke again.

"Has you not forgotten someat, sweetheart?"

Simpson, confused, looked blankly at him.

The bearded man shook something at him.

"Rifle?" he questioned, gesturing.

Simpson realised with a shock of disbelief that lying by the blanket was an antique weapon which he recognised as a Baker rifle. He picked it up and crawled out of the tent.

He now saw the bearded man wore some sort of uniform, patched trousers that once might've matched the dark coat with two broad chevrons on the sleeve.

"Yi can't be drunk. Ye awright, Simma?"

Looking down, he realised he was wearing a similar uniform.

He started to say "I shouldn't be here," when the owner of the first voice appeared, a tall, broad-shouldered older man. His uniform was no better than the corporal's with one sleeve torn and patched, carrying three broad stripes and dark stains on his trousers.

"As you gone deaf, Simpson?"

"No. I was just."

"No what?"

The corporal interceded with, "No, sergeant," loudly into his ear. Simpson looked at him blankly. The corporal responded by bringing the brass base plate of his weapon sharply down on Simpson's instep and repeating, "No, sergeant!"

Despite the pain, Simpson grasped the implication.

"No, sergeant!"

"You will join the officer at the observation post. Where you will keep observation and if necessary act as runner for the officer. Do you understand?"

The corporal shifted his rifle and Simpson responded promptly.

"Yes, sergeant!"

"Then sharpen up! Froggy won't be sending no billy doos!"

"No, sergeant! Yes, sergeant!"

"Then off with you, lad!" ordered Sergeant Springer.

Simpson replied, "Yes, sergeant! But where do you want me to go, sergeant?"

The corporal took hold of his sleeve and led him away from the sergeant.

"Pull yourself together, son. You won't win no ticket to Bedlam. Now, double time to the river and join the officer."

Simpson nodded and trotted in the direction the corporal pointed across the Great Quadrangle towards the Headmistress's Lodging. A motorcycle engine started and with a fanfare of black smoke drove past him. A man was driving in flat cap and goggles. A hooded child or woman crouched in the sidecar. Simpson stopped, tasting the oily smoke, to realise he had forgotten why he was going to the Lodging.

* * * *

The corporal joined his sergeant.

"Decent enough lad. Not the brightest. But he'll stand."

Sergeant Springer said, "Shoot any that breaks. Or they'll all bolt."

The corporal gestured with his head.

"Our young gentleman?"

The sergeant considered the question.

"Rather the boy than our absent captain. Who's always somewheres else when bullets is flying."

To the corporal's unspoken question, he answered, "The lad's scared of naught 'cause naught's ever scared him. If we can hold Monsewer two, three days..."

He left it unfinished and his corporal asked, "How do we do that?"

* * * *

A babble of voices swirled around Miss Savage. The world was both arguing and rejoicing. She was bewildered, jostled by strangers, holding on to an empty tray, struggling to hear what the big man was saying to her. He loomed over her gripping an arm to pull her close. A group of men pushed past in the passageway towards the lighted room. She smelt food, beer, the great unwashed and understood she was in some sort of public house. The Headmistress of Randall's was the sixth time walker.

In the raw cacophony, she could see his mouth moving, but couldn't hear a word. She said, "I'm in an ale house. Is that right?" It was the noisiest dream she'd ever enjoyed. She saw she wore a apron over an ankle length brown dress. Her feet were bare. Reflected in the tray, she was surprised to see not a woman of fifty-five, but a girl of perhaps eighteen. Abruptly, the big man's voice broke in upon her.

"Hast seen any coin, Nell?"

She had no idea what he was talking about. It seemed safer to shake her head.

"Norran a happney for thee?"

She shook her head uncomprehending.

"As it's a dream could you tell me where I am, please? It's historical, so if you know the date, even the year, would be a help?"

She realised he was shouting to someone down the dim passageway and hadn't heard a word. When he turned back to her, he growled, "Dost understand? No more 'til they pays someat on reckoning."

An older woman appeared at his elbow and surrendered a piece of paper. The man stood reading what was written, his lips moving as he read, counting on his fingers as he calculated the total.

She said, "If it's all the same to you, I'd like to leave, please. Don't mean to offend, but this place stinks and your customers stink worse. I'm feeling slightly sick. If I can just slip by you, I'll find myself a breath of fresh air. I'll see myself out. Bye!"

She knew you could speak like this in dreams because dreams can't hurt you. She smiled and moved to slip past the man, but he took her by the arm and lifted her onto tiptoes.

"Ow!" she cried and struggled in his grasp, "Let go! That really hurts!"

He thrust the piece of paper into her hand, speaking into her ear,

"Too much comin' and goin', Nell. Take reckoning to the gentlemen! No more nothing 'til I sees coin! Dost understand?"

She nodded vigorously and he released her. He pointed to the stairs off the passage. She began to climb away from the bedlam. On the quiet landing there were three doors. The clamour from downstairs was muffled. Being in a dream she had no idea to which door she was to offer the bill for food and drink.

Somewhere a church clock began to chime. She stood silent to count the strokes. The chimes faded into silence at eleven.

"In this dream," she said aloud. She found it reassuring in dreams to speak aloud. It demonstrated a measure of control.

"In this dream, I'm in a public house at eleven at night. I'm guessing maybe it's Shakespeare time. Good Queen Bess is on the throne and all's well with the kingdom. Though I have the weak body of a woman I have the heart of a king!"

She felt a deal braver remembering the quotation and tapped on the first door. There was no reply. She opened the door to an empty room. The second door was to a bedroom with a comfortable fire and a seductive four-poster bed. In the looking glass on the dressing table she saw Nell, a girl with tawny tangled hair and bright, intelligent eyes. There she had the first inkling that this was not a dream. She was tempted to investigate further, but resisted.

Across the landing she could see light shining under the third door. She heard laughter from the room and felt a sense of relief. Holding the reckoning as a talisman, she approached. Before she reached the door, four men came out, leaving it open behind them. The first was a tall man, handsome, clean-shaven, seemingly as alarmed as she was. His hand went to his sword, but fell away when he saw the female form. He pulled his cloak about him. The second man was short, dark, bearded and strangely familiar. The two men following pulled hoods over their heads and brushed past.

"The reckoning, sir," she said, breathless with surprise, holding out the paper to the last man...

"None of mine, but his," he declared and the men vanished down the stairs. She approached the open door.

"The reckoning, sir," she offered to the room. There was no reply and so she entered. A man lay before the fire. Blood flooded the face. A bearded man lounged in a chair by the fire, a tankard in his hand.

"God's blood!" cried Miss Savage the alehouse maid, "What foul deed is this?"

As she turned to give cry, the corpse sat up and smiled at her.

She stood frozen as the corpse raised a finger to his lips, signifying silence. Gathering her scattered wits, Miss Savage cried, ""But I see you alive, sir!"

The man sitting in the chair said, "You are mistook. He is dead. I have certified him so. Quod erat demonstrandum."

He waved a sheet of paper at Miss Savage.

"Yes, sir," she said, stumbling over logic, "If you say so. He is dead."

"Then still thy tongue," retorted the guardian of the corpse and gestured her dismissal.

"Then who shall bear the reckoning, sir?"

"None of mine!"

The corpse sat up and reached out a hand. Numbly, Miss Savage surrendered the trembling paper.

"So much for so little?" cried the corpse, "It strikes a man more dead than a final reckoning in a little room."

The dead man lay down and closed his eyes. His hand clutched the reckoning. A bewildered Miss Savage bobbed a curtsey and left the room.

"Close the door," commanded the guardian of the corpse.

* * * *

Miss Savage awoke with a start. She sat up with her heart pounding and struggled to find the switch of her bedside lamp. Something fell to the floor. The pain of angina mounted in her chest and crept into her left arm. She fumbled for her spray on the bedside table. It wasn't there. Fear flared. Then she realised it had fallen into her slipper as she switched on the light. She retrieved it and sprayed below her tongue.

She lay still until the angina subsided. She timed it at twelve minutes. The pain was becoming ever more fierce and frequent. If it doesn't stop after fifteen minutes, ring 999. One day soon she knew it wouldn't stop. In her sitting room, she poured a glass of sherry and sat sipping in her favourite chair. *Okay, it may kill me. But I like it. Why leave it for the mourners, if any?* The dream was still vivid in her head; the detail of the faked killing bewildering. It troubled her. There was a trickle of disturbing memory.

Taking the sherry decanter and glass with her, she crossed to the computer. She typed in *Murder Bull's Head Deptford* and pressed Search. . . .*the accepted version is that he and a close friend, Ingram Frizer, dined in the Bull's Head, a tavern in Deptford. The two men quarrelled over paying the bill and in the fight that followed, Frizer stabbed his friend Christopher Marlowe in the eye.*

"Oh, my word! Too much coincidence!"

Miss Savage finished her glass of sherry in one gulp and poured herself another. Sipping the second sherry, Miss Savage spoke aloud, as she often did, to the chairside photograph of her fiancé John who died on a training exercise so long ago.

"I wasn't dreaming, John. I've been time travelling. All due to that wretched man, Marlowe."

The Headmistress was the sixth time walker.

* * * *

Joan hated sheep. Before coming to the Randall, she'd never given sheep a second thought, but now she hated them. Melanie and Joan with the assistance of Harry Armstrong had spent a frustrating hour in the rain, chasing and capturing an escaped ewe. Armstrong's farm had been lived in and farmed by the family for countless generations and now it was the school farm run by manager, Harry Armstrong. When the British public had decided to reward the hero, Major General Vernon Barrett Randall, it was here on its ancient pastures and woodland that the Barrett Randall Boarding School for Girls of Military Parentage was built.

In imperial days, it was expected the girls would marry within the Army and spend their lives extending the bounds of the British Empire. Therefore, they were to be prepared as pioneer women to plough, sow, reap and harvest. They were expected to care for, medicate, milk and breed, cattle, sheep and goats. And to chase and capture wilful runaways through rain, hail and snow.

Harry explained, "Sheep is natural escapers. Goats is easier."

Melanie interrupted to say, "I thought goats were, y'know, like devilish?"

"Goats is content in good pasture. It's only when the cupboard's bare, they'll wander. But sheep in the best pasture will still be poking their noses into the hedges, looking for a way out."

"I suppose that's where it all comes from in the Bible," Joan suggested, "The Lost Sheep. The Good Shepherd who goes hunting for the Lost Sheep. You don't hear much about the Lost Goat. And the Good Goat Herder."

They were standing in the farm stores barn, aromatic of feed bins and sun dried hay, bristling with rolls of wire netting, barbed wire, bundles of chestnut paling, stacked wood of all shapes and sizes, bales of black plastic to sweat the silage and all manner of farm machinery. Harry's forge was comforting in its warmth. Leaning against his workbench, the girls, waterproofed in black plastic sacks, hole for the head, two holes for the arms, were drying their face and hair. Harry was enjoying a cigarette he had refused to share with Melanie.

"Nasty dirty habit!" he explained, "Young ladies don't smoke."

"Cows. They like order. One strand of barbed wire and they'll stay clear. Bullocks is uncertain. Spook a herd of bullocks and they'll run straight into barbed wire. Nasty business!"

Joan changed the subject; the image of cattle tangled up in barbed wire she found disturbing.

"Why do we never get poultry now? I loved collecting eggs. I didn't mind cleaning out."

"Because twelve-year-olds isn't very good at catching sheep," which silenced Joan, and provoked Melanie to complain, "We would've caught her straight away, if a certain cowardy custard hadn't let go."

"I thought she was going to bite me!"

"When did anyone ever get bitten by a sheep?"

"There's always the first time!"

The farm manager crushed out his cigarette carefully and picked up his stick.

"Let's go, girls!"

"But, I thought we'd finished?"

"No! We got to do now what we'd be doing if we weren't chasing lost sheep."

He whistled up the dogs and without another word walked out into the rain. Melanie and Joan followed reluctantly.

"This is down to you, Jo," Melanie complained.

All of which adds up to why Joan d'Urquart hated sheep.

With the rain easing off they stood in the sheep pasture; the dogs holding the noisy flock in one corner.

"Every year," Harry explained, "Farmers has to choose the ewes they'll keep to breed and those they'll be rid of."

"Wha'd'y'mean, get rid of?" Joan asked, uneasily.

"Farmers don't keep animals that don't pay."

"So how do we sort them?" practical Melanie enquired.

"First selection, the ewes do for theysels."

"How?"

"Now, this is the old way I'm showing you. Grandad's way. Before x-rays and vets."

He turned to the gate at which they stood and removed a lower spar.

"D'y'see?"

The girls shook their heads.

"To get through to the next pasture the ewes has to jump that spar. Best ewes has no trouble. Old ewes, broken-footed ewes, cannot jump. Flock passes through and bad ewes are left behind."

"But they're not bad!" Joan protested,

"They're not likely to drop good lambs."

The girls exchanged sober glances. The farm manager whistled up the dogs, Tan and Lass. The flock began to move to the gate. Joan and Melanie looked for their favourites.

"This how we end up?" Melanie commented, "Jumping through hoops?"

* * * *

It was the man's voice that made Joan look up from the ewes. The stick was firmly balanced in the hedge and one by one the ewes were jumping through, urged on by the dogs. Now and again an old ewe turned away. Grandfather was counting the ewes that cleared the mark. . "Yan, tain, eddero, peddero, pitts, tayter, layter, overy, covero, dix." Without glancing down, he notched a stick and began to count again, "Yan, tain, eddero, peddero..."

She found herself chanting in chorus and the old man turned pale blue eyes upon her and smiled. An errant ewe tried to evade her, but a movement of her stick, brought Lass to control the ewe. When she looked down at herself, she saw a hessian apron over a shabby dress and muddy bare ankles in clogs.

"Jessie!" the old man cried, "Take 'em!" and she saw the counting had finished. She whistled the dogs. Lass and Tan began to move the older ewes away. They protested against being separated, bleating loudly. Beyond the hedge the flock responded. She followed her little flock, towards the stone pen in the yard as the old man secured the hedge. She tried hard not to make favourites of their stock, but she saw sisters, Isabel and Mirabelle, limping and bleating towards the house. Separated, it was more obvious they were lame. She had raised them both as caid lambs, rejected by their mothers.

Joan bolted the pen, thanked the dogs and moved towards the house. On the threshold, she kicked off her clogs and stepped into the warmth of the kitchen. Her mother was at the hob stirring a pot.

"Where's Granpa?"

"Coming."

She sat by the hob and began to clean her ankles, rubbing the mud from feet and toes.

"Mother?"

"Yes?"

"Can's not keep Isabel and Mirabelle?"

"What did you say?" asked Melanie.

CHAPTER EIGHT

Harry Armstrong was walking ahead with the older ewes and the dogs. Melanie caught Joan's plastic sack and stopped her.

"What did you say?"

"Nothing."

"Yes, you did! You said Isabel and Mirabelle."

"If I did, I meant Isobel Tunnicliffe."

"No, you didn't! And we don't have any Mirabelle. Nobody's called Mirabelle nowadays."

Joan's legs turned to jelly. To Melanie's surprise, she sat down on the grass. Harry Armstrong, turning to see where they were, stopped the dogs and came back.

"Are you alright, Joan?"

Melanie said, "She'll be alright in a minute. Just needs a breather. Wobblitis."

"Sure you're alright?"

Joan said, "Yan, tain, eddero, peddero, pitts, tayter, layter, overy, covero, dix."

Harry Armstrong laughed and Melanie was mystified.

"That's old West Country counting. Where'd you learn that?"

"Long time ago. Sheep reminded me," she lied.

"Say it again," Melanie commanded.

"Yan, tain, eddero, peddero, pitts, tayter, layter, overy, covero, dix. That's all I remember."

Harry smiled.

"My great great granddaddy counted like that. But nobody remembers it now. Was said he counted his children into church and out again, yan, tain, eddero."

Melanie gave Joan a meaningful kick.

"Come on, Jo! I want my tea."

They walked back to school in silence until Melanie said, "You went somewhere."
Joan hesitated to confess, "Yes."
Melanie was triumphant.
"Somewhere there were sheep."
"Yes."
"You knew their names. Isabel and Mirabelle."
"I raised them because their mothers rejected them. That is Jessie raised them."
Melanie stopped.
"I knew, I knew!"
"We were doing what we were doing. Sorting the ewes. The old man, my grandfather, Jacob Armstrong."
"How do you know his name?" Melanie interrupted.
"I just know. My grandfather counted them through. Yan, tain, eddero, peddero."
Melanie said, "A hundred years ago."
She looked at her friend with a mixture of envy and wonderment.
"You went time travelling at the lecture?"
Joan surrendered, nodding.
"But you won't tell me where you went?"
"I can't! Honestly I can't bear to. I'm too ashamed."
Melanie questioned, "But were you the only one went walkies?"

* * * *

Someone tapped on the bedroom door. Joan and Melanie looked at one another. If it were a prefect, there would be no knock. She would walk straight in. Staff would knock and walk in without waiting for the ashtray to be emptied and the air perfumed with lavender. Joan shrugged.
Melanie called, "Come in, Laura."
Laura bounced in to close the door and sit on Joan's bed. At opposite sides of the small table, Melanie and Joan pretended to continue working.
Laura endured the silence until she exclaimed, "What's up? Somebody dead?"

Without looking up, Melanie explained, "We're working."

Joan looked at her watch and added, "Aren't you supposed to be in your dorm? It's after nine."

"Just thought you'd want to hear about it."

Laura was opening the door when Joan and Melanie shared a glance. Joan asked, "Wha'd'we want to hear about?"

Laura hesitated, hand on the door handle.

"Thought you were working?"

"Finished!" the girls chorused and Laura returned to her perch on the bed.

"Go on then!"

"You won't believe this."

"We'll try."

Melanie suggested, "It's not Olivia Davidson's Dad and the mess funds? That's old hat."

Laura shook her head.

"We were in biology with Ma Meadows."

Joan interrupted, "We know about the human reproductive system, thank you."

"No! We were in biology when Ma Meadows appointed me Rabbit Monitor!"

"No!"

"Yes! I nearly went mad. It was so unexpected."

"Good for you!" Joan cried, encouragingly.

"We'd just finished that disgusting business with the worms when she said, 'Stop writing! Pens down! I have a most important announcement to make.'"

"Which was?"

"'I've decided to appoint Laura MaCallaman and Patricia Davidson as Rabbit Monitors.' I thought my heart was going to stop!"

Melanie said, "For the privilege of cleaning up rabbit poo and dishing out left-over lettuce, my heart would surely dance!"

"I thought it would never happen! I know she doesn't like me. But she did! She chose me! You should've seen the jealous faces."

"So, are all your lot mentally incompetent?"

"I don't know what you mean. You get to take the rabbits out and brush them."

"Cheaper than dollies, I suppose."

"You learn to cut their nails."

"Sounds heavenly!"

"If I'm lucky, I'll be there when a doe gives birth!"

"Lucky you!"

"So if I'm not here at teatimes sometimes, you know where I am."

"We'll miss you something awful, won't we, Joan?"

Joan said, "You enjoy your rabbits, Laura. Take no notice of Mel's sarcasm."

"Was she being sarcastic?"

"After all that heart-pounding emotion, did the class carry you and potty Pat round the lab on their shoulders, chanting your names?"

"No! We cleaned up the worms. Said a prayer for them. And went to French."

Melanie scoffed, "Who says prayers for worms?"

"I do!" Laura cried defiantly, "And I don't care if nobody else does."

After Laura departed, Joan sat silent, pondering.

"Now what's bugging you?"

"So out of character for Ma Meadows. She doesn't like Laura."

"If Ma Meadows went time travelling."

"D'y'think she did?"

"There was more going on at the lecture than we know. Maybe Ma Meadows went time travelling and had a change of heart?" "I find that very hard to believe."

* * * *

The girls worked quietly until Lights Out. The footsteps of the prefect checking the bedrooms faded and Joan lay sleepless in the dark.

"Mel? You awake?"

"No. This is a recording."
"I did go time travelling at the lecture."
"I know that, Jo. I can always tell when you're lying."
"I wanted to see my Dad."
"And did you?"
"Not like I wanted to."
"What happened?"
"It was the night he was supposed to take Mum and me to the London Eye. But he had to go back to Afghanistan. He had no choice. Red alert something. But I sulked and refused to speak to him. When it came to Dad leaving, I ran upstairs and wouldn't come down."

Joan's voice ached with longing and regret.
"Why didn't he go up to you?"
"Mum would've said, don't give in to her."
"How old were you?"
"Nine. That's no excuse."
"Who's looking for excuses?"
"I watched him get into the taxi. Never even looked up at the window. Never saw him again."

In the darkness, Joan cried quietly; aching with a pain that never would be extinguished. There was silence as Melanie struggled and failed to find the right words.
"That's a lot for a kid to carry."
"I thought this was my chance. To put things right. But that stupid kid couldn't or wouldn't see me. Couldn't make her hear me. Shouted in her ear. Then he went away to die."
"The kid you were then didn't understand. But your Dad would. Nothing changed between you. He wouldn't stop loving you ever."

Joan lay in darkness and tears ran into her ears; *I wanted to tell him how much I loved him. Stupid, stupid, stupid me!*

All she could contrive to say was, "Travelling back in time doesn't change anything."

Melanie was silent for a long time and then said, " Well, we have to find this Christopher Marlowe and ask him what it's all about."

* * * *

The housing estate had been built by German prisoners of war in the Forties as they waited to go home. In the decades since, the estate had deteriorated steadily and was now the least attractive in Gilsford. There was a drab sameness about the pebble-dashed houses that was depressing. Most front gardens had vanished under concrete standings for cars. The front garden wall at 118, Springfield Park Avenue had survived, but the garden was the home of an ancient motorcycle and sidecar standing on scrubby grass. The kneeling man, struggling to tighten a nut, swore as the spanner slipped. He scowled skywards as the first drops of rain fell. As he tightened the nut, the heavens opened. Pulling the tarpaulin over the motorcycle and grabbing his toolbox, he went to the front door, only to find it closed.
"Hannah!" he shouted through the letterbox, banging on the door.
A voice answered from within.
"Who is it, please?"
The man smothered a curse, saying, "Hannah, it's raining!"
"Not in here it's not!"
"Open the door, Hannah!"
"Who is it, please?"
"Hannah! Don't be so silly!"
"Have you an appointment?"
"Stop acting the fool!"
"The voice is familiar. And the sentiment."
The man surrendered.
"It's me! Your father by adoption!"
"The father by adoption that was so rude to me?"
The man struggled with his pride and then admitted.
"Yes. I'm sorry. But you started it."
"But I'm only a child. I'm allowed hissy fits. How old are you?"
The door remained closed. Rain was running down the man's neck.
"Hannah, I'm sorry. Very sorry! Please, open the door! I'm drowning out here!"
The door opened and the man tumbled into the small hallway.

The girl struggled not to laugh, saying, "You're soaking! What were you doing out there?"

"Ha-ha!" grunted the man, passing on into the kitchen. He dropped his toolbox and found something to dry his head.

"That's a tea towel, used for drying our eggshell china or the Dresden figurines," which rebuke he ignored.

Turning away into the sitting room, she suggested, "Why don't we get rid of That Thing?"

"Because it is our mechanical horse."

"I've pushed That Thing home twice this week. I know who the horse is."

"Enough! Peace! Ilium is overthrown! I flee from the conflagration!"

Coming into the sitting room, Christopher dropped to his knees and lit the paraffin heater. He watched the blue flame run along the wick and remained sitting on the floor as the room began to warm. Hannah commented, "So like a child! You really love that stove."

"It is a wonderful invention!" he sighed, "As I remember I was never warm. Chilblains big as walnuts."

The sitting room was poorly furnished. There was a table, two unmatched wooden chairs and a sad sofa that may have been rescued from a skip. By the fireplace was an old upholstered armchair. Against the wall stood a desk on which stood a laptop. The girl went to sit at the desk.

"Anything of importance on your magical machine?"

"The ether is quiet tonight. No bookings. Just nonsense."

"Yet the isle is full of noises, sounds, and sweet airs, that give delight and hurt not. Sometimes a thousand twangling instruments will hum about mine ears; and sometime voices,

that, if I then had waked after long sleep, will make me sleep again."

"I wonder who wrote that?"

Christopher stretched out on the floor, hands under his head.

"Mock my poor wit if you may, but we are free of the world for a moment's grace. Be grateful for they won't leave us alone forever."

"Just how do we eat?"

The man was silent.

"Your government will give us money."
"You mean charity? You refused when they offered."
"I cannot have them find me."
The man began to snore, pretending to sleep. Hannah sat back in her chair watching him. When he stopped snoring, she knew he was asleep. Hannah took the rug from the shabby couch and covered him. She did this because she loved him. The room was warm enough. Then Hannah went into the kitchen and ate the remainder of the cold beans in the can.

CHAPTER NINE

Under a fitful moon the two men waded across the ford holding their rifles above their heads. The water was above knee level. The short man cursed as he blundered against one of the wooden spikes set under water to deter cavalry. When they reached the farther shore they halted, water draining from boots and trousers, as if they were waiting for something. The challenge came crisply, but hushed.

"Halt! Who goes there?"

"Sergeant Springer. Private Simpson. Third Rifles."

"Advance to be recognised."

The two Riflemen advanced five paces.

"Give the password, sergeant."

"You know who us is, Taffy!" cried Springer, "Stop playing the fool!"

"Password, sergeant!"

"Sausages?"

"Wrong, sergeant!"

Springer and Simpson heard the click of rifle locks.

"Pork sausages!" cried Private Simpson.

"Pass, friend!"

The disappointment in the sentry's voice was clear.

As they passed the fire point in the willows, the sergeant threatened, "When I has some shut-eye remind me to kick your vile Welsh backside, Taffy."

"Only does what you learned us, sergeant."

In the makeshift camp in the dead ground above the river, Springer related what he had learned on the scouting trip.

"They're so cock-a-hoop, sir. You'd think war were won."

"Not yet it isn't."

"They see British Army in retreat, sir. That's what they see."

He stopped speaking, waiting for the officer to contradict him. "In orderly retreat, sergeant."

"There was more cavalry coming in both days we was there, sir. Never seen so many. Maybe ten, twelve thousand."

The Ensign countered, "Then he has to find the provender."

The sergeant continued equably, but determinedly, to get his message through.

"Them cavalry will come through our ford, sir. Followed by the foot. They will ride over us as they shall ride down the rearguard. Then, once the panic starts, sir."

He was interrupted by his officer who asked, "How do you know this, sergeant?"

"Monsewer has parked his artillery. Tarped and plugged. They has no battle to fight."

In the firelight the sergeant watched the young man's face. He saw only resolution. *He has no notion what carnage Monsewer will bring when his horses cross the river.*

"When may we expect them?" asked the Ensign.

"Reckon three days, sir. Two days forced march for me and Simpson. Marshal Massena is not with them. Still in Frogland, I expect. If they waits for him, we has, mebbes, four days."

"If we hold them three days," the Ensign decided, "Wellington will be in Lisbon. And the evacuation will be underway."

"Didn't seem river was rising, sir?"

"It has slowed," the Ensign admitted, "But three days will be enough."

The sergeant thought otherwise, but held his tongue. *Three days? Nine rifles? When Monsewer Froggy rides across the ford it'll be all over in three minutes.*

"Horse and rider 'proaching, sir!" the voice cried.

"Where from?" the Ensign shouted.

"South, sir!"

Ensign and sergeant rose to their feet.

The sentry cried again.

"'Tis the Captain, sir!"

"There's a surprise," said Sergeant Springer.

The Ensign urged, "Let's pray there's a battalion behind him."

* * * *

"Why did I ever let you talk me into joining, Mel?" Joan asked.

Her body ached. They were sitting in a rapidly emptying changing room. Joan was nursing a bruised knee. Melanie at the steamy mirror was trying to develop a new hairstyle and failing. She was now accustomed to the two Riflemen who were sitting on a bench. Wherever Joan was, one or more Riflemen was always present, but they were neither seen nor saw. She turned to Joan, brush in hand.

"Wha'd'y'think?"

"I think karate is the stupidest thing ever invented. I am sick of being thrown on the floor by these kids. I can think of better things for a Saturday."

This wasn't strictly true as the karate mats absorbed most of the violent energy.

"I didn't mean that. I meant me. My hair?"

Melanie postured and indicated her hair.

"How long is this ridiculous course?"

"Christmas."

Joan groaned.

"I don't want to throw these kids about. But they happily knock me down. And it hurts!"

"You've got to get tougher, Jo. Then, Mister Curtis'll move us from Beginners. The kids know you're a soft mark. I don't care if they're twelve years old. Rub their noses in the mat!"

Laura's face appeared round the changing room door.

"Why don't you start with her? Our own Charlie Chuckles!"

Laura entered, smiling, uncomprehending.

Joan said, "You're going to tell us something we don't know. Right?"

Laura was surprised.

"How'd you know that?"

Melanie answered, "Because you tracked us down to the gym, waited while we knocked eight bells out of one another. And when we didn't bolt from the dressing room, you came in to see if we'd climbed out the window."

"That's very clever, Mel," Laura agreed. She came to sit on the bench by Joan.

"Don't call me Mel!"

"Joan calls you Mel!"

"Joan's my friend."

Laura's sunny face clouded over.

Joan hastened to say, "And you're my friend, Laura!"

"If you're my friend and Mel is your friend, doesn't that make Mel nearly my friend?"

Melanie said, "Would you like me to throw you to the floor, kneel on you, twist your arm up your back until you scream for mercy?"

Laura paled and said, "No, Mel, please, no!"

"Then tell us what you're dying to tell us!"

"Norma, that's Ma Savage's housekeeper."

"We know that!" interrupted an impatient Melanie.

"Well, she's got awful lumbago in her knee again. It comes on with the weather. The pain, she says, is excruciating."

"Wow! That's quite a word for a kid like you."

"It's what Norma said."

"Norma has a pain in the knee? While you are a pain in the posterior. You, Laura, are excruciatingly irritating!"

Joan begged, "Laura, please, just tell us what you think we should know!"

"Because of her knee, Norma let me take the letters to the post box."

"Go on!"

"She says I'm a treasure."

"People bury treasure," Melanie threatened.

"Remember Ma Savage wasn't going to pay Mister Marlowe?"

"She's changed her mind!" Joan rejoiced.

Melanie queried, "You've posted off the letter?"

"Yes."

"I'm glad," Melanie continued, "I suspect they really need that money."

"There's more," Laura chirped.

"What?"

"I know where they live."

Joan and Melanie looked to one another in wonderment.

"We think, when we look at her pretty dolly face and her sweet girlie curls...."

"Thank you!" Laura interrupted, "You've never said anything nice to me before, Mel."

Melanie pressed on, "You might think Laura's another cud-chewing bovine destined to live out a pointless existence as a life-sized brain-dead mannequin."

"You might," Joan agreed.

"But behind the mascara and lipstick."

"I don't have any mascara and lipstick," Laura protested.

"There is a quick-witted, intelligent, funny human being whom I rejoice to call friend!"

Laura complained, "Why are you always making fun of me?"

Melanie seized her in a crushing embrace and swung her round and round, shouting joyously, "She knows where he lives, she knows where he lives!"

Joan, alarmed, cried, "Don't throw her on the floor!"

* * * *

Miss Savage said, "If you give an undertaking that you will accept a service commission on successful completion of your degree, the Ministry of Defence may offer you a scholarship for the duration of your university course."

Sandra Collins sat silent in the chair, fingers of both hands fiddling with the chair arms.

"You're predicted to do well in your A Levels. I've no doubt your university career will be successful. Your family are service people."

Miss Savage stopped speaking because something remarkable happened. In one swirling movement, she found herself sitting on a wooden chair in a cellar stinking of damp and alcohol. With a tremor of panic, she recognised her surroundings. She knew when she looked down what she would see, stained hessian apron, shabby dress and bare feet.

"Look at me, Nell!"

She raised frightened eyes to see four men. Todd, the alehouse keeper, she recognised. The function of the two brutish men in doublet and hose was obvious. But, what terrified her were the eyes of the short man in expensive clothes. His jewellery caught the candlelight. She saw in his eyes that he would maim, cripple, blind or kill anyone who stood in his path without a second thought. She struggled not to soil herself.

"You went to the upper chamber bearing the reckoning from our admirable host, Todd?"

"Yes, milord."

"I know you to be a good girl. A truthful girl. A girl who would cry out against heresy."

"Yes, milord. On my soul, I would!"

"Be careful what you answer. Let it be the truth."

"Yes, milord."

She was trembling as she spoke and recoiled when the gentleman bent to brush back her hair. He smiled at her terror.

"Did you meet anyone on the stairs as you ascended to the upper chamber?"

"No, milord."

"Did you see anyone, man or woman, on the upper landing?"

"No, milord!"

In the farther darkness of her mind, a voice screamed, *What're you doing? Why're you lying? Tell him the truth! It's not too late! Tell him what you saw! When he finds the truth he will kill you!*

"You saw no one?"

"No one, milord."

"Then what did you do?"

"I opened the chamber door to present the reckoning."

The girl stopped.

"Continue!"

"I found a dead man on the floor."

"Was there anyone else in the room?"

"No, milord."

"Did you know the dead man?"

"No, milord. But his mother would not have recognised him."

"How so?"

"His face was drownded in blood."

"How was he killed?"

"Don't know, milord."

The gentleman stared at Nell for an eternity. From below filtered the racket of the alehouse. A man shouted. A woman screamed. Uproar exploded. The landlord fidgeted. The gentleman nodded. Todd bowed and left the room. The gentleman never took his eyes from Nell.

"When I find you have lied, my pretty Nell, I will cut you piece from piece until finally, I will cut off your head. Better to tell me the truth now. You saw no one, but the dead man?"

"No one, milord, I swear!"

The gentleman turned and nodded to his bodyguards. One man opened the door and preceded the gentleman to the stairs, his comrade following behind. Nell began to weep as much from relief as terror.

* * * *

Sandra Collins said, "Are you alright, Miss?"

"We'll continue this discussion on another occasion," said the Headmistress.

When Sandra had departed, Miss Savage went into her washroom to refresh her face. She looked in the mirror. The face of frightened Nell who worked in an Elizabethan alehouse stared back at her.

Miss Savage said aloud, "What if I don't come back?"

Nell said nothing.

* * * *

Heads were raised as the three girls tumbled into the computer room. In this area, humans did not converse with humans, but with machines. Appearing duly chastened, the trio sought and found an empty carrel. Laura borrowed two extra chairs.

"What now?" asked Laura.

"Google," said Joan.

A prefect appeared at Melanie's shoulder.
"What are you researching?"
Melanie said, "Geography. Wiltshire."
"You haven't signed in."
"Sorry, Barrett. I'll do it now, shall I?"
"That's the idea."

When Melanie returned to the carrel, Gilsford, Wiltshire, was on screen and Joan was searching for the district of Springfield at Laura's direction.

"Here we are!"

Springfield Park Avenue appeared as the main artery of Springfield.

"What number?"
"A hundred and eighteen."

At street level the drabness of the estate became clear. The girls' spirits drooped. Too many of the households appeared to have dismantled one or more vehicles on what must once have been a front garden. As they passed along the avenue, they paused at a house where a burnt-out caravan adorned the frontage.

Laura spoke for the trio when she commented, "Wouldn't want to live there."

"Which side is a hundred and eighteen on?"
"No idea,"

The trio exchanged glances.

"How do we find the house?" asked Joan.

Laura suggested, "Start at one end and count along?"

"How do we know which end to start counting?"

Silence.

Melanie said, "We find the motorbike."

In an hour's painstaking search of Springfield Park Avenue they found five motorcycles. But not one with a sidecar. The trio struggled to hide their disappointment.

Joan put up a map of England and they studied it.

Laura regretted, "We're a long way from Wiltshire."

"You're thinking of us going there? To Gilsford?"

"Isn't that what we need to do? Find Christopher?"

Melanie offered, "We're not far away. Only a bus ride."

"Are we looking at the same map?" queried Joan.
"I don't mean from school. We're just over the border in Berkshire."

Laura asked, "Which we is that?"

"My family. From home, I would take a bus to Gilsford."

Laura squealed so loudly the prefect stood up and launched an icy glare. Three heads were bowed in shame.

Joan whispered, "Do you think your revered mother could be persuaded to invite two jolly chums to visit on a weekend or Half Term?"

"I reckon she's guilty enough."

"Then it's agreed? We pay a visit to Christopher Marlowe, man of mystery."

"And gorgeous," added Laura.

The prefect ushered the trio to the door for laughing.

But Melanie's words lingered, disturbing echoes for Joan.

"I reckon she's guilty enough."

She heard again the girl, Hannah, on the steps of the Lodging.

"What is this dump? An orphanage?"

"Boarding school for Army brats."

"Same thing. Parents dump unwanted kids in boarding schools."

"So you say."

"You ever noticed boarding school is not an anagram for orphanage?"

"No," Joan said, completely confused.

"That's so as to fool you."

CHAPTER TEN

The Rifleman held the bridle of the belathered horse as the officer dismounted. The Ensign saluted. Sergeant Springer called, "Atten-shun! Riflemen, pre-pare to present arms! Riflemen, pre-sent arms!" With discipline and precision, four Riflemen paid due courtesy to the Captain of Cavalry.

"These scarecrows are posturing as his Majesty's Riflemen, sergeant?"

Springer stiffened at the insult and recited, "Private Simpson on observation at the ford, sir. Private Evans on observation to our rear, sir. Private Flanagan at your horse, sir. All present or correct, sir."

Simpson in a hole in the ground, besieged by flies. Evans, suffering vertigo, precariously wedged in the upper limbs of a tree. Flanagan, fearful of horses, hanging on to the Captain's horse.

"This man is bareheaded. Where's your shako, private?"

"Lost in a wrestling match with a Froggie, sir."

The Ensign apologised, "We haven't seen a quartermaster for some months, sir."

"No excuse for slackness, sir," decided the Captain, "Your corporal has no backside to his trousers."

Which was not strictly true and unfair, as the corporal had exchanged trousers unwillingly with his sergeant. The inspection of the squad was not a success.

The Ensign offered, "You wish to inspect rifles, sir?"

"Indeed, I do, sir!"

The Bakers were immaculate. Spare flints and patches were produced from the heel box. Cartridge boxes were full and dry. Needle-point bayonets, sharp as razors. All was in order, which disappointed the Captain.

When the Riflemen were dismissed they vanished silently, which was not their usual custom. The Corporal and Rifleman Flanagan accepted the care of the Captain's horse.

"A sullen bunch," judged the Captain.

"I have not found them so, sir."

The Captain looked hard at the young officer.

"How long have you been in Portugal, sir?"

"Since April, sir."

"Who bought your commission?"

"My father."

"Who is?"

"A country parson, sir."

"He couldn't afford a decent regiment?"

"The Rifles are a decent regiment, sir."

The icy silence startled the young man.

"On the contrary, they are not, sir. They are a new-fangled notion. Rifles? Nothing can better the musket."

The Ensign rebelled despite the inner voice that counselled caution.

"The musket scarce reaches a hundred yards, sir. A good Rifleman will kill at thrice that range."

The captain replied, "The Rifles do not stand in the line. They do not wear the red and white. They do not bear the enemy's volleys. They shoot from hiding and run away. Like Americans."

The Captain was red in the face and his voice had taken on a near-hysterical tone. He wiped away spittle as he repeated, "They shoot and run away, sir. Like Americans."

"Were you in America, sir?" the Ensign offered.

"Shall we withdraw somewhere private?"

They sat in the Ensign's tent. The Captain on the chair, the young officer on his ankles.

"You're too close to these men, sir."

"I am, sir?"

"I do not believe you may rely upon them."

"During the retreat they have been very steady, sir."

"Doubtless senior officers were close at hand."

The Ensign was silent.

"Have you yet flogged a man?"

Shocked, the Ensign cried, "No, sir! Never!"

"From the dumb insolence I have perceived today, sir, I would find reason to flog at least one of them."

"Dumb insolence?"

"We shall talk later, sir."

The Ensign rose, saying "Yes, sir."

"Before you go, what have you to drink?"

Bewildered, the Ensign faltered, "To drink, sir? Water."

"Fetch me my saddlebags."

"Yes, sir."

The Ensign left the tent to find Sergeant Springer in attendance.

"Is there a battalion behind him, sir?"

"The captain's asking for his saddlebags?"

The sergeant grimaced and mimed drinking a glass of spirits.

All this Joan Flete d'Urquart observed as she stood at the Ensign's shoulder. But no one took notice of her presence.

"Rifles?" she said aloud, but no one was listening, "They're Riflemen!"

* * * *

Gillian Meadows was standing in the checkout queue, ignoring the woman who was trying to enlist her support in complaining how slowly the queue was moving. To her relief, the woman turned to the customer in front of her. Then, with a sudden lurch, Gillian Meadows was no longer in a queue holding a wire basket. She was standing by a fresh graveside.

It was raining and the wind was cold. By these elements, Gillian Meadows knew it was not a dream. Her childhood family stood about the grave. An elderly clergyman paused to clean the rain from his spectacles before continuing the burial service. Her mother and father, sister and brothers were clustered together. She saw her childish self struggle to escape her mother's grasp.

As Gillian Meadows walked around the grave, she saw Eleanor's death had struck the family a grievous blow. Her weeping mother was old and fragile; her father pale and drawn. Her siblings wavered between grief and bewilderment. The child Gillian bit her mother's hand to free her own. The service completed, the family dropped soil that turned to mud on the little coffin. Her childhood self threw a pebble that bounced sharply off the wooden lid. No one seemed to notice this spiteful action. As the family turned away, her childhood self smiled sweetly at Gillian Meadows.

"She can see me," she cried aloud, "She knows I'm here!"

Miss Meadows stood alone, looking down into the grave where muddy rain gathered in puddles on and about the little pink box painted with cherubs. A large teddy bear sat on the coffin lid awaiting the darkness the gravediggers would bring. She was shocked when a voice disturbed her meditation.

"You got away scot-free with that one, sweetling," said the short man standing at her side. A tall man flanked her on the left. Both men were oddly attired in full-length transparent pink plastic raincoats and pixie hoods tied neatly in a bow beneath the chin. She suddenly felt faint and may have fallen into the grave, but the tall man put a strong arm about her. He lifted her away from the muddy edge.

The short man, sharp-featured, bearded, eyes unreadable, produced an umbrella. The second man opened and held it over Miss Meadows' head. The rain beat a sharp tattoo on the fabric.

Struggling to retain some measure of calm, Miss Meadows asked, "Are you the police?"

Without waiting for an answer, she continued, "Yes, I killed her. I'm glad to have it over and done with. Her death has haunted me all my life. I won't make any trouble."

The rain drummed louder on the umbrella and tumbled from the pixie hoods.

The short man asked, "Do we look like the police?"

He plucked up and dropped a muddy portion of soil. The teddy bear fell over. He wiped his fingers on the grass.

"Do you mean you're not the police?"

The tall man made a rumbling noise that may have been laughter or bronchitis.

"If you're not the police, then?"

She was interrupted by the short man who asked, "How many more souls have you sent to judgement without anyone noticing? If that's not a impertinent question."

Miss Meadows was visibly shaken.

"Jealousy of my baby sister may have temporarily deranged my mind, but...."

The tall man rumbled again and his companion interrupted, "Our experience in these matters suggests if a lady or gentleman escapes detection of a first murder, she or he tends to repeat the crime."

Miss Meadows tried to free herself from the tall man's embrace, but failed. She noted the umbrella advertised Campari and Soda the Nation's Super Summertime Drink.

"If you are not...."

Again to be interrupted by the short man.

"I do apologise, Miss Meadows! I only asked out of professional curiosity. Murder is a particular interest of mine."

The unexceptional manner in which he made this statement chilled Gillian Meadows' blood.

"However, no matter! We're only interested in whether you can assist us in finding a man."

"I teach in a girls school. I have very little contact with men."

"A particular man."

Miss Meadows shook her head slowly.

"I rarely come into contact with tradesmen."

"A visiting lecturer, perhaps?"

Miss Savage's words rang clearly in Miss Meadows' head. *This evening has been lamentable! Time travel, indeed! That man and his daughter have never at any time visited the Randall! Do I make myself clear?*

"Oh, yes! There was a retired Merchant Navy captain. Came recently to lecture on knots. A big success with the girls! They asked him to come again!"

Not police? Private detectives? How much do these men know?

"We're looking for a younger man? Dark-haired, bearded?"

"Ah, I may well have met your man! An Italian gentleman came last term to lecture on the Renaissance! A very good speaker!"

* * * *

Then suddenly, as if a telephone connection had been broken, Miss Meadows found herself at the checkout with two discounted mangoes, one pack of spicy chicken wings, two tins of rice pudding, one kipper fillet in a bag, a chicken korma, four bananas and four fruit yoghurts.

"Well," asked the checkout operator, "Gona put ya stuff on the belt or just stand there admiring me hair do?"

The queue laughed. Miss Meadows smiled and the till operator was pleased with her banter. But Gillian Meadows could not dispel the image of two men, oddly attired in transparent pink plastic raincoats and pixie hoods. She knew she would see them again.

* * * *

"They were Riflemen," Joan explained, "Which is why I suppose I was there."

The girls lay in the familiar darkness of Lights Out. Footsteps receded in the corridor. A fretful moon offered a pale face at the window.

"Though I don't know why."

"Does there have to be a reason?" Melanie questioned.

"Then it's all rather pointless, isn't it? Mystery Tours by Time Travel. Book now! Dissatisfaction guaranteed!"

"Tell me more."

"A squad of eight riflemen. Baker rifles, not muskets. An Ensign not much older than you and me. Everyone's bigger than him, but they all have to salute the officer. The Sergeant and his Ensign look like father and son. And a rather unpleasant Captain arrived to make life miserable."

Melanie interrupted, "All Captains are unpleasant. They've failed their majority and take it out on the men."

"Not my Dad!" Joan protested, "He loved his men. Sometimes I think he...."

Interrupted by Melanie who said, "This is the nineteenth century. Joan. They bought their commissions. If they had money they didn't have to be any good at soldiering."

"The Sergeant knows what he's doing."

"What else did you learn?"

"They're in Portugal. Guarding a river crossing. Army's in retreat. The French are advancing."

"It's the Peninsular War. Us against Napoleon. Wellington and Nelson. We can look it up first chance we get."

They lay silent as the images replayed in Joan's head. The water pipes burbled and grumbled in the walls.

Melanie said, "If you want to know. I'm jealous of you time travelling."

Joan laughed, "Don't be, Mel! It's just random. I don't control it. There's only one thing I'd do, if I did."

Melanie was silent. If Joan was going to say something important she didn't need coaxing.

"I was nine years old! A stupid, spoilt kid. I hate her! She let him go without a kiss. Without saying, I love you. I must've hurt him so much. But I didn't know he was going to be killed."

Melanie was silent, struggling not to weep for her friend and failing.

"Tore up all the photographs. My mother didn't understand. She was very angry. But so was I!"

To Melanie her friend's pain was almost unbearable, awakening the agony of countless partings from her own father; the constant unspoken fear of all military families. Will he come back this time?

"If I controlled this time travelling, I'd go to that time and place where my Dad died. I wouldn't let him die. I'd make sure the bullet or whatever missed him. Then I'd bring him home to Mum and I'd never let him go again."

There was nothing Melanie could say.

"If I get the chance, that's what I'll do. Otherwise none of this time travelling makes any sense."

The Crimea clock struck twelve before either of the girls fell asleep. The Rifleman outside the bedroom door eased from foot to foot as the chimes sounded.

CHAPTER ELEVEN

Hannah jumped down from the 23 bus at the end of Springfield Park Avenue and turned to assist the heavily pregnant young woman wavering on the platform. She handed her down to the pavement and with the conductor, unloaded the buggie wherein sat a chubby child solemnly regarding the world. The bus drew away as the conductor called cheerfully, "Toodle-oo, ladies!" Hannah responded with a smile and a wave.

As the pregnant young mother took the buggie handle, Hannah asked, "How long now?"

The young woman said ruefully, "Couldn't be soon enough!"

Hannah took the carrier bag from her, despite protest. She indicated her own bag of library books.

"Balances me nicely."

They walked in a companionable silence until the young woman asked, "You the girl with the motorbike and sidecar?"

"Yes. Hannah. Live with me Dad."

"Mira. You wouldn't believe me Mam stuck me with Mirabelle?"

Hannah didn't know what to say, so she tried, "Lovely old-fashioned name. Probably family."

Mira asked, "D'y'know any longer road than this?"

Hannah agreed, "It's a bit of a slog."

"D'y'know I'm trudging along one day when I hear a drumming noise?"

Hannah indicated interest.

"When I looked round, it was raining, mebbes fifty yards behind me. Next thing I know, it caught up with me and I'm dripping wet."

"Never!"

"Fact!"

The young woman stopped. Hannah glanced behind half-expecting to see rain advancing on the pavement. The young woman knelt down to tuck in the baby who immediately shook off the cover.

"Don't look now," she said, quietly, "But that's a Council car and van. Trouble with a capital T!"

Hannah knelt down and the baby chuckled at the absurdities of life. But he was game for a game. He immediately threw out the teddy bear to the pavement. Hannah fielded the teddy. The baby threw out a pink mouse from his secret store.

"Outside yours," the young mother judged.

Hannah groaned.

"I can't trust him to do anything."

There were three men on the pavement. A fat man in a shiny suit; a skinny teenager and grey-haired man in overalls. A tall man came out from the open gateway with a clipboard in his hand. He shook his head.

"Next, they'll force the door."

"They wouldn't dare!"

"They will!"

Hannah stood up and started walking. The young mother followed, saying, "Don't stop! Keep walking!"

As they approached number one hundred and eighteen the next-door neighbour appeared; Mr. Stanley, a small man behind a large moustache and a pipe welded to his jaw.

"Why don't yi just bog off and leave people alone? They's a decent couple! Leave people alone!"

The man with the clipboard replied loudly, "We are here on Council business! I'd be glad if you'd keep your opinions to yourself, sir!"

His voice faltered as Mr. Stanley's two large sons appeared.

"Don't you talk to me Da like that! Another word and ah'll deck yi!"

"Don't you threaten me, sir! I am a compliance officer and I will..."

The compliance officer and his entourage retreated swiftly to the centre of the road as the younger Stanley advanced on to the pavement.

"My colleagues are taking note of your behaviour, sir!"
Brother joined brother.
"Come on then! Wi'll deck the lot of yis!"
The invitation to have their facial features restyled, however tempting, was not accepted, but the commotion was attracting attention in the Avenue.

Neighbours were appearing on their concrete car stands. Out of nowhere appeared a group of loud teenagers who began to rock the Council van, singing, "Come out, come out, whoever you are!" The driver appeared alarmed as the van began to rock. He blew the horn vigorously. The teenagers cheered and redoubled their efforts to overturn the van. The driver opened his door and fell out. The compliance officer complied.

"All right, all right! If that's how you wish to behave! But we will return! I assure you!"

To jeers and laughter, the Council crew scrambled to their vehicles. To a discordant hammering on car bonnet and van flanks, Authority disappeared at speed. The crowd dispersed as rapidly as they had assembled. Hannah and Mira stood alone on the pavement by number one hundred and eighteen, Springfield Park Avenue.

"I am amazed!" cried Hannah, "That they'd do that for us!"
Mira laughed.
"They didn't do it for you. We won't have nobody messed about in Springfield."
Hannah was suitably humbled.
"Where's your Dad then?"
"Probably hiding in the airing cupboard."
Mira laughed.
"Catch ya later!"

* * * *

The Captain filled the silver cup from the flask. He gestured vaguely as if to invite the Ensign to drink and then emptied the cup in one swallow. The Captain was relaxed on the Ensign's camp bed and the young man sat on the chair. He had tried twice to excuse himself to walk the rounds and failed. He knew Sergeant Springer would've done duty in his place. The Captain continued to denounce every senior officer whom he complained, failed to promote him on merit alone. The Ensign wisely did not ask why he had not purchased his majority. The Captain would've had to admit the regiment refused his money.

The Captain was steadily becoming drunker. The Ensign struggled to hide his disgust as his senior officer continued to abuse the Duke of Wellington.

"I tell you, boy, it'll soon be every man for himself. The artillery is stuck at that damn river. Foot and cavalry too. I've never seen such incompetence! He can't leave his guns for Massena. But he'll be lucky to see half across that flood. He'll be disgraced! And I tell you something else, boy! He won't rescue the foot neither. I've been in Lisbon. Seen with me own eyes! There's not enough ships to carry a division! Never mind an army! You can forget an evacuation."

The Captain refilled the silver cup and drank it down. The Ensign regarded him with barely concealed contempt.

"What're you thinking, boy? Have I got some magical solution up my sleeve? You're thinking a chap of my experience must have an answer! Well, I have!"

The Ensign was surprised.

"You have, sir?"

"I have, indeed, sir!"

The Ensign awaited the answer to Wellington's dilemma.

"Spain, sir!"

The Ensign considered the problem.

"We can't transport the whole Army to Spain. What purpose would that serve?"

"Who said anything about the Army? When it's every man for himself, boy, it's onto a good horse and tally-ho for Spain! Trek to Bilboa! Press gold into an eager hand and we're on our way home to jolly old England! Or do you want to rot in a French prison?"

The Ensign could barely conceal his anger. He rose to his feet, proclaiming, "I must walk the posts, sir."

He left the tent without waiting for permission.

In the cool darkness, he swore aloud until he ran out of breath and curses. At his elbow, Sergeant Springer commented, "Take it, there's no battalion behind him, sir?"

"Wellington has more to worry about than us, sergeant."

They walked towards the river together.

"Mays I speak, sir?"

"You may not blackguard senior officers, sergeant."

"Things may not be half so bad as the captain says, sir. He's panicking like my Aunt Fanny. I'd put my money, if I had any, on old Nosey. Panicking is not his game."

The Ensign felt strangely comforted by his sergeant's speech.

"We shall continue to do our duty, sergeant."

"Amen to that, sir!"

And I'll do my best to stop you getting us all killed, sir.

* * * *

Hannah was wrong. Christopher was not hiding in the airing cupboard. He was lying under the front window of the sitting room where anyone who looked in the window would not see him. As the house was designed on the non-parlour system anyone who troubled to look in from the back garden would have seen him lying under the front window. If the compliance officer had peer in through the back window, he must've assumed what he saw was a bundle of rags.

Christopher Marlowe was pretending to be asleep, snoring loudly. Hannah kicked him smartly in the backside.

"Ow! Was that necessary, my sweeting?"

"I enjoyed it."

Christopher climbed sourly to his feet.

"How did I take on board such a cruel daughter?"

"How did I get stuck with a cowardy custard for a father?"

He regarded her soberly.

"I am not a coward. A custard does not frighten me. But I am wary of spilling my blood unnecessarily. As I constantly remind you, there are men who want me dead."

"If I believed you."

Christopher followed her into the kitchen. Hannah measured water into the kettle and set it to boil.

"Let's pretend I believe you. That there are evil men set upon finding and killing you. Would they come disguised as the Council? By van and car in broad daylight?"

When Christopher attempted to interrupt, Hannah raised a stern finger and continued.

"Why didn't they bring the Gilsford Silver Band as well?"

Christopher persisted, "There are men searching to kill me. When they find me, they'll kill you too."

"Well, today they kicked up such a row a minor riot erupted!"

Hannah regarded her adopted father sadly. The kettle whistled mournfully.

"Don't you think it's time we got some help for you?"

"Incarcerated, I am an easier target."

Hannah sighed and shook her head.

"There's medication can help you."

Impulsively, she kissed his cheek and stroked the hair from his brow. Stirring two mugs of coffee, she asked, "Why didn't you answer the door and just show them the cheque from that school? You could've signed over the cheque and they'd've been satisfied we'd paid something off the arrears?"

Christopher shrugged and sipped hot coffee.

"Instead you hid."

Embarrassed, he avoided her gaze.

"If old man Stanley and his pet gorillas hadn't interfered, they would've bust in the front door and taken my lapdog, thank you!"

Her father brightened up.

"Then I must go and thank him for his kindness."

"I wouldn't, if I were you."

"Why not? It would be discourteous otherwise."

"He hasn't forgiven you for burning the piano he gave you."

"I didn't know it was his deceased wife's instrument."

"He thought you were a musician and would treasure it. He didn't recognise you as a vandal."

"We needed to keep warm."

"Speaking of which. That front door is one of only two doors still standing in this house. I'd rather they didn't find that out before we're gone."

Hannah finished her coffee and nudged her father.

"Come on! Bring your guitar. We'll do the rent office first. Then the Haymarket. I'll be your skinny dog on a string."

* * * *

Melanie and Joan banged heads together as Joan scrolled down the history of the Peninsular War. Between the two friends,

Laura struggled for a view of the screen

"Slow down, slow down!" Melanie demanded, "I can't keep up."

The screen slowed and peace reigned. Two heads, ear to ear, viewed the screen, with Laura's breath disturbing their hair as a breeze through a willow coppice. When they finished reading, they stared at one another in disbelief.

"That boy, the Ensign, knows nothing!"

"And the captain's a liar."

"I didn't understand it," Laura complained.

Joan explained, "Wellington is pulling off the cleverest trick ever. The Army is retreating into the peninsula.

"Think of a sock. No way out."

"Only way to evacuate the Army is from Lisbon. At the toe of the sock. But he hasn't the ships."

"French think they're on a winner. Wellington pretends to panic. Slows down the artillery because the French are not coming fast enough."

"But it's all a trick. For two years he's built a line of strong fortifications across the peninsula."

"All in secret."

"Wow!" cried Laura, "Old Wellie Boots doesn't look all that bright in his pictures."

"The soldiers and guns will suddenly vanish."

"And the French will be in real trouble, a long way from home."

"But it's gone wrong. The artillery is snagged. That ford has got to be held to save the Army!"

"That boy and his men are going to die!" mourned Joan.

Laura suggested, "Don't let's read any more until we find out what happened."

"Or what will happen," decided Melanie.

* * * *

For one moment, Mary Savage believed she was drowning, struggling for breath. Then she realised she was drowning in people, a great swirling mob of boisterous, stinking, laughing men and women dressed to take part in some Hollywood hysterical drama. When she looked down, she saw a tidy ankle length brown dress and around her shoulders a green shawl. Her feet were bare. The crowd roared with laughter; her neighbours turning amused mouthfuls of broken teeth upon her, wiping eyes bubbling with tears of mirth. Then, just as abruptly, the mob jeered and booed and Mary Savage knew where she was.

She was watching Christopher Marlowe's The Jew of Malta played by the Admiral's Men at The Theatre. She was in the pit with the groundlings while richer patrons filled the boxes about the stage. Sitting on stools on stage were three well-dressed gentlemen, not actors, but the audience among the action. Mary Savage surrendered to the drama and laughed, jeered and booed with her fellow groundlings. From time to time, an actor attired as the Devil with horns, dressed in a flaming red costume complete with spiked tail, entered to cries of fear and open unease among the audience. He would appear suddenly in a box with the gentry, among the groundlings and even sitting with the gentlemen on stage. His appearances, Mary assumed, symbolised forthcoming disaster; a premonition of tragedy.

The Devil finally came to rest, sitting on the edge of the stage, searching among the groundlings with a satanic mocking smile. The groundlings moved uneasily to avoid his gaze as if the Devil himself sat in judgement on them. He beckoned a young girl to him. Her mother threw a shawl over the child and moved as far away as she could. The Devil laughed and a chill ran down Mary's spine.

Then his eye fell upon her. She struggled to breath and was consumed by unnameable terror. She fought her way into the street to make her way home to Deptford where Nell lived and worked. From time to time, she saw the Devil following behind. As the latch of the alehouse door lifted, she breathed a sigh of relief. She pushed through the busy bar, ignoring patrons who called to her. In the passage beyond, Mary Savage paused outside the parlour door.

* * * *

Joan should've recognised something was wrong when Melanie took out a packet of cigarettes. Joan refused. Melanie lit one for herself. They were sitting on the grass in a quiet corner between the squash court buildings. Joan presumed that was why Melanie had suggested it as a good place to talk. Joan had only one topic in mind.
"When d'y'think your Mum can invite us for a weekend?"
Melanie blew a smoke ring and studied her nails.
"The sooner she does, the sooner we can surprise Christopher."
"I haven't asked her."
Joan was shocked.
"Why not?"
"Tina says I'm spending too much time with you. And Laura."
Joan felt the first inkling of unease.
"What's it got to do with her?"
"It's not Tina. It's the Angels."
"I don't understand."
Melanie studied the ash on her cigarette.
"They want me to drop you."
The iron words rang sharply.
"Or?"
"They'll drop me."
Joan struggled to speak calmly.
"Is it a difficult decision to make?"
"You don't understand, Jo."
Joan bit down a rising anger.
"Then explain it to me. In simple words. I'm a simple girl."
Melanie hesitated and then said, "My mother would be very upset if the Angels dropped me."
"What's it got to do with her?"
"Most women in executive positions belong to the D.A."

"What's D.A.?"

"Dangerous Angels."

"You're kidding? More like Desperate Angels!"

"Scoff away! Whatever career I choose the Angels will help me."

"A secret society? Like the Masons?"

"They don't advertise. They choose the best."

Joan tried to laugh, but didn't succeed.

"So I'm not the best?"

"You turned them down, Jo. They don't ask twice."

Joan couldn't find an answer.

"In the best universities you will always find D.A. members. They have influence. They promote each other. Most women M.P.s, television presenters, business executives are Dangerous Angels."

"I thought 'Angels' was pretty tacky. But Dangerous Angels, that's really gross!"

"Think it started as Angels. Then they added Dangerous. Some sort of joke."

"A Mafia for women?"

"Why not? Men have their old boy networks. Women must stick together. Help each other."

"Dump their friends?"

Melanie pinched the ash from her cigarette and dropped it.

"I've never really liked smoking. But they smoke."

"So you're not going to help us find Christopher Marlowe?"

"I'm moving in with Natalie. She's been a single since Beatrice moved to Switzerland."

"What about your stuff?"

"I've moved it."

"Then there wasn't any decision to make, was there?"

Melanie rose, saying, "I'm sorry. I really am. But you can see why."

Joan bit back an angry response. Melanie vanished. Joan couldn't restrain her tears and wept openly. She heard her lamentation echoing off the brick walls around her. The pain in her chest was beyond bearing. *I love Melanie. How stupid! If this is love it hurts too much.*

CHAPTER TWELVE

Fortunately, no one saw Joan weep and when she was dry of tears, she cleaned her face with spit and a handkerchief. Randall girls don't wear tearstained faces. She picked up Melanie's cigarette and dropped it into her shoulder bag. It was foolish of Melanie to leave it lying in open sight. Smoking was a capital offence at Randall. Which was why some older girls persisted in the pernicious habit. Randall girls were expected to face up to challenges and defy oppression. If they had been prohibited from shaving their heads . . .

When she reached their empty room, Joan was oddly disappointed. In some rose-tinted corner of her mind she hoped Melanie had changed her mind and rushed off to restore the room. She was praying to walk in and find a shamefaced Melanie putting her Rough Teds back to glower from the windowsill.

"I'm sorry. I realised I didn't want to leave you. Forgiven, Jo?"

She was ready to say, "Nothing to forgive, Mel. I'll put the Nice Teds back, shall I?"

They would work together happily and the absurd notion of Melanie moving out would never again be mentioned. The realisation that they belonged together would bind them closer still. Always they would bring their hot cocoa from the kitchen, hugging the mugs, happier than ever to share this quiet time together, sitting at the open window to watch the summer bats hunt the Lesser Quadrangle or watch the blackness of the Quad turn white with the first slow drift of winter snow. Together, they would turn all Melanie's creatures to regard the window, guard the door or worship any of their latest artistic creations.

It was unbearably empty without Melanie, without her sprawling untidiness. Gone were all her teddies, chickens, dogs, mice, and the blue duck that had perched on or clung to every conceivable edge or ledge. All gone. Suddenly, she realised how accustomed she was to their idiot faces, the Rough Teds, the Nice Teds, Charlie Chuckles the Duckle, Cat-Cat, so fat they named him twice and Little Kit, the smallest, most timid of all the gang who lived behind the radiator valve.

Suddenly, it was all too much for Joan. She dropped to her knees and crawled under the bed for sanctuary. She lay on her back, staring at the underside of the mattress. With her shoulder against the wall, she was as far away from the world as she could contrive. At the loss of Calais, the greatest jewel in the English Crown, Queen Mary declared when she was dead they would find Calais engraved on her heart. The Queen then turned her face to the wall and died. Joan tried lying to face the wall, but found it uncomfortable. It all seemed so silly, but then, heart-broken, she wept again. Someone knocked on the door. Joan lay still and silent. To her annoyance the door opened and someone entered.

* * * *

In the passage of the alehouse, Mary Savage hesitated. She struggled to remain calm. Her heart was racing.

She said aloud, "I am the Headmistress of Randall's School. I am fifty-five years old. I must hold to that. This is another reality."

A serving girl passing with her tray of ale mugs looked at her curiously.

"Get about your business, girl!"

The girl scurried off.

"I am also the girl Nell who lives and works in the Bull's Head, Deptford. In the fifteen nineties. This cannot be, yet I find everything familiar."

A burst of laughter from the noisy bar was truly familiar to the Headmistress of Randall's who had never in her ordered life entered a public house.

Taking a deep breath, she opened the parlour door and screamed at the Devil sitting in Todd's chair. A man pulled her into the room and silenced her with a blow that sent her sprawling to the floor. As she struggled to her feet, Mary Nell saw it wasn't the Devil. Todd's face was running with blood and he was tied to the chair. He hung unconscious on his bonds.

"Todd, my heart, what have they done to you?"

There were two men in the parlour, the tall man and the short man.

She cried out to them, "Why have you done this? What harm has Todd ever done you?"

The taller man struck her again with force enough to send her to the wall. She stayed on her feet.

"Why? What can you want from Todd?"

He would have hit her again, but the short man said, "Desist! There is something adrift with this woman. Bring her into the light."

She was brought forward where the weasel-faced short man lifted the candle to study her face. Mary Nell could also study him. He studied her face closely, examined her teeth, lifted up into candlelight her foot to examine broken nails and hard calloused yellow soles.

The taller man with the scarred face asked, "What do you look for, master?"

Studying her strong, hard-palmed hands and bitten nails, the Weasel answered without looking up, "A different woman."

Scarface was puzzled.

"This is Nell, no doubt. I swears to it! Knows her well."

"This is Nell, but more than our Nell. Do not contrive to understand for I do not either."

Returning the candle to the table, he asked, "Where would you go to purchase the best of Belfast linen, Nell?"

The girl shook her head.

"I know not what to answer, sir. I know not where Belfast is. So I have never purchased the best of linen, sir. There is a chapman sells remnants."

"You see?" interrupted the Weasel to his accomplice.

"What, master?"

"When did our sweet Nell ever come out with such a pretty speech?"

Todd began to wake, moaning, coughing and spitting blood. Mary Nell knelt down and tried to clean his face.

"What have they done to you, Todd? And why? What do they want?"

"We want some questions answered, woman. Some true answers. Not the lies you have spilled before."

Todd looked to Nell imploring, his mouth torn, teeth broken.

"What would I know, sir? And what about?"

"Who comes here? Who goes from here? What gentlemen consort here? Who is killed here?"

Mary Nell read in Todd's eyes the desperate plea to resist. Not to give the answers they were sworn to protect.

"Then I knows not what to answer, sir. I does me work. Never listens at doors. Bears no grudges to none. I knows me place, sir."

"Commendable, my dear Nell! But what you know may not be of interest to you, but is most important to us. We will help you to remember."

The parlour door opened and the Devil stepped in. Mary Savage, a sophisticated twenty-first century woman, could not stem her cry of terror.

The Weasel said, "We have the girl, milord. I wager she will tell us what the man would not."

With a clarity of mind that surprised her, Mary Savage realised the Devil whom the thugs addressed so respectfully was not the Devil from the playhouse. This man was taller, broader and beardless. He wore a sword that marked him as a gentleman. His painted face was a disguise. That the visage might frighten was not its first purpose. His voice, quiet, insistent, polite was frightening enough. He waited as Mary Nell cleaned Todd's face and comforted him.

"This girl has an affinity to this man. See how she nurses her child. The poor lamb has taken a tumble in the street and scraped his knee. The sad mite has fallen out of favour with his playmates and blows as well as sour words have been exchanged. Alas, he has come off worst, but woman by her nature will always comfort the fallen. She will cosset him with Esau's pottage, lamb for her lamb."

The thugs didn't know whether to laugh. At the first squeak the Devil turned to look at them and they were silent.

"May we all meet such tender care when we fall amiss. However, our business cannot linger here. Dear Nell, I am to ask a question or two of you. Each lie you tell will cause poor Todd to lose a finger. Do you understand me?"

Mary Nell nodded, aware of Todd's grip on her wrist tightening.

"Gentlemen of the playhouse frequent this house from time to time. Is that so, Nell?"

Mary Nell nodded.

"A nod is not enough."

"Yes."

"One of these gentlemen is the notorious heretic, Christopher Marlowe. Sometimes goes by Kit Marlon. Is that so?"

"Yes."

"Then you have seen this Christopher Marlowe?"

"Yes."

"Then you know this man by sight?"

"Yes."

"If I were to produce Marlowe among others could you lay a hand upon him and say this is the man?"

The girl hesitated. The Weasel moved as if, but the Devil raised a hand.

"Would you know him?"

"Yes."

"How many fingers does Todd have?"

"Eight fingers and two thumbs, milord."

"You see how easy it is?"

"Yes."

"On Friday, the twenty-seventh of May, there were gentlemen enjoying supper in the upstairs chamber."

"Yes."

"Gentlemen coming and going. And you were bringing them victuals, ale, wine, in quantity?"

"Yes."

"Todd, being a cautious man would've liked to have seen some money from these gentlemen."

"Yes."

"And you went upstairs with the reckoning? But there was no one there to meet the request."

The woman was silent, striving to find some acceptable response.

"You told my associates earlier that you met no one on the stair or the landing. Only a dead man in the chamber."

"Yes, milord."

"My associate will now cut off Todd's right thumb. Because you lied."

Todd's right wrist was forced to align with the wooden arm of the chair and the Weasel prepared to cut off the thumb. He looked to the Devil and waited, blade in hand.

Todd mumbled what might have been a plea to Nell not to speak.

"Wait!" said Mary Nell, "I lied."

The blade hesitated. The Devil shook his head.

"I met two men on the landing. They passed me to the stairs. I did find the dead man on the floor in the chamber."

"Was the dead man Christopher Marlowe?"

The girl shook her head.

"Answer, please!"

"No. It was not Marlowe. I had never seen the dead man before."

"And the two men on the stairs?"

"One man I did not know. The other man was Christopher Marlowe."

"So Christopher Marlowe did not die in this house that night?"

"No, milord."

* * * *

The class was working quietly, heads bent over dissection trays. A bored Miss Meadows prowled the room. She knew the girls didn't like her. If a student looked up, the girl didn't smile. She had seen this interchange of smiles between girls and her colleagues. She envied the trust they shared. The class worked well. Many fathers had paid the ultimate price for their daughters' education and the girls were aware of sacrifice. At best they tolerated her, but when the bell rang to end a lesson they didn't linger to ask a last question.

They would walk out talking together, barely aware of her presence. She resented this deeply and seethed with anger.

The bell rang and the class gathered up books and belongings to depart. Only two girls stayed to clear the dissection trays. They worked in silence. She tried to engage them, saying, "Thank you for clearing up."

"Yes, miss," they said in chorus. As a reward for cleaning up after a lesson she allowed the volunteers to visit the rabbits kept next door on the flat roof adapted as a small animal area. Once it had been the site of the astronomical telescope that now had its own observatory. The tray cleaners vanished to cuddle their favourite rabbits. The volunteers were not appreciated by the Rabbit Monitors.

As she sat at the desk adding to the notes she had made during the lesson, a shadow fell over her. She looked up and froze. She knew her visitors. They were a tall and a short, thinner man, dressed in pink plastic raincoats and plastic pixie hoods. She knew if she looked at their feet they would be wearing yellow duck Wellington boots.

The short man said, "A very creditable exposition."

"Indeed," agreed his companion, "A creditable exposition."

"But then our dear Miss Meadows is a very good teacher. Did you not find her explanation of the digestive system of the worm absorbing?"

"Indeed, I did. I shall always regard worms differently now."

"But, of course, our dear Miss Meadows is skilful at many different trades."

"Yes, indeed, a mistress of many trades."

Gillian Meadows stood up slowly on trembling legs.

"What do you want?"

The short man ignored the question and continued.

"In truth, her teaching ability is only surpassed by her skill at murdering children without being discovered."

"What do you want?"

She heard the restless sound of the next class assembling outside the door.

"A moment of your time."

* * * *

Before she could draw breath, she was standing on the cliff at Land's End looking down at the Atlantic surge pounding the rocks below. The men stood either side of her.

"The fashion in which the ocean drives over the rocks is most frightening. Not for all the chocolate in Africa would I climb down to stand in the spray. Pray tell us how you did it, dear Gillian?"

"Tell you what?"

"How you enticed the children to their deaths? How you murdered seven children who were a nuisance to you."

"It was an accident."

"No, no, it wasn't! The Headmaster and his wife walked away for a cup of tea, foolishly believing they were leaving the children in sensible, responsible hands."

"I did nothing wrong."

"They paid a terrible price for that mistake. You know, of course, the Headmaster resigned and committed suicide. His wife was dead within the year. They felt responsible for the tragedy."

"It was an accident."

"Perhaps you are right!"

Gillian Meadows turned to look at the hard face rimmed by the ridiculous pink plastic hood. What she saw froze her blood.

"Perhaps the Headmaster and his wife were the real targets, Gillian? And the children merely the means to an end?"

The short man appeared horrified.

"Is that the truth of it, Gillian, dearest heart? Perhaps the Headmaster had offended you? Was your intention all along to destroy the Headmaster and his wife?"

The tall man shook his head sadly.

"Tell us, sweet Gillian, how you coaxed the children to their death?" the short man coaxed.

"It was an accident."

"Then, I shall tell you what you already know. With you and the unfortunate young assistant teacher, who left teaching after the tragedy, the children were happy to clamber down the cliff. But at a certain level they stopped. But you knew how to motivate them."

Gillian whispered, "This is all fantasy."

"All week on this so-called 'Adventure Trip' they had been disobedient and rude to you. They weren't in school. They took advantage. So what did you do? You ordered them not to climb down. And they disobeyed you."

Miss Meadows' temper flared.

"They were unpleasant, foulmouthed children. Do you think children should make a crude display of their backsides to a teacher?"

"You followed them down. They didn't realise you were driving them into danger. They ignored you and seven children died. In the confusion, the Atlantic nearly got you."

"I jumped in to help them!"

"You didn't jump in. The wave took you as it took four boys and three girls. You were lucky. But you taught them a fine lesson, didn't you, Gillian? They wouldn't be disobedient to you again!"

"What do you want?"

"A simple task. We want you to kill three children."

"And if I won't?"

"We will kill you."

The tall man pushed her hard and she fell screaming from the cliff onto the foaming rocks.

Shocked, terrified, trembling, Miss Meadows stood against the desk. From the doorway of the classroom, the taller of the two departing children asked politely, "Are you alright, miss?"

* * * *

Someone knocked at the door. Joan lay still and silent. To her annoyance, the door opened and someone entered.

"Joan?" whispered Laura, "Are you there?"

Joan began to feel more irritated than heartbroken.

"Jacqueline saw you come in."

Joan removed fluff from her nose.

"I'll go away if you like."

Joan started to count to a hundred.

"If you're in the wardrobe, you'll soon get short of air and die."

Fifty-six, fifty-seven.

"I know what's wrong. Everybody does. But I know what it feels like. You just want to die."

There was a ring of truth, a wistfulness of the heart in Laura's voice; *I know how dreadful you feel. I too have been hurt so badly I wanted to stop living.*

"I'll go then. I hope you'll feel better soon."

Joan said, "I'm under the bed."

She waited for Laura to laugh, but she didn't. Instead, Laura knelt down and slid under the bed to lie beside Joan. She lay in silence. Because she was Laura she didn't say all the wrong things. After a respectful silence, she commented, "It's not as dusty as I expected. In fact, it's really clean."

"I'm the tidy one," Joan admitted, "Melanie's not. Melanie's."

Melanie's gone.

Laura said, "I know Mel was really keen on you. You could've said you'd drop me. I know she thinks I'm too young. But I am getting older."

Joan said, "When you're sixty-eight and I'm seventy, will it make that much difference?"

Laura chuckled. *You're the only girl I know who chuckles. Everybody laughs, but you're the only one who chuckles.*

They lay under the bed in a comfortable silence until Joan began to search for a handkerchief and Laura provided hers.

Laura said, "Wha'd'y'think Early Man used before he had a handkerchief?"

"Early Woman's?"

Laura chuckled. Feet and voices sounded in the corridor.

"Time to rejoin the world?" Joan suggested. She took Laura's hand and said. "Thank you, Laura."

She blinked in the sudden daylight. They were standing in an unfamiliar street outside a newsagent's shop. Laura was the seventh time walker.

CHAPTER THIRTEEN

Laura gasped aloud and Joan cried, "Oh, no! Where are we now?"

It was totally unknown to her; a pleasant avenue of semi-detached houses.

Laura said, "I know where we are! This is Morpeth Avenue. That's Mister Patel's shop. He's my friend. We're not far from home! We could go to see my Mother!"

She pulled at Joan's arm, her face flushed with happiness.

"Whoa! We're not supposed to be here. Let's just think it through first."

They looked at one another, two English schoolgirls in neat, tidy uniform; black skirt, white shirt and tie, black blazer.

"Do we know the date? Today could be ten years ago. Twenty? Fifty? We end up on a stranger's doorstep looking very silly if you haven't been born yet."

Laura took a newspaper from the rack outside the shop.

"Today's today!"

Laura put the newspaper back tidily. Her Year teacher would've smiled upon her.

"I'm not sure we should be doing this, but if you want to go visiting?"

Joan felt uneasy. Yet it was hard to refuse Laura's imitation of an eager, bouncing ball.

"How about you say hello to your friend? Mister Patel? I can't see any harm in that."

As they were about to enter, a shaven-headed young man pushed them aside. A voice behind them called, "Make it snappy, Mick!"

There was a motorcycle at the kerb with a similar youth aboard, flexing the accelerator.

Turning back to the shop door, Joan said, "He's robbing the shop!"

The young man was threatening Mr. Patel with a club. The shopkeeper was not intimidated. He was threatening the thief from behind his counter with a stick. His wife ran into the back of the shop. As the girls were about to rush in a tall man appeared behind them.

"Ring the police! Please! He's robbing Mister Patel!" cried Laura. Surprisingly, the man obeyed. An older man appeared behind saying, "Excuse me!"

"Robbery!" said the first man.

The older man thrust his stick through the handles of the door.

"That'll slow him down. Have you got the police?"

The tall man nodded.

"Hurry, please! We've got him trapped in the shop!"

Joan said, "He's in it as well."

She pointed at the youth on the motorcycle.

The two men approached the motorcycle.

"Your mate robbing Mister Patel, is he?"

The youth's answer was a flood of obscenities. Angered, the older man kicked the bike. The rider was caught by surprise, lost control and the bike fell over, engine roaring. The two men struggled to hold the rider, but he was too strong. He ran away as the sirens sounded. In the shop the thief was pulling at the door. Mr. Patel was beating him with his stick.

The police car screeched to a halt.

"They don't need us," said Joan and took Laura's hand. The sunlight vanished and they were under Joan's bed, hiding from the world.

* * * *

They talked while Laura burnished her hair with Joan's expensive brush.

"It's okay. I haven't got nits," Laura reassured the brush's owner.

"But I have."

Laura almost stopped brushing.

"Mister Patel won't even know we saved him!" complained Laura.

"We didn't save him." Joan explained, "His customers did. They like him. They weren't going to have him robbed."

Silence.

"But we were there at the right time!" Laura rejoiced.

"Yes," Joan agreed, "We were there at the right time."

"I think it was meant to be."

"No, it wasn't! It was an excruciatingly serendipitous event!"

"You can be as rude as you like. But I know Mister Patel needed me and I was there!"

When Laura had departed, hair shining like liquorice, Joan wondered why this time travel episode had lasted so long and not broken off. She had taken Laura's hand. It wasn't something they normally did. Randall girls didn't wander about holding hands; they were to be Empire wives, ready to stand at the Residency window, musket to the shoulder, capable of shooting any upstart without hesitation.

She had taken Laura's hand because she had been so decent and they arrived at the newsagent's. When she took Laura's hand to lead her away, they were back under the bed. It was nothing to do with the robbery. *Did I initiate the time shift by taking Laura's hand? If this is a true, does this mean I can travel in time when I wish? And take someone with me?*

* * * *

Melanie was tired. She was tired when she rose in the morning and ached for bedtime, although she slept poorly. She was now writing unreadable notes at panic speed as Miss Salomon explained the importance of the Congress of Vienna, 1815. A certain Klemens Wenzel von Metternich, a belligerent Austrian, was bullying the major European states into accepting something called the status quo. Melanie had no idea what or who this might be. Two desks in front of her, Joan was writing steadily, untroubled by the status of the status quo. When the two were one, Joan would've explained anything and everything to Melanie.

Melanie stopped writing. She was overtaken by a sadness that would from time to time surprise her; the simplest object, memory, sound, voice would spark a terrifying loneliness. She was watching Joan's hair moving in the classroom sunlight as she wrote, listened, looked up to Miss Salomon and bent again to write. Then the teacher's voice stopped although Joan continued writing; as did the rest of the class.

When Melanie looked to the teacher, there was no Miss Salomon. In her place stood Hannah, the girl who had accompanied Christopher Marlowe. She was speaking urgently to Melanie, but she could not be heard. Hannah moved from the whiteboard, making her way around the room from desk to desk. Always looking to Melanie, her mouth moved in urgent speech. Words that Melanie couldn't comprehend, words spoken under water that almost made sense. Then Hannah was gone and Miss Salomon came to Melanie's desk.

"Melanie, why have you stopped taking notes?"

Melanie shook her head in confusion.

"If I am speaking too quickly, then you must tell me. I will speak more slowly. I do not like the sound of my own voice so much."

There was a ripple of amusement around the class. Joan had turned round, but she wasn't smiling or laughing.

"When I was at University we had a tutor who entered the lecture room spouting his wealth of words. As he called it. We had to grab whatever of his pennies we could."

I know she's being kind to me. She is trying to find out what is wrong. And she starts with herself.

"I don't like to see you giving up like this. Is there something you don't understand?"

I don't understand anything. Nothing makes sense any more. .

"I don't understand what status quo is, miss. What or who it is."

The class laughed, but Melanie saw anger in Joan's face.

"Are we all so clever we can afford to be cruel?"

The class was subdued and Melanie saw Joan lower her head.

"Here is an honest girl who when asked, says she does not understand the phrase status quo. It means simply to keep things the same. That is what Metternich wanted."

"Nothing stays the same, miss," Melanie denied, "Everything changes. You can't keep things the same. It all goes wrong. That's what I don't understand. Why?"

Miss Salomon regarded Melanie thoughtfully.

"What is your next period?"

"Study period. With you, miss."

The class laughed, but it was a warmer laughter. Joan smiled.

"Perhaps I may help you understand? Would you like me to try?"

"Yes, miss! Thank you, miss?"

What was the girl Hannah trying to tell me? She was warning me. But about what?

* * * *

Someone was singing to a guitar; a clear, strong voice that carried the tune well. The guitar was played skilfully. The man knew his instrument. He played and sang because he enjoyed it. His songs weren't familiar to the ear, not soft rock or lugubrious ballads, but passers-by stopped and lingered to listen.

Christopher Marlowe, midnight hair, trimmed moustache and beard, a handsome man, stood by the underpass that led from Gilsford Market to the High Street, singing to a constant river of

humanity passing from the Market to the High Street and from the High Street to the open air Market.

Hannah, dirty face, scraggy hair, open-knee jeans, sat with a biscuit tin that she played as drum when empty. Now that it bore some coins, she rattled it occasionally as families passed. It was a tentative rattle that suggested there's-not-enough-coins-in-here-to-buy-us-a-cup-of-tea-cough-cough.

Children like buskers. They will stop and listen. Young children will squeeze money from the tightest pocket. Children especially like buskers with dogs. No child can resist a flea-ridden dog on a string. It is rumoured some buskers take their dogs to specialist groomers who prepare them for the street.

Christopher Marlowe didn't need a dog. He had Hannah who would make faces to send the children into fits of giggles. Every time a coin dropped into the tin, Hannah would give a loud cocka-doodle-doo that encouraged children to prise even more coins from reluctant parents.

When Christopher was taking a break, Hannah would perform her scarecrow dance or play the robot. Together they were an entertaining couple, doing no harm and creating good humour. Christopher's songs enchanted listeners who had never heard them before. University students came to listen, but dropped very little in the tin. Local enthusiasts came to persuade him to join their drama groups, but he fell about laughing, which left them puzzled.

"He's a natural," they would complain, "He should be on stage," and Hannah would explain how he had once fallen from a stage and broken his thespis which had never healed. They were very sympathetic. Hannah was Christopher's skinny dog.

A man in his thirties, academic, bespectacled, wearing a haversack, polar neck sweater, jeans and sandals, came up the underpass and stopped to listen to Christopher singing.

"O, mistress mine, where are you roaming? O, stay and hear; your true love's coming, That can sing both high and low:

Trip no further, pretty sweeting; Journeys end in lovers meeting, Every wise man's son doth know."

Every teenage girl listening, knew Christopher was singing to her. If he was mocking himself it was difficult to tell. The polar neck listened, applauded, chose a pound coin from his purse, changed his mind and dropped fifty pence into the tin. Hannah gave him her most heartbreaking face. He changed his mind and produced the pound coin. Hannah rattled the tin. He released the coin. He looked as if he wished to retrieve his fifty pence piece.

Hannah said, reproachfully, "We have no procedures to return money."

He smiled and walked on. And then returned to speak to Christopher.

"Minstrel, do you know what you're singing?"

Christopher smiled, struck a chord and sang, "Forsooth, I did not choose the life of a delinquent. Alas, the life of a delinquent chose I!"

"I'll take that as a yes. You know your Shakespeare."

Christopher smiled sourly. Hannah raised a warning hand, but in vain.

"Indeed, I do, master! A more devious little toad you'd hope never to meet. I would gladly pay for the pleasure of hanging him. And for the rope to break his scrawny little neck!"

The polar neck laughed to say, "What have we here?"

He bent to Christopher's open saddle bags. He had hardly a glimpse of handwritten yellowed sheets before Hannah snatched away the treasure.

"That's very old," observed the polar neck, "Very old indeed!! Perhaps as old as. May I enquire where you found it?"

"It's mine," said Christopher.

"Yes, it is! I wondered where you found it? An auction? Boot sale? House clearance?"

Hannah intervened, "He means it's his work."

"Indeed? I wonder if I might take a peek?"

"He's very private," said Hannah, in warning.

The polar neck nodded agreement.

"As I am myself."

"He would come and sing for you," offered Hannah, "At a private party?"

The polar neck smiled, saying, "Farewell, thou art too rich for my possessing."

He saluted Hannah and ambled away only to return again.

"I know not where I command," mocked Hannah.

Donald Mason said, "I'm at the University. Elizabethan England is my obsession. There's never any money, but perhaps you'll keep this? You never know! If I had money for more than pencils."

He handed Christopher a business card and wandered away to be lost in the market crowd. Christopher glanced at the card and was about to flick it at the waste bin when Hannah intercepted.

"I'll have that, if you don't mind."

She was scanning the card when she realised Christopher was gathering their possessions together.

"What are you doing?"

"Too much of a pokenose. Don't trust him."

"He's perfectly harmless. From the University."

"Indeed! Snakes take many shapes. I met them at Cambridge. A nest of venomous vipers."

He slung his guitar to his shoulder.

"Coming?"

"This is ridiculous," Hannah grumbled.

"I scent danger. And I am never wrong."

"You're wrong this time. Mister Polar Neck is harmless. But we're more obvious by not being here when we are expected to be here."

"That's woman's logic, is it? If we're not here, we're more to be noticed?"

Christopher was hustling Hannah through the underpass into the town centre, biscuit tin rattling like a fire alarm. He didn't slow down until they arrived at the motorcycle and sidecar.

"You're crazy!" Hannah complained, "We were going to have a really good day. We must have ten quid already."

Christopher carefully stowed the guitar and saddle bags aboard. Hannah counted the takings.

"Fourteen quid thirty seven pee. And what could be a Roman sesterce or a button. Today we might've taken enough to hang your friendemy."

"Friendemy?"

"Shakespeare. I can never work out if he's friend or enemy."

"For such a childling, you make too free with the English language!"

Settling herself into the sidecar, Hannah laughed.

"Listen to yourself! Pot calling the kettle black. How about *seas incarnadine*? Show me incarnadine in any dictionary!"

"Peace, peace! I hear you, Robin Goodfellow! If you'll cease nagging, before we go home, we'll stop at the pub you like."

"The Falstaff!"

"The landlord thinks it's Shakespearean."

"It's themed."

"If it's more than Saint Audrey's fair, I'm the Bishop of Peckham."

"If he wants you to sing, my lord Bishop?"

"Not if he gadzooks me one more time! I never met the word."

Straddling the bike, Christopher said, "Just make sure of the coinage first."

"You are the biggest coward ever," Hannah decided, "You want the money, but you shy from asking."

"Money is woman's work," he rejoined and kicked the starter.

* * * *

The market crowd drew aside, amused or curious, as two men made their way through the market aisles. A short and a taller man dressed most oddly in pink plastic raincoats and plastic pixie hoods. But the children liked the yellow duck wellies. Whatever they sought in the market, they failed to find. At the entrance to the underpass they hesitated.

Donald Mason, Renaissance Man in a polar neck sweater, lecturer in English Literature, Gilsford University, was standing against the wall, taking photographs of the market. When the men in pink plastic swam into his lens, he photographed them.

Donald Mason asked, "Doing it for charity, are we?"

The tall man questioned, "What do you mean?"

"Dressing up?" he offered placatingly.

There was but the merest trace of menace in his voice when the short man answered, "Is there something amiss with how we are attired?"

"No, no, not at all," said Donald, wishing he hadn't spoken, "Quite fetching actually."

The tall man scowled and the short man asked, "We were told there was a minstrel here on market days? Quite singular."

"No! Never heard him. I think I would've. I'm fairly regular, if not singular."

As soon as the words left his mouth, Donald Mason knew he had made a mistake. He hesitated just a moment too long. He saw in the short man's eyes that he knew he was lying. Why he was lying, Donald didn't understand, but he knew there was something very wrong about these two men. Perhaps an echo of the bullies who had destroyed his childhood happiness?

Donald blundered on to say, "There was an Irishman. I think he was Irish. At Christmas. Two of them, actually. Otherwise, no singer. Certainly, no one singular. The Irishman could barely hold a tune.

Most of the time I don't think he was sober. He was often sick in the underpass."

He listened to himself jabbering on and tried to stop.

"Black Horse on the High Street. That would be the place! They have music nights. They might know. Sorry I can't help."

Smiling inanely, Donald Mason moved away, taking photographs of anything and everything, camera clicking aimlessly. He felt very cold and shivered in the summer sun. *God, I'm scared of those two. Why on earth, I don't know. Just let me get clear!*

CHAPTER FOURTEEN

When Donald Mason looked up too casually from a stall he saw both men were watching him. He pretended to consult his watch, shook his head and moved off smartly. To his horror, he saw his wife, Sandra and their daughter, Eleanor, coming towards him. Ellie had her nose in a paper bag; absorbed by something she'd bought.

In mime, Donald struggled to convey to Sandra not to acknowledge him. Sandra stopped, bemused, but catching his urgently mimed 'please', turned into a side aisle with Ellie in tow. Breathing a prayer of relief, Donald walked on, heart pounding. He knew without knowing that the two men in pink plastic must not become aware of his family. Deep within his being, he knew they were very dangerous.

Donald stopped at a bookstall and spent twenty minutes browsing. To his surprise and pleasure, he found a shabby copy of Tamburlaine by Christopher Marlowe. He suspected the foxed pages had not been opened in a hundred years. He bought the volume. Wandering away from the stall, he saw no sign of the predatory pair.

His wife and daughter were in the car; Ellie asleep in the back seat, Sandra was already deep into a paperback Maeve Binchy.

"What was that all about?"

Donald recited his prepared statement.

"I'd just had half an hour of the Forresters. Hard enough to get away from them. I didn't want another basinful if they'd spotted you."

"And the last half an hour?"

Donald offered his Tamburlaine as excuse.

"Look what I found!"

"A dirty old book, smelling of the Plague? You dug it out of a cesspit?"

"A masterpiece from a playwright who has never received the acclaim he deserves."

Sandra started the car.

"Put your seat belt on. Then I know you're mine."

She leaned across to kiss his cheek.

"For such grace of mouth, much thanks."

"For such grace of speech, much thanks," his wife corrected him.

There was no sign of pink plastic on the streets of Gilsford. Once they left the town behind and drove between green hedges, Donald Mason began to forget.

CHAPTER FIFTEEN

It was the only sunny day that Joan remembered as a sheep day. In Joan's scheme of things sheep meant rain. Therefore, it was a memorable day. The only thorn was the absence of Melanie. They shared classes and saw each other frequently. Joan tried always to speak. Melanie ignored her, but once, Joan had seen her erstwhile friend hesitate before turning away. It was an unceasing cause of unhappiness. Joan observed Melanie seemed quieter with the Angels. There was less laughter.

Joan was now teamed with Naomi Bowman Phillips for Environmental Studies. Naomi was a tall, pleasant girl who was delighted to be assigned to sheep.

"You're kidding?"

"Anything that takes me outdoors."

Joan knew one day on television she would hear the words, "Clear round, Miss Bowman Phillips!" and there would be Naomi and horse flying over enormous obstacles to applause.

As the trio met in the stores barn, Harry Armstrong, the farm manager, asked, "D'y'know anything about sheep, Naomi?"

"A bit," the girl confessed modestly.

"Which bit?" Joan chipped in, "The dirty end or the dirtier end?"

"My grandfather has sheep," Naomi explained, "I go there on holiday."

Harry said, "A sizeable flock?"

"A hundred and fifty thousand, I think."

"You're kidding!" cried Joan, "Where'd you hide that lot?".

"New Zealand."

"I wouldn't have thought it was big enough!"

"How do you manage a flock that size?" asked Harry.

"We have space, I guess. Once it was horses and dogs. Now it's buggies and the helicopter. He still keeps the horses. What we wouldn't use is barbed wire."

She gestured to the hillock of barbed wire bales stacked in the barn.

"Grandfather won't have the wire. Ewe or lamb becomes entangled, they may not be found for days."

That afternoon became a delight for Joan. Naomi wasn't a great conversationalist, but as they were wearing masks for sheep dipping it was of no consequence. Joan would give the ewe a quick dip in the chemical brew, but Naomi kept the ewe under until Joan feared she would drown. To Harry Armstrong it was as if he had been blessed with an unexpected daughter. Joan found herself demoted to counting the ewes coming from the dip. *Yan, tain, eddero, peddero, pitts, tayter, layter, overy, covero, dix.*

When Joan looked up from her counting, she found the Captain of Cavalry standing over her. She stifled a cry of surprise. She was sitting on the big stone in the Rifles encampment, but shot backwards as the Captain planted a polished long boot on the stone. He was not aware of her. The Ensign stood beside the Captain. His jaw was set and his eyes smouldered with resentment. Joan went to stand beside him.

In the full heat of a very hot day, Sergeant Springer was putting the Riflemen through every page of the British Army drill book. They wore full equipment, loaded like donkeys with everything including the guardroom sink; a pack load of eighty pounds weight. They were exhausted. Counting the sweating, red-faced Riflemen, she realised there was no man on observation. The Sergeant came to a fine flourish and ended the drill, standing the men at ease. Their resentment was apparent.

"You have become very sloppy," the Captain barked, "Very sloppy indeed! Lounging in the sunshine! Not one of you is earning his pay. While not very far away there are real soldiers preparing to risk life and limb in the service of Crown and Country. While you sit on your backsides like prize pigs. Well, my shysters, that is finished! You have taken advantage of your officer and you will pay the price!"

Joan felt the Ensign beside her, close to bursting with anger.

"Every day I am here, we will burnish our drill! In a week, I shall have you drilling like soldiers. Although you are not real soldiers! Real soldiers hold the line. Riflemen run away."

Joan realised the Captain was trying to provoke one man at least into insubordination. She feared the Ensign might be that man.

"Sergeant!"

"Yes, sir!"

"You may dismiss the men!"

The Ensign called, "Riflemen! Stand fast!"

The Captain turned on the boy.

"Sir, I have dismissed the parade."

"So you have, sir. And as their officer, I am resuming command of my men, sir."

The Captain hesitated for a moment and then, "Very well, sir."

"I wish to show you, sir, what Riflemen are trained to do, if you will indulge me, sir."

Reluctantly the Captain agreed.

"Very well!"

The Ensign spoke to the hot weary men.

"You will dismiss and drink water. You will return in ten minutes with unloaded rifles only. No kit, no useless impedimenta! Rifles! Carry on Sergeant!"

"Officer on parade! Dis-miss!"

The Riflemen saluted, turned and vanished.

The Captain sat in his campaign chair, sipping from his silver cup. The Riflemen stood at ease. The Sergeant and Corporal had cleared every rifle twice. Joan decided it was to dissuade any Rifleman from shooting the Captain.

"You have your watch, sir?"

"If you insist."

"Each man is paired with another. Two rifles. One man is the shooter. His comrade is the loader. Both are skilled tasks. The loader must not fumble and the shooter must not miss. You aspire with the musket to fire four times in a minute. A good squad of Riflemen will kill ten enemy in a minute."

The pairs spread across the open encampment, four pairs of two Riflemen.

"Each man will do exactly as they have been trained. At some two hundred yards distance and on a clear day, three hundred yards, the infantry begin to advance. The Riflemen begin to kill officers, sergeants and corporals."

A steady clicking of rifle locks began. Shooters picked a target, changed the rifle, shot again. The loader worked smoothly and speedily. Every time the shooter extended his hand there was a rifle to fill it. The steady click of locks continued at a rising speed.

"At a hundred yards, the enemy are finding their officers, sergeants and corporals gone. The men are dying in the ranks. At fifty yards, the Riflemen will fire a final volley and run back to prepared positions to begin again their deadly fire."

The Riflemen vanished.

"If it were a troop of cavalry, sir, men and horses would be dead now. Riflemen do not stay standing for you to ride over them, sir. They run away so they may have the satisfaction of shooting you another day."

A ripple of amusement ran through the Riflemen that the Sergeant and Corporal couldn't suppress.

"Eight determined marksmen will stop ten times that number. If you counted by your watch, they were killing at least ten men a minute."

The Captain said nothing.

"If you have any further orders, sir?"

The Captain shook his head. Taking his liquor, he vanished into his tent. The Corporal followed with his chair. The Riflemen, beyond exhaustion, were dismissed and retired smiling.

"Went the day, well?" the Ensign said to his Sergeant.

"Better than some, sir. But you have made a very bad enemy, sir. The Captain won't forget this day. He'll do you down whenever and wherever he can, sir."

Sitting on her stone, Joan nodded agreement, trying to make sense of what she had read and what she was learning firsthand. From reading, she knew Wellington's strategy was to draw the French under Marshal Massena onto the defensive line of Torres Vedra. Her thoughts were interrupted by the Ensign who said, "Well, is Springer correct, have I made a grievous error incurring the enmity of Captain Dandy? He's not a Colonel or a General. He is, after all, a mere Captain!"

Astonished, Joan said, "Are you talking to me?"

The Ensign sat down beside her, saying, "I see no one else. Is there anyone else?"

"You can see me?"

"Is there anyone else?"

"No. I'm alone. And you can see me?"

The Ensign waited until the Corporal had passed.

"I've seen you around the camp. At first, I thought you were a Portugee come to steal."

"I'm not a thief!"

He smiled at Joan's indignation.

"We have nothing worth stealing. Then I thought you were my Guardian Angel."

Joan laughed, but tried to smother her laughter.

"Laugh if you may! No one will hear you."

He was a handsome, earnest boy. She wasn't very good with boys, but Joan felt comfortable with this Ensign.

"You look like an Angel, but you're not, are you?" he asked, wistfully. A battered shako on his head, patched and dirty coat and trousers all contrived to make her want to hug him. She did not because Randall girls did not hug strange officers and Wellington's officers did not hug strange girls. Or Guardian Angels for that matter.

"Are you my Guardian Angel?"

"No, I'm not. I don't have wings. See?"

"My father is divided on that issue."

"Your father is a clergyman?"

"A country parson. Small parish of three villages. Wardley, Alexton and Belton in the County of Rutland."

"And he isn't sure about Angels having wings?"

"As God's messengers, why would they need wings?"

"Perhaps I am a demon?"

The boy laughed.

"No, you're not. I know a demon when I see one. This Captain Dandy is a demon. He flourishes on cruelty and malice."

"Then you've answered your own question. Yes, that unpleasant man will do his utmost to damage you."

In the unquiet silence between them, Joan looked at the encampment. Three Riflemen sat outside their shabby tents, sewing at shirts or coats. Two wet white figures in shabby drawers came running from the river to shake water at their comrades, drying themselves on shirts, rags or grass. There was a sense of peace, of simple contentment among the Riflemen that humbled Joan who knew how close they were to death.

"But you haven't come to discuss theology?"

"Nobody else sees or hears me?"

"No."

"I'm not going to try to explain where I'm from. I'm not sure how or why anyway. What I know is I am here to help you."

The Ensign smiled.

"It's going to be very unpleasant here shortly."

"I know. I also know the French are pretending to rebuild the bridge at Sorino. They're moving an army of foot there. That is not where the attack is coming. Here they have built an underwater roadway. Here thousands of cavalry will cross to destroy the retreating Army in a brilliant stroke."

The Ensign was amazed and speechless. He seemed about to rise, but Joan took his hand.

"There's no point in telling the Captain. He won't believe you. He wouldn't believe you if the French cavalry were crossing now and offered him a lift to Lisbon."

It was a long speech for Joan, but she needed to restrain the young officer. His training told him he should pass such information to his superior officer.

"What you must do is hold this ford. No one need know more."

She released his hand and he sat silent.

"I can't hold the ford."

"You will hold the ford. I've come to help you."

"How?"

"I don't know yet."

"Can you set the river on fire? Conjure up a battalion? Raise the river? But that wouldn't stop them. Cavalry horses swim to saddle depth. And there's no battalion here to stop them."

"You're here."

The Ensign smiled.

"Have you counted my squad? Eight men and a boy. I know they think of me as a boy."

"But you have to hold the ford. Wellington needs you to do so. Three days will be enough."

The young officer was surprised.

"You've spoken to him?"

"No, but I've read about him."

"Read about him?"

"What can I do to help?"

"Stop the cavalry crossing the ford. Can you do that?"

"I'll find the answer."

* * * *

Joan smiled and vanished. She was tempted to kiss him, but was relieved not to have given way to temptation. The Ensign was startled when Joan vanished, but recovered to greet his Sergeant who came to make sure his officer was still in his right mind although talking to himself.

"You alright, sir?"

"Yes, sergeant. Why shouldn't I be?"

"The lads noticed you seemed to be talking to yourself, sir. If you'll pardon the impudence."

"I was recalling poetry I learned at school, sergeant," said the Ensign reciting his prepared lie, "Very soothing to the spirit."

"Yes, sir. I'll give it a try sometime, sir."

When pigs fly, sir.

"How many extra rifles have we?"

The Ensign knew there was no better picker-up of unconsidered trifles in the regiment than Sergeant Springer. The Sergeant, if asked, would have said he was a picker-up of unconsidered rifles.

"Nine, sir. Two with damaged stocks, but useable. Locks in good order. Ample flints."

"Let the men bring the rifles up to scratch. I want to see nine, clean, oiled, lock-free rifles, last call tonight."

"Yes, sir."

* * * *

The prefect in the Computer room was surprised to find Joan d'Urquart in a computer carrel when she would have sworn the girl had never entered the room.

"Why are you not in the book, d'Urquart?"

"My mother never buys a parking ticket before she finds a space for the car."

I never even asked his name. Silly me!
I never asked her name. Angels must surely have names?

CHAPTER SIXTEEN

It was too hot a day for a funeral. The small procession wended its sorrowful way down Southern Lane, Stratford upon Avon, to Holy Trinity church. No one took any notice of the solemn progress. If they had looked twice they may have noted the lack of mutes, bereaved women and professional mourners. There were no flowers carried or displayed on the coffin. The cheap pine box wobbled on the shoulders of four men of disparate height: one bearer tall and thin, a fat man, an Herculean figure and a man of dwarfish proportions. The coffin bobbed as a dinghy on a fractious tide. The funeral procession was led by an unsteady, bearded priest. One might have suspected him of being drunk. He walked with one hand on the shoulder of a boy dressed in black with painted tears on his face. Without the young mourner's support the reverent gentleman might readily have fallen.

Behind the plain coffin, followed two mourners, one man, not short nor tall, bearded, well-set with his friend, a handsome man with a good face free of hair, a confident walk and an admirable figure. At the lichgate to the churchyard, they stopped to lodge the coffin to free the bearers to groan, grumble and wipe away honest sweat. The priest propped himself against the nearest sepulchre to take comfort from a small bottle. The boy with the painted tears fought to take the bottle from him, but failed.

Christopher Marlowe asked, "Am I paying for this fiasco?"

"Regrettably, you are," said Edward Alleyn, "And I know how much that hurts you, Kit! To part with coinage."

Raising his voice, Christopher cried, "This is the worst funeral I have ever attended! Call yourself actors? If I were not already dead, you would've banged out my brains in that box! I would've done better to borrow a crew from Bedlam!"

The Time Walkers

"Never played no rehearsal," grumbled Billy Brakspar, "It's all been done on the trot, so to speak!"

"A little dignity is all I crave, Billy. How often is a man buried?"

Alleyn laid a hand on his friend's arm to silence him and drew him aside. Into his ear, he whispered, "Leave off, Kit! Or it will be just thee and me to drag this box to its hole."

The funeral party contrived to reach the open grave where the coffin was dropped onto the grass without ceremony and the party flopped down similarly. To prove a parable, ale miraculously appeared from nowhere and the funeral party settled to toast the deceased's health. Birdsong filled the graveyard, but failed to placate Christopher Marlowe.

"Up, up, ye lazy dogs! Or I will kick thee, one after another into that grave!"

"Ease off, Kit!" cried Billy, "Give time to take breath. We's steaming like puddens in an oven! Give we time!"

Edward Alleyn nodded agreement, drawing his friend aside from argument.

"Who are we burying today?" Christopher asked, "I presume we have not carted a box of bricks all the way to Stratford?"

"You may remember him, Kit? Yorick Haye?"

"Alas, poor Yorick! I knew him well, Edward!"

"Fortunately for us, he is deceased. Escaping from the bailiffs. Quite the acrobat. Taunted their reluctance to follow him across the rooftops. Did a little jig to enrage them."

"How can one forget his tedious jigs?"

"He fell into a dung cart and drowned."

"Alas, poor Yorick!" commiserated Christopher Marlowe, "The unfunniest jester of them all. He had a host of jests that made one weep, not laugh. He could neither sing nor act. Nor tell a tale to set the table on a roar. Fancied himself an acrobat, but broke his bones or an innocent other's. Yet he insisted on doing all five badly."

Alleyn laughed and Christopher continued, "He found The Massacre of Paris, too short and a trifle grim. He offered to fill it out and brighten it with his capers! He was sublimely blind to his failings. Indeed, I knew him well, that damned Yorick!"

As the grave was short on measure for the coffin, which lodged awkwardly, the fat man jumped up and down on the box to ensure all was fair and square. When it was seen to be pleasurable, the pall bearers began to dance a jig on the coffin. The afternoon took on a pleasurable turn. The dwarf was a particularly proficient tap dancer and earned generous applause as he sank slowly into the earth.

The priest was too far-gone in liquor to dance on the coffin, although vigorously prodded into service. He was voted worst caperer. It was proposed by unanimous vote to bury him with Yorick Haye. But Edward Alleyn, ever the diplomat, persuaded the sportsmen instead to hang him upside down from a tree.

"Who will now carry the service?" enquired Billy.

"I will," decided Christopher Marlowe, "as it is my funeral."

"Make it short, master!" pleaded a voice, "The sun splits me skull."

Christopher began, "The gentleman who we have interred in spirit today was a unique creature. A fine playwright. A generous friend. A most handsome gentleman."

"A miserly employer," came a voice.

"He has been wrongly judged by the world. He is no heretic. He is no traitor to his Queen. He has fought for Queen and Faith as a valiant man and true. He has only done his duty as a man is bound to do. His reputation is besmirched beyond measure. His work discarded. His very name erased."

Christopher paused and continued, "And as I perceive none of you is listening to a word I say, I will cease to proclaim the virtues of this peerless gentleman."

A volume of cheers startled the rooks from the elms. A blown raspberry stained the ensuing silence.

"One would expect no more from rascals who call themselves actors," complained the interred.

"Where is the headstone/" asked Edward Alleyn, hoping to distract his friend.

The stone was brought forward. The Herculean began to fill the grave. The tall thin man joined him.

"Here lies Christopher Marlowe? Is that all?"

"That's all there were room for. If the mason had cut Kit, there might have been room for He has left the stage. But as this is where you lie, in both usages of the word, it is self-evident!"

"I didn't understand that, master," said Billy Brakspar.

"Don't worry about it, Billy," Edward Alleyn reassured him, "As long as we are agreed that Kit has snuffed it and is under this very sod."

Billy and the funeral party agreed.

"What do you say, Kit?" enquired Alleyn, "Has all been done well to celebrate your passing from this vale of tears?"

"The scurvy mason has spelt my name wrongly," said Christopher Marlowe deceased.

CHAPTER SEVENTEEN

The gentleman said, "You should be ashamed, Nell, for what you have brought upon Todd. The good man Todd who waters his ale no more than a quart to a gallon. No more does he to his spirits than a sprinkle of pepper to spice sour wine or nightshood to his brandy to induce slumber."

Mary Savage, Headmistress of Randall's, sheathed in the body of Nell, drudge of the Bull's Head, crouched by the chair to which the beaten Todd was tied. With her dress hem she tried to wipe clean his bruised face. His mouth was torn and he bled from brow and ear. *And yet he refused to tell them what I told them so willingly.*

"What should I do to our sweet Nell, friend Todd?"

Mary Savage felt her bladder fill to overflowing. Terror made her tremble openly.

"Please!" she begged, but said no more when the gentleman raised a finger to his lips.

"She has betrayed you, my friend. As you tried to deceive me. I have only to say the word and you will hang from your own lintel."

He turned to Mary Nell who flinched, unable to meet his eyes.

"What say you, Todd? Do I hang you? Or the drudge that betrayed you? Someone must pay the piper's price."

In the silence of the chamber, Mary Savage cried out, "I did betray him! Then hang me! Hang me! Leave Todd be! You've tortured him enough!"

The gentleman smiled at Nell.

"Come, come, friend Todd! I have better uses for my time! Be quick! Tell me your desire! Or I shall hang you both!"

The broken mouth opened and said, "Hang me. Let Nell be."

Mary Savage began to weep until silenced by a kick from the Weasel. The gentleman looked upon the man and girl in wonderment.

He quoted, "Tell me, where is fancy bred, In the heart or in the head? God's truth, Todd, I'd never have dreamt you were a man of passion! She must have some quality I cannot see, must our pretty Nell!"

He turned to his confederates.

"We have what we came for. The heretic Marlowe is not dead. We must snare him to ensure he shuffles off this mortal coil in the least time."

The parlour door opened and closed. The chamber was silent.

To the beaten man, Mary Savage said, "Thank you," and rose to bring a knife to cut his bonds.

Mary Savage sewed precisely, neatly as a machine. Just as she once demonstrated the Art of Sewing to classes of girls. She tied off the thread. Snipped off her loose ends.

"How is that? I fear I may have hurt you for my hands are shaking."

Todd essayed a smile with a freshly sewn mouth.

"You have the touch of a butterfly."

She dabbed away the slightest leakage of blood and regarded her handiwork.

"You were never a handsome man, Todd, but..."

He snatched the looking glass from her and examined his swollen face.

"But," she continued, "I consider my work an improvement upon Nature."

"Done well," whispered Todd, painfully.

The torturers had cut his mouth back almost to his ears. Nell had sewn without anaesthetic to restore his mouth; fine stitches from a skilful, unhurried hand. Dabbing again at the sealed wounds, she wondered how she had had the courage to begin. It wasn't fragile, frightened Nell who threaded the needle. It wasn't frightened, skilful Mary who put the needle through the flesh and drew the raw wounds together. It was a new person, a woman born out of the trauma of past days.

"Why did you ask them to hang you and not me?"

Todd tried to speak and failed. He took her hand and kissed her fingers. The woman, neither Nell nor Mary, kissed his tortured mouth gently.

* * * *

Joan waited until the prefect, Isobel Morgan, was immersed in helping a younger girl sort out her electronic chaos and then pressed print. She walked without haste to the printer, gathered her pictures into a folder and signed the print book. On her way to the door, she smiled sweetly at a suspicious Morgan and signed in and out of the Computer Room. In the corridor, Joan drew a deep breath of relief. All Randall girls learn to outwit prefects. All prefects expect to be outwitted.

At the bedroom door where *MELANIE DUNCAN MACKENZIE* remained in its slot, Joan looked to left and right before she entered. She dropped to her knees to slide under the bed where she examined the pictures by torchlight. Three pictures she discarded.

With the chosen pictures safely in a satchel, Joan slid out of her hidyhole. She tore up the unwanted pictures. With a delicious sense of disobedience, Joan lay on her bed, clutching the satchel. Randall girls do not lie on their beds before bedtime. Randall girls stand or sit. Randall girls do not lean, slouch or prop themselves on or against furniture. A Randall girl learns that how she behaves is the measure of how she will be perceived by the world. No doubt if time travel became commonplace, the Randall would prohibit travel without a chaperone.

Joan focussed her thoughts on the boy Ensign and his Riflemen, waiting at the hidden roadway for the French cavalry to pour across the river.

* * * *

The sun was hot on the small animal area. The doe and her kittens in the open pen were stretched out napping in the sun. Laura could hear girls' voices from the quadrangle far below. She was reluctantly putting her favourite rabbit, Randolph, back into his hutch when

Miss Meadows appeared. The other Monitor had gone on to her next class.

Latching the hutch door, Laura apologised, saying, "Sorry, miss, he's too sweet to part with. Going now!"

She didn't like Miss Meadows, but a few stolen moments of affection with Randolph were worth the price. Randall girls were taught to regard affection with suspicion as Russian girls learn smiling is weakness. Randall girls were encouraged to smile.

"I quite understand, Laura," said Miss Meadows who didn't understand, "What is your next lesson?"

"Free study period, miss."

"Then, if you'll give me a hand, I'd be grateful?"

"Yes, miss. What would you like me to do?"

"Buck Seven needs a vitamin and mineral injection."

"You mean Randolph, miss?"

"Yes. Randolph, if you wish. Buck Seven."

Laura brought the rabbit out of his hutch, gently stroking him. Randolph, a fine Flemish Giant, sat calmly on the roof of his hutch.

"Splendid! Now if you will hold him, one hand on his neck and one hand on his hind quarters, I will inject his rear right leg."

Laura held the unresisting rabbit as requested.

"I don't like injections, miss. If you don't mind, I'll look away when you tell me."

"Look away now," said Miss Meadows and stabbed Laura's right hand with the hypodermic needle. Laura cried out in pain and instinctively shook off the needle violently. She began to suck the wound, but with admirable presence of mind, retained her grip on Randolph.

"Laura, I'm so sorry! What can I say? The rabbit moved just when I was about to inject him. I'm so sorry!"

As Laura sucked the microscopic wound, she knew Miss Meadows was lying. Randolph had not moved. Miss Meadows rescued the hypodermic.

"Let me try again. I'm afraid I let my nerves get the better of me. I must confess I'm not at ease giving injections."

Laura reluctantly agreed. She forced herself to watch the injection. Randolph didn't react beyond a twitch. Miss Meadows did not empty the hypodermic, which Laura considered odd.

"I have other rabbits to treat," Miss Meadows explained.

In the biology lab, she insisted on washing and disinfecting Laura's hand. She added a neat Elastoplast strip. Miss Meadows' parting words were, "I'm so sorry, Laura, a most regrettable accident. May I hope we are still good friends?"

"Yes, miss," lied Laura.

* * * *

When Joan came out of double French, she found Laura waiting for her. They went to tea together. Laura was quiet. Finally, Joan couldn't bear the silence any longer. She chewed and swallowed the crust of her sandwich. Randall girls always eat the crust.

"Is there something you want to tell me, Laura?"

"No. I just enjoy having tea with you."

"Skip the nonsense about how wonderful it is to eat tuna sandwiches with me. What's wrong, Charlie Chuckles?"

Laura said, "If I'm right there's something so very wrong it really frightens me. I hope it's me that's wrong. You won't laugh at me?"

"I promise. Now spill the beans."

"I think Ma Meadows just tried to kill me."

Joan suppressed the urge to laugh. She swallowed the last of her tea and picked up what was left of her sandwich.

"Come on! Bring your sandwich. But don't say another word."

Lying in the secret bunker under the bed, Joan asked, "Why would you think a crazy thing like that? I don't like her, but..."

"After biology I cleaned up and went to see Randolph."

"Who is Randolph?" Joan interrupted.

"Randolph is a rabbit."

"A rabbit. Okay!"

"Ma Meadows came out and said he needed a vitamin injection and would I hold him while she did it. So, I held Randolph and I looked away because I don't like needles and she stabbed me in the hand."

Joan laughed. Laura looked upset.

"What's so funny?"

"I'm sorry, but it is funny."

"Not to me, it wasn't. I'm the one got stabbed! You try it and see how funny it is!"

"What did you do?"

"Yelled. Sucked it like you do when a snake bites you."

"Did she inject anything into you?"

"Don't think so."

"Did she finally inject the rabbit?"

"Yes. But she only gave him a little bit. There was plenty left in the needle."

"Did you ask her why?"

"She said she had other rabbits to do."

"Did you hold any other rabbits for her?"

"I'm not completely loopy!"

"Did she ask?"

"No."

"Why do you think she was trying to kill you?"

"I don't know. It just felt all wrong. Her face was pale. Her hand shook."

"Which is why she stuck you."

"No. From the moment she got out the needle, none of it felt right."

Joan was silent, thinking it through.

"How would it have worked? This murder?"

Laura hesitated and then said, "The injection knocks me out. Ma Meadows pushes me over the wall and I fall to the Quad. Oh, dear me! An accident. Goodbye, Laura! And by the way, I don't want to be cremated."

"Why do you think she wanted to kill you? I know you can be irritating, but..."

Laura shook her head.

"Dunno! Does she have to have a reason?"

"Most murderers do. I'm sorry, but I think you're way off. Teachers can be cruel, mean, unfair and ignorant. Ma Meadows is a prize winner in all categories."

She looked to Laura for a response. She was silent.

"But you can't go around the school telling people Ma Meadows tried to kill you. You still think you're right, stay away from her."

"But I can't! I'm a Rabbit Monitor. I have her for Biology. And some private study."

"Give up being a Monitor."

Laura interrupted to say, "I can't do that!"

"Then see to the rabbits when she's not there. Sit at the back of the class in Biology. Don't draw attention to yourself and never be alone with her."

Laura was silent.

"Teachers don't kill children. They just don't."

Laura said, "Would you like to see where she stabbed me?"

Joan switched on her torch to examine the grievous wound.

CHAPTER EIGHTEEN

Dimly aware of the buzz of university life outside his door, Donald Mason in a polar neck sweater, sat at the desk in his office, defeated by the crumpled sheet of paper before him. It constituted the weekly essay of a fresher who boasted of A Levels in Language and Literature. Donald had struggled to find anything positive to say about the dismal piece. He wondered why the schools had given up teaching English children to speak and write their native language. The foreign students spoke and wrote better English. In all conscience he couldn't grade this essay even at the lowest level. He put a large red question mark at the bottom of the paper and put it aside. He reached for another essay and someone knocked at his door.

"Come in!"

The door opened and two men entered; a short and a tall man, each dressed most oddly in a pink plastic raincoat and pixie hood. Donald Mason struggled not to wet himself. He had never ever been more frightened than he was now. In the Cairngorms he had fallen thirty feet; fortunately to lodge on a ledge where he lay overnight awaiting rescue. He had been frightened then. Now he was in fear for his life. He rose unsteadily to his feet.

"What can I do for you?"

His voice sounded wrong. The tall man stood with his back to the door. The short man came round the desk to him and Donald edged away.

"What d'y'want?"

The weasel-faced man sat down at the desk and ruffled through the stack of essays. Finding nothing of interest, he dropped them to the floor.

"Do you mind?"

"Do I mind what?"

"Not throwing my students' work on the floor."

"I dropped. Not threw. This is throwing."

He picked up Donald's treasured fragment of Roman mosaic and threw it at the wall. The fragment dissolved into a handful of tesserae.

"There was no need for that."

"Indeed, there was. You lied to me."

"I'm sure I didn't."

The tall man moved so swiftly, Donald was bent over the desk with his arm thrust painfully up his back before he could protest. He cried out in pain.

"Splendid! I have your attention."

Donald said nothing.

"We know you spoke to the man we seek. Others have told us so. What conversation did you have with him?"

Donald was silent.

"Those who saw you together said you spoke like friends."

The tall man forced the arm farther up his back and Donald cried out in pain.

"A man who knew you worked at the University said you shared a particular interest. The songs he sang. Very old songs."

Donald Mason knew the two men would kill the busker and the girl.

"We have no interest in harming you. Tell us where we may find this man and we will part good friends."

Somewhere Donald Mason found a reserve of strength, of obstinacy that surprised him. He had hated the bullies in school who despised the glorious literature he held dear. He abhorred fellow students in University who had no real interest in study and saw it as another three, four years of idleness. It astonished him they didn't understand what a privilege it was to be at University.

Donald Mason said, "If I knew where he lived, I wouldn't tell you."

The grip on him relaxed and the short man said, "In our excursions we have met many marvels. But in our particular trade, this is a most splendid device."

A cigarette lighter appeared within Donald's vision. There was a click and a flame of two, three inches appeared. The tall man held his left arm behind Donald's back. His right hand was pressed onto the desk. The short man applied the flame. As the skin sizzled and smoke arose, Donald Mason began to shout. He knew it was unlikely anyone would hear, but it was his only weapon. The flame vanished. Donald nursed a burnt hand.

"Imagine if I were to apply this toy to your eye."

"Then I would shout louder."

"We must take him from here."

The short man picked up the photograph of Donald's wife and daughter, Eleanor.

"I would very much like to meet your delightful family."

"In a pig's ear!"

"But we must continue our conversation."

"I've nothing to say."

"We cannot continue here. If you continue to refuse, I will kill the girl first. If you take us to your home, I promise your good wife and daughter will suffer no harm."

Donald pretended to consider the options.

"If you refuse, I would remind you that we found you. We will find your home and family."

"Do I have your absolute word you will not harm my family?"

"On my oath, God's blood, I swear."

There was a tap at the door and a young man put his head in to say, "If it's convenient, I'd like to."

"Later," said his tutor, "I'll be free later."

The door closed reluctantly.

"We will kill anyone who enters," the short man warned.

Donald Mason shrugged his surrender.

"Do you have a carriage without horses?"

* * * *

Driving along the road between the dykes to the solitary cottage where he knew his wife and daughter would be tortured and murdered, Donald made his decision. He pulled the steering wheel sharply to the left and drove off the road into the dyke.

As the car sank into deep water the two men in pink plastic screamed and pulled at their safety belts. Donald Mason sat impassive, grasping the steering wheel with one hand. With his free hand he pressed the button to lock the doors.

* * * *

Sitting at the table to catch the early evening light, Joan showed Laura the photographs she had printed.

"They're gross," Laura complained, "I don't want to look at them. And anyway, where're you going to get gunpowder?"

"If you help me I can get what we need. Don't you want to help the Riflemen at the ford?"

"You have a pash for this boy."

Joan blushed and said, "They'll be killed if I don't help them."

"They're dead now, Joan. They've been dead for centuries."

"Not if you look at All Time is Now."

Interrupting, Laura said, "Okay! All Time is Now! Then, this boy is two hundred years too old for you. Your mother wouldn't approve."

"That's not funny."

"Wasn't meant for funny. We were going to find Christopher Marlowe who actually is here. What happened about that?"

"Well, we know who put the kibosh on that!"

"To be honest, Joan, I don't want to go time travelling."

Joan tried to interrupt but Laura ignored her.

"All I'd want to find is my Dad and stop him going to that bomb. And if I did, it would mean somebody else would be killed. But not my Dad. I want that so much. My Dad alive. They can have the silly medal back! But then I think, do I want some other girl to feel like I do? Tomorrow there would be another bomb anyway."

Joan was suddenly humbled.

"You must've had to grow up quick. I don't know anybody who thinks like that. You're really something else, Laura."

"So, I don't want to go time travelling with you. Why don't you ask Melanie?"

"You're kidding?"

"No. She might be waiting for you to ask."

* * * *

Girls in the corridors of the Wavell Wing looked on Joan with curiosity as she wandered along looking for the right door. It had not occurred to Joan to ask Laura who knew where everyone lived, in whatever nook and cranny. There were voices, music and laughter behind doors as she walked, checking name labels, determined not to ask directions. Joan walked into the prefect, Julie Morris, coming out of a bedroom door.

"Aren't you on the wrong turf, d'Urquart?"

"Isn't this the Randall, Morris?"

"Where are you going?"

"Melanie Mackenzie."

"With Natalie de Meliere. Twenty seven. Turn right at the corridor end."

"Thank you."

Joan hesitated to knock on the door. A girl passed, almost walking backwards to watch Joan. She tapped on the door.

"Go away!"

Joan tapped again. There was a muttering and the door opened. Natalie, visibly surprised, stared at Joan.

"Wha'd'y'want, d'Urquart?"

"A word with Melanie, please?"

The door closed. The muttering resumed. The door opened. Melanie came out closing the door behind her.

Joan was shocked at her appearance. She had lost weight she didn't need to lose and looked tired. Melanie brightened at the sight of Joan and smiled.

"Wow! A real surprise! Mahomet has arrived at the mountain!"

"The cavalry will cross the ford any time now. Will you help me stop them?"

"Now?"

"Tomorrow? Saturday for us, whatever day it is for them."

The light went out in Melanie's face.

"I'm sorry. I can't."

"Can't or won't?"

Uncertainty flickered.

"We're going to Paris tonight. Eurostar."

"Of course!"

"Natalie's been invited by this Marquise. Family friend. There's a gallery tour tomorrow. And a fashion show. She can take a guest and I've said yes. I'm sorry. I can't let her down."

"Not like you let me down. I'll tell the Riflemen you were too busy to help."

Walking away, Joan turned to see Melanie standing at the bedroom door. She felt mean and furious.

"That was unworthy of you," she rebuked herself as she walked through the double doors between the wings, "There was no need to say that."

"I didn't say anything," complained the puzzled girl Joan had brushed aside.

* * * *

Laura climbed the silent stairs to the third floor, only her solitary feet echoing in the stairwell. When she stood still to listen she could hear herself breathing. On the landing, she walked past Chemistry labs, One and Two and Physics labs Alpha and Beta, holding her breath, daring not to look left or right. No one challenged her. At the Biology lab door, she hesitated, but it was unlocked. She entered into its curiously surgical atmosphere and was startled when a voice asked, "What're you doing here?"

The cleaner stood leaning on her mop. Laura was shocked to silence.

"Cat got your tongue?"

"I'm the Rabbit Monitor. I've come to check on a rabbit."

"Why?"

"He wasn't very well this afternoon."

The cleaner said grudgingly, "Never known any of you to be so keen."

"May I?"

"No skin off my nose."

"Thank you."

Laura moved across the lab to the door to the flat roof.

"What's your name?"

Laura hesitated.

"You don't know your name?"

"Laura. Laura MaCallaman."

Why am I giving her my real name?

Inquisitive noses brought rabbits to hutch doors as Laura wandered down the row. Her heart lurched at the empty hutch, but opening the sleeping half, she found Randolph, opening a drowsy eye to her. He stood up to grasp the dandelion leaves she had brought him. When she lifted him out onto the hutch roof she saw he was shaky on his feet. All the occupants of the hutches she had passed were lively. *Was it a vitamin and mineral injection? Or something to put him to sleep?* The door from the lab opened to surprise Laura. The cleaner came to join her.

"Gosh! He's a big 'un! What's his name?"

They took turns stroking Randolph.

"Ya right," observed the cleaner, "He's a bit off colour."

Laura agreed.

"Best put him back? I'm sure he'll be alright tomorrow."

As they parted the cleaner said, "Nice you come see how he was doing."

She returned to her mop and Laura walked down the stairs thinking. *Why would she want to put me to sleep?*

* * * *

Robert Simpson was a happy man. He enjoyed being Miss Savage's Man Friday. Whatever she asked of him he performed with a good heart. He was also pleased to be Rifleman Simpson at the French-made underwater road on a Portuguese river in 1810. He didn't know why he was there, but he accepted his situation. It was like being called out from Reserve. He understood his weapon, the Baker rifle and knew the rifling in the barrel spun the ball giving greater accuracy and range. He had worked hard to become as good a marksman as his comrades and not rely on the skill of the Rifleman whose body he occupied. He liked his mates, trusted his Sergeant, could eat anything and wasn't surprised the Army had changed very little in two hundred years.

He was lying in the fire pit among the willows watching the ford. In the warm evening sunshine it was a pleasant duty. The chorus of birds, the quiet voice of the river, the silence of the camp in the dead ground behind him all contrived to lull the senses. Rifleman Simpson was too wily a bird to fall into a doze. A sharp stone under his stomach was a constant irritation. The passing fly was an ally. A soldier who fell asleep at his post was flogged. But it wasn't fear of punishment kept Bob Simpson alert. He respected his officer and would never let his mates down.

At his right side lay his rifle, loaded, primed, with a new flint. The lock was loosely wrapped in a cloth to keep off any stray sand. To his left lay a second rifle, similarly prepared. Under his nose was a knotted cord that wound back to the camp where a stick would fall over if he pulled, signalling the squad to arms.

Something moved on the farther bank beyond the screening willows. Simpson automatically slid his rifle to his shoulder, the dust cloth falling away. This was what they had been waiting for during endless, airless days. He froze and watched. He was bareheaded. His battered shako lay somewhere behind him. This was something he had taught his mates.

"Ya shako's meant to make you look eight feet tall. Here you want to be three feet nothing so Monsewer cannot see ya. Ya meant to be a nasty surprise to the Froggies."

Saying this he hadn't known Sergeant Springer and Corporal Thatcher were behind him. Neither contradicted the Rifleman. The Sergeant had nodded. *I suppose once a sergeant always a sergeant. Watch yourself, Bob!*

Nothing moved for an eternity. He released his breath slowly. His hand relaxed on the trigger guard. He had begun to believe he was mistaken when the willow curtain moved again. He decided not to pull the cord. Embarrassing if deer or donkey stepped out onto the shingle. If this is a Frog, he knows his business.

A fine bay horse stepped out onto the shingle. The Rifleman took aim at the rider. The horse stood still as the officer surveyed the farther shore through his telescope, the tube moving steadily along the shoreline.

Simpson had time to study the Frenchman. He wore a high blue shako with gold trimming and a red and white plume. His tightly fitting tunic was of imperial blue with gold facings. His white breeches were immaculate. His boots were knee high and dazzlingly polished. Some poor squaddie worked a lifetime on those. He wore a curved cavalry sword; a young officer of the Imperial Dragoons. Robert Simpson, porter at the Randall, prepared to kill this young man.

CHAPTER NINETEEN

There was scarcely a whisper of a breeze, the light excellent, the target stationary. The Rifleman aimed for a breast shot, the easiest and the deadliest. The Dragoon nudged his horse into the water and moved out twelve, fifteen paces. He's making sure the ford is untouched. He surveyed the farther shore again. Simpson remained immovable. He knew it was movement that was detected. The horse drank from the ford. When his mount had filled his belly, his rider jerked the reins and his horse shouted. His neigh was loud and imperative. The officer sat silent, listening. Simpson prayed the Captain's horse wouldn't respond, wouldn't answer the cavalry mount. The moment was endless. The Captain's horse didn't answer. The Dragoon returned to the shore.

There again he tugged the reins and the horse shouted loudly. Simpson found himself sweating with anxiety. His rifle was aimed to project an ounce of lead that would break through the gold and blue to shatter the heart within. His finger was curled about the trigger. Bob Simpson took a deep breath and prepared to kill the Frenchman. The Dragoon snapped shut his telescope. Horse and rider vanished into the green willow.

Bob Simpson breathed a sigh of relief and wiped sweat from his brow. He uncocked his rifle and put it to one side, wrapping the lock in its cloth. He groped for his water bottle, drank deeply and recorked it. Then he pulled the signal string. He seemed only to have taken a single breath before the Ensign and Sergeant slid silently into the fire pit beside him.

"Yes?" said the Ensign.

"A French Dragoon officer, sir. Young man. On his own. He surveyed our shore. Did it twice. Checked the ford was still here. Caused his horse to neigh twice. The Captain's horse didn't answer, sir."

"Why didn't you shoot him?" asked Sergeant Springer.

"He came to see if we were here, sir. If we had discovered the ford. He rode away believing we aren't here. That we haven't discovered their ford. That's what he'll tell his Captain. If I shot him, sir, they'd know we was here."

The Ensign and the Sergeant looked at one another in surprise.

"You worked this all out by yourself, Simma?" asked the Sergeant.

"While you were preparing to shoot the officer?" the Ensign asked.

Bob Simpson nodded.

"Yes, sir. Just commonsense, sir."

When addressed by a Sergeant and an Officer address every answer to the Officer.

"They're coming, sir. But it's us that'll be the surprise, sir."

Throw in as many sirs as you can stomach.

"Well done, Simpson," said the Ensign.

The Sergeant nodded approval.

"I'll send your relief, Simpson."

"Thank you, sir."

As they walked away, Sergeant Springer confessed, "Never thought Simpson had any wits whatever, sir. He's no Isaac Newton. Apple hit Simma, he'd eat it."

The Ensign smiled, responding, "Good sergeants make good Riflemen. Bad sergeants waste good Riflemen."

"Thank you, sir."

He'll make a proper officer yet. He's learnt how to oil a sergeant.

"That was a compliment well-earned, Sergeant. Not a load of flannel."

"Yes, sir. Thank you, sir."

* * * *

With a bang, clatter and enough black smoke to rouse the Sioux nation, the motorcycle and sidecar racketed through the gateway arch of Gilsford University Old Campus to park in a Disabled space. The porter came as far as the archway to glare across the car park at the riders. Christopher Marlowe limped about the bike unconvincingly as he retrieved his saddle bags. Hannah jumped out nimbly with the guitar. Reassured, the porter lost interest.

"Do we always have to drag those about with us?" Hannah complained, indicating the saddle bags.

"Tell me where is safe?"

Wrapping a chain and padlock about the front wheel, Christopher said, "Tell me again why we're doing this?"

"Gilsford Council think we should pay some rent. Or they'll evict us. I like to eat. You just eat. Polar Neck should hire you to lecture on Elizabethan England. Nobody knows more than you. Or just to sing?"

"They'll find and kill us."

"Homeless, we can die in a ditch."

"Do you take nothing seriously? They will kill us."

"Who's this us? Who did I upset in the sixteenth century?"

The middle-aged receptionist smiled sweetly at this handsome man. Hannah suppressed a scowl and produced Donald Mason's card.

"We met Mister Mason and he suggested."

The sweet smile vanished.

"You don't know?"

Christopher asked, "What should we know, please?"

Hannah interrupted to worry, "Please don't tell us he's had the boot?"

"I wish I could say he'd been terminated," intoned the receptionist, unconscious of the irony, "The fact is, Donald Mason is in intensive care."

The receptionist fought back her tears. Christopher and Hannah knew not what to say.

Hannah tried, "What happened? His heart? A road accident?"

"His car went off the road into Drayton Dyke."

Recognising their uncomprehending glances, she continued, "You're not local? The dykes are deep. If a police car hadn't been passing, Donald would've drowned."

"Any reason why?" Hannah asked tentatively, "the car would?"

"Nothing wrong with the car. I don't know what comfort it might be to his wife, but Donald didn't seem to have struggled. I'm told he was sitting, hands on the steering wheel, safety belt still secured. He smiled at the policeman who dived in to release him."

"Anyone else in the car?" Christopher questioned.

The receptionist shook her head.

"Just Donald. Wasn't he lucky?"

As he unwrapped the chain from the front wheel, Christopher said, "Now you believe me, Hannah?"

She was silent.

"He spoke to us. Others would see he spoke to us. Those that seek us found this poor man. He had nothing to tell them. They intended to kill him just the same."

"He doesn't seem to have struggled."

"There are substances that would quieten him."

"It could be a simple road accident."

"Then again, it may not be so, my dear Hannah. It may be attempted murder. Fortunately, our dark friends are not at ease with modern magic."

Hannah laughed.

"But you are, of course! The man who's afraid of the immersion heater."

Christopher kicked the motorcycle into life.

"Remember! The dykes are deep."

"Not yet so deep as my foreboding."

"Ever the cheerful word as we trust our lives once more to This Thing!"

How have they tracked us this far? A moment of insight. *That damned school! Those girls!*

* * * *

In the midst of the screaming and shouting of men in fear and anger, Hannah defied the flailing of clubs and knives to win through to where she had seen Christopher fall. He lay on his back in the mud, unheeded by trampling boots. Hannah fell to her knees beside him. Blood was pouring from his neck. He smiled at her weakly.

Tearing at her dress, she knew she couldn't stop the bleeding. Christopher Marlowe had only moments to live.

Devastated, Hannah cried out in her agony, "My God, is this how it will end? Dying in the mud?"

She awoke weeping, to stifle her sobs as she recognised the steady breathing from the other bedroom. She lay listening for some minutes as her pain and terror subsided. Then she arose and went silently to stand at the open doorway of Christopher's bedroom.

They had burned the upstairs doors to keep warm in the winter. She had said jokingly, when they dismantled the last door, the bathroom door, "Next winter we burn the rafters."

Reprovingly, Christopher had replied, "After the furniture."

She noted he was always somewhere else when she used the bathroom and became accustomed to bathing, knowing she wouldn't be interrupted. Similarly, she paid him the same courtesy. It was easy to spot when he was in the bathroom from the noise, the reciting, the singing. He never entered her doorless bedroom.

He was breathing easily, steadily, buried in the duvet that he regarded with alarm when first he met it. Christopher had an easy grace, a carelessness of action. Hannah had concluded it wasn't that he was careless by nature, but that he saw less to care about. It didn't trouble him that they burnt the doors. It was necessary to keep warm. His discovery of the paraffin stove, which amused Hannah, was more important.

"If there were a fire, what would you save, Kit?"

He thought for a moment and answered, "My writings, my stove and my instrument."

"What about me?"

Puzzled, he responded, "What about you?"

"Wouldn't you save me?"

"You would be carrying my stove."

Hannah stood watching him breathe.

Almost silently, she whispered, "Is this how it will end? Dying in the mud?"

She went back to bed. It took a long time for her to fall asleep.

* * * *

The Ensign, with Sergeant Springer and Rifleman Simpson in attendance, related to the Captain the incident of the French Dragoon. The Captain sat in his campaign chair, toying with his silver cup. The young officer ended by saying, "I have commended Rifleman Simpson, sir."

"I fear, sir," said the Captain, "that I have been stricken with an affliction of the ear. I don't believe I heard your last remark correctly. Please, repeat what you said, sir."

"I have commended Rifleman Simpson, sir."

"How odd! My order is to have the Rifleman flogged. Twenty strokes should be sufficient."

The three Riflemen stood frozen in shock and disbelief.

"I don't understand, sir."

"Furthermore, the Sergeant is relieved of his stripes and returned to the ranks. I would hesitate to flog a sergeant before the squad."

"Sir, I must protest."

"Protest away, sir. You will be reported to the Office of the Provost Marshal and face a court martial. You will be stripped of your commission."

The Ensign was pale with suppressed anger. The Sergeant's face was unreadable. The Rifleman looked bewildered.

"Sir, I cannot understand why you are behaving in this fashion."

"You have broken the primary rule of the Army in the field, sir."

The Ensign stood speechless.

"In the British Army, sir, private soldiers do not make decisions. Officers make decisions. Your Rifleman made the decision not to shoot the enemy. He decided how the situation should be resolved. Your Sergeant is as guilty because he didn't instantly rebuke the Rifleman."

In the silence the simple noises of the encampment sounded loudly.

"What do you think would happen if every soldier made his own decisions?"

"Rifleman Simpson is not every soldier."

"When you took your post what were your orders, Rifleman?"

Bob Simpson pondered for a moment.

"Well, man? I presume you had orders?"

"Yes, sir. To observe, report and oppose any attempt of the enemy to cross."

"Do you believe you carried out your orders?"

"Yes, sir."

"Wrong! You observed an enemy approach. You should've reported his presence and prepared to oppose him crossing."

"If he had attempted to cross I was prepared to shoot him, sir. But there wasn't time to report to the officer, sir. I did what I knew he would do, sir."

"Of course, you knew what your officer would do. I presume you have had many a fireside chat with him? Good chums, eh?"

"No, sir. I have never spoken to the officer, sir."

"You and your chum, the Ensign, calculated that the enemy thinking you weren't here would expect no opposition if, as you believe, their cavalry will cross tomorrow. On the other hand, I believe shooting the Dragoon would tell the enemy his ruse was working and we were splitting our forces to cover both the rebuilt bridge at Sorino and the mythical ford."

The Ensign insisted, "It took a vast volume of labour to create this crossing, sir. It is an underwater roadway. The bridge is a feint, sir. The French cavalry will cross here and overwhelm our rearguard..."

"When were you attached to Lord Wellington's staff?"

The Ensign was silent.

"Decisions, sir, are taken by officers, not private soldiers. Prepare to flog the Rifleman. And we will strip the Sergeant of his plumage. Time for your merry little gang to learn some hard lessons."

When the Ensign hesitated, the Captain demanded, "Well, what are you waiting for, sir?"

"Sir, I reject your order as unreasonable. I will not flog Rifleman Simpson. Sergeant Springer will retain his hard-won stripes."

The Sergeant began to say something, but changed his mind.

"Simpson, you are dismissed. Your commendation stands."

"Thank you, sir."

The Rifleman saluted and vanished.

"Do you understand what you are doing, sir."

"My duty, sir. The enemy will try to cross the river here and we will oppose them. Tomorrow the matter will be settled. Your views, sir, are irrelevant. I regret to say you are the calibre of Officer who is the enemy within the Army. You do not care for your men. I doubt whether you perceive them as human. To you, they are no more than cannon fodder. Your only concern is your own self-interest. You, sir, are a disgrace to your rank and your uniform."

The Captain spluttered his disbelief, indignation and anger.

"Then, before you are court-martialled, I demand satisfaction. I will not accept an apology, sir."

"No apology will be forthcoming. I will be delighted to give you satisfaction."

The Sergeant's face almost expressed dismay.

"But first we must face Monsewer tomorrow. Will you be joining us, sir? When we have disposed of his little gang, I will be delighted to accommodate you, sir."

"The next time you see me, I shall carry a warrant for your arrest. Sergeant, my horse!"

"Yes, sir! Corporal, the Captain's horse! The officer is leaving us."

The Riflemen turned out smartly to salute the departing officer. As they watched the Captain and his valise of complaints trot away, Sergeant Springer said, "Begging your pardon for the impudence, sir, but that took some nerve. He won't rest at the Provost Marshal. He'll seek a body dressed in gold braid."

The Ensign snorted.

"I was not to have you and Simpson treated so outrageously."

"He'll seek to have you out of the Army, sir."

"Alas, my poor father's savings! But then Monsewer may manage it for me tomorrow."

The Sergeant saluted and departed to tell his Riflemen what a cracking officer they had. Brave, but mad, quite mad.

"I'd prefer it if Monsewer didn't manage it for you tomorrow," said Joan.

"I'd prefer it if you didn't make faces at a senior officer, miss."

"Yes, sir!"

Joan patted the rock beside her.

"Sit down, please. I've some photographs to show you. Pictures. Then I'll tell you how we'll stop the French tomorrow."

* * * *

Mr. Mortimer intercepted Melanie's hand holding the bishop and smiled at Irena Mahashwari Frobisher.

"Think again," he advised Melanie and apologised to Irena, "Forgive me."

If Randall girls are to be of use in the world it follows they should be taught chess. The girls soon realised they were learning an invaluable skill: how to think beyond the moment. Mr. Mortimer's classes were more popular than some European languages.

Irena Mahashwari Frobisher's family was destroyed in an hotel in Mumbai, India, when terrorists demonstrated the quality of freedom the people would enjoy if they succeeded. Her father went to face the murdering thugs because that's how Ghurkha officers behave even when on holiday. With the help of others he organised successful opposition and drove them from the fourth floor saving many lives. However, the grenade thrown into the bedroom killed Irena's mother and stole her daughter's left arm. Irena Mahashwari Frobisher was unmatched at chess by students or staff. Meeting Irena one would never guess the trauma she had suffered. There were a number of similarly afflicted girls from pointless wars in sanctuary at Randall's.

"Take a moment to study Irena's pieces," advised Mr. Mortimer and walked on to the next table.

Melanie was bewildered when Hannah said, "You are in danger. You put us in danger. Leave us alone."

Hannah?

Before she could grasp what was happening, Hannah vanished and Irena smiling, waited for her next move.

Melanie said, "Sorry, sorry. Going for a pee."

Irena said, "Get one for me, Mel!" which was wasted on the empty air. Melanie hid in the cubicle until the bell rang and went off to Biology with Miss Meadows.

Hannah? What did she mean?

* * * *

Corporal Thatcher's Statement; "When it was near dark, our Officer, Sergeant Springer, Riflemen Simpson, Flanagan and me bound every hand securely in hessian and canvas strips.

When I asked Sergeant what the bindings was for he said to me, "Has yous ever tackled tigers afore, Tommy?"

I answered him, "I seen them in India. Nasty brutes. But, no, Sergeant, I have not had the privilege."

"Then you're in for a rare treat," the Sergeant replied.

I did not know whether he was jesting so I resolved to see how he tackled a tiger before I took one on myself.

We went in company with a local girl who spoke better English than Paddy to a barn at a nearby farm. There we took back to camp fifty bales of wire I had not seen before. It was armed with hooks. Sergeant was right. It was wicked stuff. Worse than tigers.

We spent the rest of the night in the river, ending up with cut hands and legs, weaving this murderous wire in and out of our stakes. Once we grasped what this would do to the Frogs we worked like demons, filling their ford with killing wire to catch boots and hooves. Then the officer swam across below the ford and we laid more wire from shore to shore. He done the same above the ford so there was no escaping from this evil wire. I hopes never to see this again.

False dawn was on us as we was done. We was frozen through. Bleeding like that time we pulled out the hundred and one leeches we got wading through a swamp. Best to come was Sergeant brought out two bottles of liquor that had accidentally fallen from the Captain's baggage. We all supped a good draught, but not the Officer who was not too proud to drink with us, but had promised his Father, a Clergyman. We drank the Captain's health. Then we cleaned up and waited for the Frogs. Signed Thomas Thatcher, Corporal, 273, 3rd Rifles.

This was the Corporal's rationalisation of his time walking experience. It was the first time Joan had ever tried to time walk in company. It had worked when she took Laura's hand. Looking at the ferocious Riflemen, Joan baulked at the thought of asking them to hold hands. They had appeared puzzled when ordered to stack rifles, leave shakos behind and pick up unlit torches. But she had seen them, on command, shuffling into line with right hand on a comrade's shoulder. The Ensign stood as marker, the Riflemen shuffled into line and Joan took the young man's hand. They were plunged into darkness. Joan released the boy's hand reluctantly. There was the scratch of flints on iron and the darkness was suddenly illuminated.

To Joan's relief they were standing in the store barn of the Home farm at Randall's. The Riflemen were looking about them. Much of what they saw was familiar. They were in a barn. At the Ensign's order they brought out the bales of barbed wire, each two hundred yards wound around a stout stake. With two men to a bale they made a growing pile of wire. Joan felt little conscience. She left four bales for emergency use.

At Joan's direction the Ensign ordered every man to lay a hand on the wire. Joan laid two hands on the nearest bale. Instantly they were standing in the little encampment in the dead ground above the river. The barbed wire glimmered in the torchlight. Joan gave a great sigh of relief, but was surprised there was so little reaction among the Riflemen. They were not sophisticated men. The Officer gave an order and events unfolded. If he was a good Officer, the outcome was positive. If he was a bad Officer, men died. Such is the power of faith.

The Ensign, Sergeant Springer, Rifleman Flanagan and Corporal Thatcher were Time Walkers eight, nine, ten and eleven.

CHAPTER TWENTY

It was one of those days touched with honeyed sunshine. From breakfast everything had gone well for Joan. She returned to her room to find the cleaner had left a commendation for tidiness. This confirmed her decision to try to win back Melanie. The room was too tidy. She longed for Melanie's shotgun approach to decoration. Morning classes went well. She received an A for her Geometry prep. At lunch she looked for Melanie and couldn't find her. Afternoon classes included her favourite, European history. The bell rang to end school. It was as she was packing her shoulder bag that everything went catastrophically wrong. Melanie's cigarette fell from the bag. It rolled across the floor to lie under the feet of Miss Savage as she entered the classroom. Joan was devastated.

Miss Savage said, "Come with me, d'Urquart."

Joan followed the Headmistress to her office. Miss Savage sat in her chair. Joan stood in front of the desk with knees strained hard enough to break.

"Have you anything to say?"

Joan was tempted to deny ownership of the cigarette, but knew she couldn't betray Melanie. She shook her head.

"Although the figures are decreasing, thousands of women die every year from breast cancer."

"Yes, miss."

"Then you will understand why Randall's views this matter so strictly."

"Yes, miss."

The Headmistress hesitated and sighed. It was a genuine sigh of regret. Joan d'Urquart was not a child she would have thought to smoke.

"You are suspended from Randall's. You will go to your room and pack your immediate belongings. You will wait in your room until I arrange for Mister Simpson to escort you home. Your mother will be informed to expect you. If you have any other cigarettes, please, give them to Mister Simpson."

"But," said Joan, "But, I...."

Yet to save her soul she couldn't find the words to say, it is not my cigarette. It belonged to Melanie. My friend Melanie. True love is a prison to which neither has the key,

"How long you are suspended is a matter for me to decide. Your mother will be informed of my decision in due course."

She hesitated and said, "I must admit, Joan, I am very, very sorry to see you in this situation. I am both shocked and surprised."

The Headmistress looked to Joan who said nothing.

* * * *

The blue flame spread both warmth and reassurance. Christopher sat on the floor. Hannah sat in the chair.

"Well?" asked Hannah, "What're we going to do?"

"Do? I propose to do nothing. I will sit here until my nose turns red. You are going to serve us, prithee please, those delicious little fish from inside the tin box on top of slightly burnt bread."

"Toast," interrupted Hannah, "But first we must decide how we will pay for the little fish and the bread. And for the roof over our heads."

She kicked the silent Christopher.

"I'm serious. They will come in force and not even Mister Stanley's gorillas will stop them seizing the house."

She kicked him again somewhat harder.

"Hard knocks and kicks are all of love's dowry."

"I don't want to be living on the street. I've grown accustomed to a roof over my head."

Instead of weeping, she kicked him harder. Christopher moved the saddlebags to shield his legs.

Hannah complained, "We lug those saddle bags around twenty four seven. We haven't got a horse! Is there nothing in there we can sell?"

An offended Christopher protested, "This is what of my papers I could salvage when I ran."

"Collectors are keen on historical documents. Is there nothing we can sell? A pardon from Queen Elizabeth?"

"Her Majesty only ever considered a pardon after she'd executed the miscreant."

Christopher pondered.

"There's my burial certificate."

"Your what?"

"When they bury you they give you a certificate."

"Let me see."

Christopher unlatched one pannier and burrowed into the ancient, yellowed sheets, jealously guarding them from Hannah's view.

"I don't want to see what you've got."

He handed over a tired yellowed sheet with faded writing.

Silence fell beyond the purring of the paraffin stove.

"You were buried in Holy Trinity Churchyard, Stratford upon Avon in something smudged fifteen ninety three?"

"A very salubrious place to lay one's head."

"But as you haven't lain your head, who did you bury?"

"A miserable creature. Yorick Haye."

"You're joking? Not alas, poor Yorick, I knew him, that one?"

"He drowned in a dung cart. Stank to high Heaven. We got him for sixpence."

"You bought the poor man?"

"They don't give corpses away for free."

"And who's this? Ambergris Templetwist? That's not a real name."

"I doubt he was a real priest. Never knew his name. Drunk beyond any measure."

"Looks as if he signed it upside down!"

"He was hanging from a tree at the time."

Hannah rose from the chair bearing such a look of disbelief upon Christopher as would've singed a ferret.

"Enough! I don't know what to believe."

She vanished to the kitchen.

Fumbling in the saddle bags, Christopher cried, "I have a letter from her Majesty. And the original cast of Tamburlaine. A drawing of me sweet Edward made. What a truly handsome man I am!"

Hannah reappeared.

"Let me see!"

Christopher sat in an awkward silence.

"It's thought to be a good likeness."

Hannah snorted and then surprised, said, "Her Majesty is thanking you for faithful service! She commends your loyalty. What did you do for her?"

"Another time. Another story."

"Oh, this is payday for the cast! Did you really pay so little? Shame on you! Actors here who can't write their names! How did they read their lines?"

"You mistake. They wouldn't sign their names. Safer not to."

A brighter silence.

"I know who will buy these."

Christopher laughed.

"Bobby Bedlam?"

"John Lambert. The Shakespearean nut? The Falstaff? The themed pub you scoff at? He'll buy these. Are you going to ride me over?"

"What will he do with them?"

"Frame them. Hang them on the wall with the other rubbish."

"What about the little fish on burnt bread?"

"Fish and chips on the way back?"

Christopher picked up the saddle bags,

"Please?" Hannah suggested, "Just this once?"

He replaced the saddle bags by the chair.

* * * *

Joan accepted the brown envelope from Miss Savage.

"You will give this envelope to your mother."

"Yes, miss."

"You may go."

The Time Walkers

Joan left the office with Miss Savage's eyes boring into the back of her head. In the deathly silence of the entrance hall, it seemed a hundred years passed before she reached the double front door, every footstep echoing and re-echoing. Joan opened the front door.

It was a long flight of steps down to where the Mitsubishi 4X4 Shogun with the school crest on the polished panels awaited. As she descended, she knew there were eyes at every window of the Great Quadrangle watching her. Symbols have immense power.

Every Summer she had watched with envy the gathering on the steps of the successful O and A level candidates to be photographed with celebrating staff. She had never imagined she would descend these steps alone and in disgrace, She felt small, humiliated and frightened.

The porter, Mr. Simpson, opened the rear door for her, but she objected, saying, "I'd rather ride in front with you."

"Sorry! Better off in the back."

He stood holding the door.

"I'll be driving, not talking. I know you've broken the rules, but that's all I need to know. What I can say is, I'm sure I've done worse. It's not the end of the world, girl. Nothing lasts forever. Not even feeling sorry for yourself. End of lecture."

It was a long speech for Bob Simpson. He felt sorry for the child, but if lessons were to be learned, sympathy was not the right ointment.

Joan got into the rear seat. The driver closed the door. The car moved out of the Great Quadrangle and Joan felt she was dying. Through the country lanes, she fought not to weep, but once they were on the motorway she let tiredness overcome her and she slept. When she woke up it was dark. The driver spoke to her.

"Would you like to stop for something to eat or drink?"

She shook her head,

"Sure?"

She nodded affirmatively. Mr. Simpson drove on. Watching all the whirligig of lights near and far, she thought through what she had done. She discovered she didn't regret her decision. She couldn't have betrayed Melanie and would not do so.

She dozed off again and woke with a start when the car stopped outside the familiar house.

"Home. It cannot be all bad to be home. Your mother here?"

Joan nodded.

"Stay there!"

He walked round the car and brought her bag from the boot. He opened the passenger door.

"Out you come, as the pin said to the winkle."

Joan almost smiled. She exited the car and they stood on the pavement, an ill-assorted couple. Mr. Simpson looked at her as if awaiting her instructions.

Joan requested, "Please don't come to the door. Like a parcel being delivered."

I don't want you to see me crying,

"I've got to see you safely into the house."

"You can see me from here. I'll wave as I go in. You'll see the door close."

Mr. Simpson nodded, satisfied and handed over her bag.

"Good luck! Remember! The sun will shine again."

Joan walked up the garden path to the front door. She turned to see Mr. Simpson standing at the gate. She pressed the bell. Nothing. She pressed it again. Footsteps in the hallway. The door opened. Joan's greeting died in her throat. She was looking at a strange girl of about her own age. Joan was rendered speechless. The girl turned and shouted into the house, "She's here!"

To Joan, she said, "Are you coming in or not?"

Joan turned to wave to Mr. Simpson and entered the house. The strange girl stood regarding Joan, summing her up.

"You got the order of the boot?"

"No. I'm suspended."

As the stranger was regarding her, so was Joan regarding the stranger. Red hair well groomed. Eyebrows not natural. Lipstick and nail polish. Joan thought she could smell tobacco.

"Where's my mother?"

"Pamela?"

Pamela?

"Yes, my mother!"

"She's in the bath. They're going out to dinner."
Joan struggled not to say with whom.
"What's your name?"
"Cherise. I know you're Joan."
Joan couldn't smother her curiosity.
"What're you doing here?"
"Doing here?" blanked Cherise, "I live here."
Suddenly, Joan wished she was within the security of the Shogun with Mr. Simpson driving anywhere, but here.
"I don't know what you mean? You live here?"
"Me, Dad and Pamela. Not counting Bisto. He's my cat."
Joan became aware a white cat was sitting on the stairs watching her.

* * * *

Outside the Falstaff Arms, Christopher Marlowe was sitting astride the motorcycle, washed occasionally by gusts of music and voices whenever the doors opened and closed. When they had arrived, Christopher assumed he would go with Hannah to sell the historic documents to John Lambert.
"No, you don't!" Hannah insisted, "Stay there!"
"Why?"
"We need to sell this stuff."
"Then, better the two of us."
"You'll antagonise him and he won't buy."
"Indeed, I won't!"
"You can't help it, Kit! You don't like the man. He'll ask if they're real and you'll have him by the throat."
"You judge me harshly. I'm sweet-tongued as the honey bee."
"Bees are not noted for their sweet tongue, but the sharp bit."
Christopher protested, but Hannah insisted, "Stay there! Don't follow me. If you do, I'll tell the bouncer you're bothering me."
"How sharper than a serpent's tooth it is to have a thankless child!"
Hannah blew a raspberry and walked away.

The car park began to fill. A car drove into the slot next to the motorcycle. A party of four exited, looked at Christopher curiously and entered the Falstaff. The bouncer ambled over to the motorcycle.

"This isn't doing the Falstaff any favours, mate."

Christopher stared at him blankly.

"I'm sorry. I don't understand."

The bouncer looked at Christopher and realising the man was in earnest, explained, "The Falstaff is a classy joint..."

Christopher interrupted to agree, "Indeed, a favoured establishment."

"With a class clientele. Your wreck stuck out front says otherwise."

"I understand! I would move it immediately. But my daughter is inside talking with your boss, John Lambert? I need her to see I'm here when she comes out."

The bouncer hesitated.

"Okay! Let's give it ten minutes."

"Thank you! You're a gentleman."

Ten minutes later the bouncer opened the door for Hannah. He spoke to her and she replied. Hannah came dancing to the motorcycle.

"What did he say to you?"

"Did I get the job?"

"And you said?"

"Even better than that."

The engine started on the third kick.

The motorcycle drew into the layby and the engine stopped.

"Why we stopped?"

"I want to know what happened."

"Can't you wait 'til we get home?"

"Tell me."

"You won't get upset?"

"Why should I?"

"I got two hundred pounds."

"Is that a lot of money?"

Hannah hesitated.

"No. But it is to us."

Christopher was silent.

Hannah said, "I hate the way we live. No money. Threatened with being evicted. Doesn't it worry you?"

"Are you not happy with me?"

"That has nothing to do with it!"

"Nonsense, my dear girl! It is the only matter of concern."

He looked to her as if expecting an answer.

"Well?"

Hannah said, "You're the most annoying person I have ever met. You have little acquaintance with truth. But, yes, I am happy with you. But it would be nice to pay the rent."

"Then I shall go and shake more money from that slippery little toad."

"But two hundred pounds isn't all!"

"Tell me."

"John will have them valued. If they're genuine they're worth a lot more."

"My burial certificate! My cast pay sheet! My commendation from my Sovereign lady! A splendid likeness of myself! How more genuine can they be?"

Hannah repeated with emphasis, "If they are genuine. Then he'll give us half the professional valuation minus two hundred pounds."

"Do you trust the scheming little cleg?"

"I don't think we have much choice."

Christopher pondered.

"Do we get to eat fish and chips?"

"We get to eat fish and chips."

CHAPTER TWENTY-ONE

Angie Armstrong came from the kitchen with the tea towel in hand. To her husband who was watching television, she said, "Harry, I just caught sight of two men crossing lower pasture, heading up to the school? Shouldn't be anybody this time of night, should there?"

Harry stood up.

"You sure?"

Angie nodded.

"I'll take a look."

"Give Bob a ring,"

"He's taking a girl home. London, I think."

He went to the hall and brought his jacket.

"Don't open the door."

"Take the dogs with you."

"I'll take the cattle prod."

Angie stood at the kitchen window listening to the buggie drive off. They were rarely bothered, but the theft of the barbed wire had left them more aware.

* * * *

Harry parked by the milking parlour and was waiting for the intruders as they climbed the pasture slope. He hushed the dogs to silence. He stepped out in front of the trespassers.

"How can I help you gentlemen?"

The way they were dressed surprised him; in granny raincoats of blue plastic and plastic pixie hoods tied under the chin. His first reaction was to smile at a prank, but the short man said, "By stepping out from our way, fellow!"

The dogs were circling the pair, growling, showing teeth. They weren't impressed by the visitors.

"And if I don't?"

Out of the darkness stepped two big men in fancy dress, Tweedledum and Tweedledee. Harry called the dogs to him and felt for the button on the cattle prod. Tan and Lass came to heel, growling quietly.

"Then I must ask you gentlemen to turn about and retrace your steps to the road. As it's dark I'll be happy to escort you."

Harry found himself sweating, but unafraid. *More fool you! These are nasty people.*

The short man laughed and the tall man echoed him dutifully. Tweedledum and Tweedledee shifted from foot to foot and growled.

"I have to inform you that my wife has phoned the police and the school is now aware of trespassers."

As he spoke, Harry was judging the opposition. They would not expect the cattle prod. Whoever came at him first would receive the full charge. If it would stun a bullock it would certainly put down a man and shorten the odds. Then he would seize the leader and threaten him with the empty prod.

The short man laughed again, a dry, brittle laugh.

"What impresses me most, fellow, is your impudence. No one impedes my passage. But you amuse me. Step aside and no one will harm you."

"Turn about and no harm done, sir," said Harry and the leader stepped aside. Tweedledum came at him so quickly Harry was caught on the back foot. The dogs were quicker. Lass leapt for the hand that held a knife,. Even as Harry recovered, Tan went for the man's ankle. The blade flashed, but Lass held on like fury, shaking and tugging. Harry stepped in to discharge the cattle prod into Tweedledum's chest. The prod fizzled and failed. The man brushed the useless weapon aside, but struggled to free himself from the dogs. To Harry's dismay, Tweedledee came at him with a club.

Then, to his absolute disbelief, four soldiers in antique dress entered the melee. They carried rifle and bayonet reversed and began beating the trespassers with brass-plated rifle butts. Harry had time to recognise how efficiently they went about their business; head and groin, head and groin. In no time all four intruders were on the ground, groaning and squirming with bayonets at their necks. The older soldier grinned at the farm manager and said, "How's that, Harry?"

A bewildered Harry started to say, "How do you....?" as victors and vanquished vanished in the blackening of an eye. Harry, bewildered, confused, was alone with the dogs.

"How did he know my name?" Harry puzzled, but turned to the more practical concern as to what he should say to Angie. He decided the safest thing to say was, "No bother! They were lost. Sent them back to the road." *Why trouble her?*

He was able to rationalise the appearance of the soldiers from the past quite easily. *God bless Major General Vernon Barrett Randall! Obviously he still keeps an eye on his school. But how did that soldier know my name?*

* * * *

Replete with fish and chips, the singing motorcyclist rode the bike into the open gateway and stopped the engine on the scrubby grass beneath the bay window of number one hundred and eighteen. He was rising from the saddle when Hannah tugged his arm.

She whispered, "The front door's open."

Christopher got off the bike slowly.

"Stay there!"

Hannah ignored the advice and followed him to the front door. Christopher gave it a push and the door swung open. The house was silent. They entered cautiously. There seemed to be no one downstairs.

"Stay down here!"

Christopher went upstairs and returned.

"They didn't find my instrument."

Hannah said, "They've stolen your saddlebags."

"Oh, God's blood, no!"

"And your stove."

"Not my stove! My sweet stove!"

A desolated Christopher buried his face in his hands.

"Dear God, what sort of world do you live in where the poor rob the poor?"

"And they stole my laptop."

Christopher slammed the front door.

"You told me to leave my saddle bags! You told me! I did what you said! Now see!"

"I'm sorry. So sorry. It's all my fault."

"If I had my saddle bags, I swear to God I would never let them out of my sight again. Not even to relieve my bowels! And my sweet stove! Light of my life! Gone forever!"

Christopher stormed about in agitation. He kicked a wooden chair and broke a leg. The chair fell over.

Hannah said, "I didn't tell you to leave your stove behind."

To her utmost relief, Christopher burst out laughing.

"No, you didn't! Why didn't you? Saddle bags round my neck and my stove in my lap! We would have them safe!"

He laughed again and to her surprise hugged Hannah, which he rarely did; explained by reason of his coming of Spartan stock that despised shows of affection...

"God's truth, truly, truly you never did tell me to take my stove."

"I'm sorry, Kit. I can't tell you how sorry. I would give my right arm to get them back."

"You didn't steal them," said Christopher, "It's not your fault. And you will need your right arm for opening the baked beans."

"But it is my fault!"

"If I say it is not your fault, it is not your fault. And they didn't steal you. That is a small blessing."

Hannah went to the bathroom and cried quietly. When she came downstairs, Christopher had dismembered the broken chair to start a fire. When they were settled, Hannah in the big chair and Christopher on the floor, drinking tea, soaking in the warmth, Christopher said, "We can't stay here much longer."

"There's still the kitchen cupboards and fittings to burn. The skirting boards. And I suppose we can live without a back door."

"My enemies will find us soon."

Hannah asked wearily, "Who are these enemies, Kit? Do they have names?"

And was surprised to have an answer.

"I am accused of heresy which means nothing to you. But Richard Baines hates me with such virulence, he would light my fire himself. Whitgift is a foolish old noddy of an archbishop, but his scrawl on a scrap of paper would have me tortured and cut in four pieces. As those creatures did to my dear friend, Thomas Kidd. A Spanish Tragedy indeed!"

Hannah said, "Are you telling me the truth?"

"I stand condemned to death for believing the Earth goes round the Sun and not vice versa."

"What sort of world do you live in?"

"We must go to the school. There is a child there who has the power to free us."

"Can I say I'm not happy about this idea?"

They were startled by a tapping at the front door. Christopher picked up the brass poker and gestured for Hannah to open the door.

* * * *

Joan picked up her bag and started to the stairs.

Cherise said, "Where're you going?"

"To my room."

"I think you mean my room."

Joan stopped as if she'd walked into a brick wall.

"Your room?"

"Yes. My room. If you hadn't been so stupid getting copped smoking, it'd all been worked out, end of term. Like Pamela planned."

A tired Joan fought to make sense of her situation.

"Your father's going to marry my mother?"

Cherise laughed.

"Who gets married these days?"

"My father and mother did."

The silence was painful. There was a whisper of traffic from the street. From the kitchen a kettle complained of neglect.

"Look, Princess," advised Cherise, "We're both in the same Skoda. Your Dad is. Not here any more. My mother went off with my Dad's best friend. Scumbag Uncle Ronnie. If you think that's not a heart-breaker."

"Nobody told me."

"Nobody told me."

"Where do I sleep?"

"We made up a bed for you in the spare room. Want me to show you?"

"I know where it is."

"Give me your bag."

Joan surrendered her bag and followed Cherise up the stairs. She found she was very tired. Cherise waited on the landing.

"How come you got busted?"

"I didn't get busted. I hate smoking. It was someone else's cigarette. Fell out of my bag. In front of the Headmistress."

"Why didn't you tell her it wasn't yours?"

"I really don't know. Melanie used to be my best friend. But she isn't any more."

"You're more of a friend than she knows," Cherise commented.

Passing the bathroom door, Cherise knocked and called out, "Delivering the prisoner to her cell, Pamela."

A female voice said something. Joan couldn't think of anything to say.

* * * *

Someone shook the Headmistress of Randall's School roughly and Nell awoke, confused. She knew it was Todd by the size and smell of him.

"What's up?"

"They're putting fire to the house."

She sat up with a start, reaching for her dress. Against the moonlight she saw Todd wrap his fist and break the attic casement.

Buttoning her dress, she said, "I'm not going out on the roof."

"You ain't got too many choices, Nell."

"I can't do heights."

"I'll see you don't fall."

He held out a hand as big as a shovel.

"I can't! I can't. I'm frit!"

She heard the first sounds of the fire swallowing the dry wooden building. She smelt smoke and heard the voice of a gathering crowd.

"Go on, Todd! Save yourself! Leave me. Just leave me!"

Despite her protest, the man pushed her headfirst through the broken casement on to the slates. She heard a stray slate hit the street below and screamed. Todd slapped her hard. Her face stung.

"Hold your noise!"

He forced Nell to her feet. She whimpered with fear as he dragged her over the roof to where the alley lay below.

"Hark to me, girl! We are gona jump..."

Nell interrupted by trying to break away.

"Stop it! We are going to jump across the alley onto Finnegan's Lodging House and break into that casement."

"I can't! I can't! I'll fall!"

"Nell, I'm losing patience! All you done is jabber, I can't, I can't! If I was to say, will you wed me, would the answer be the same?"

Nell stood shocked, mouth gaping wide. Todd picked up the girl. He threw her like a roll of carpet across the alley onto Finnegan's roof and followed by jumping himself.

Among the growing crowd they watched the Bull burn. They stood together for warmth. Todd's massive arm was about her shivering shoulders. Nell was wrapped in the blanket Todd had borrowed as they passed through the Lodging House. When Nell wept, Todd chided her.

"Why the tears? By Fortune's grace, we are not within!"

"It's just. Oh, I cannot say why! It was the Bull. It was where we lived."

"A verminous, rat-ridden, pile of rotten timbers! Come, us must be away from here! Those poxy villains meant to kill us! We must leave them believing so!"

They walked away from collapsing rafters and a sky full of flames.

"Where are we going?"

"Somewheres us be less likely to be roasted in our beds."

"Am I going with you?"

"God's tooth, girl, are your wits so addled? We're quitting this sewer of London. We're going home to my father's house."

"Your father has a house?"

"Great steamin' puddens, Nell! Did you strike your noddle?"

"I don't understand anything, Todd. I don't know why you did not leave me to burn."

"Then let me tells you! You are my sweetest, bravest Nell! I wouldn't part from you, my dumpling! Your stitching is admirable."

"It had to be done."

"Nor did you flinch away, my brave! So us to take livery from Grant's yard for Cullompton in Darkest Devon. Nigh on is Armstrong's farm. My father's there, my mother too. My sister's buried by the bee hives. Dost thou know how to count ewes, sweet Nell?"

"I could learn if thee would teach me."

"Yan, tain, eddero, peddero, pitts, tayter, layter, overy, covero, dix," chanted Todd Armstrong.

* * * *

Hannah was refilling their cups of tea when they were both startled by a tapping at the front door. Christopher picked up the brass poker and gestured for Hannah to answer the door. In the light from the hallway stood Mira engulfed by the familiar saddle bags.

"Never seen the horse."

The bags were snatched unceremoniously by Christopher. He gave a cry of utmost joy and ran up the stairs.

Hannah said, "I cannot thank you enough for finding his stupid bags, Mira. They mean everything to him."

"I didn't find them. They threw them into our garden."

Hannah produced four five-pound notes and offered them to Mira.

"We sold some stuff. You have to take it. Life with Kit would be unbearable without his blessed bags," and by sudden inspiration, "And you need to buy loads of talcum."

"A baby girl. Marilyn. She's with me Mam."

"How wonderful!" Hannah cried with the merest tinge of envy. "Fancy swapping for Kit?"

Hannah shook her head and laughed. Christopher was singing upstairs, a song of pure happiness.

"He really can sing, can't he?" admired Mira, "He should be on telly!"

"Heaven forefend!" Hannah cried, "He's unbearable as he is!"

"What else did they take?"

"His paraffin stove. And my laptop. I'm going to miss it."

Mira said, "I know where there might be one for sale."

* * * *

Out of the predawn darkness Sergeant Springer ran from the woodland into the silent encampment. The sentry didn't challenge him. The Riflemen were at dawn stand-to.

"Dear God!" the Ensign said to the empty air, "how fast that man runs towards his death!"

The Sergeant arrived breathless to salute his officer.

"All quiet, sir?"

"All quiet."

The Sergeant nodded his relief, struggling for breath.

"Have you run all the way?"

"Now and then, sir. Needed to get back."

"You thought we couldn't manage without you?"

Springer looked as hurt as a Sergeant allows himself to show.

"No, sir! If there was fireworks I didn't want to miss it."

"You are in good time. Monsewer keeps us waiting still."

"Prisoners delivered to the Captain, sir. Fair and square."

"Let's hope he gets some intelligence from them."

"Don't think so, sir."

"Don't think so?"

"He hanged them all four, sir."

The Ensign was silent, struggling with rage and frustration.

When he recovered himself, he asked, "Did he bother to question them at all? Even ask for names?"

"He decided they'd escaped from some local Bedlam. One maniac took five men to put him down. And one calling hisself, Sir John Puckering, Lord Counsel. Privy to, he said, Her Most Gracious Majesty Elizabeth. Without any doubt, insane, sir. Or pretending. He demanded to be treated as her Ambassador Extraordinary."

"The Captain wouldn't like that!"

"When he called the Captain 'fellow' I've never seen anyone more purple in the face, sir. I thought he was going to explode, sir."

"And he hanged them?"

"Yes, sir. He seemed to enjoy it. Sir John Puckering changed his tune and begged for his life. He wept and screamed, which the Captain thought most amusing."

"But you didn't?"

"No, sir. Brothers under the skin, our Captain Dandy and Sir John Puckering. Or whoever he was."

Thus perished four creatures who relished bringing pain and sorrow on others. They delighted in terrifying the innocent. They would've tortured and killed Donald Mason's family if they had laid hands on them. They tortured Todd Armstrong and terrified the girl Nell. They fired the Bull to silence them. They would've tortured and murdered Kit and Hannah if they had found them. They would've killed Harry Armstrong and fired the school if Bob Simpson and his mates had not interfered. So run the tangled tides of time. But the Devil's army never lacks recruits.

CHAPTER TWENTY-TWO

They stood at the mouth of the dismal cul-de-sac. The street light was extinguished. It was an area of the estate Hannah avoided even in daylight.

"D'y'know what you're doing, Mira?"

"Walk as if you owned the place. And don't look round."

Dogs barked as they walked.

"Wish we'd brought Kit."

"No, you don't."

They walked almost to the end of the cul-de-sac before Mira stopped and lifted aside a broken gate. Unlike most of the houses there was no abandoned machinery in the front garden. A dog barked and a chain rattled.

"Stand still!"

Hannah was beginning to wonder if she'd ever see one hundred and eighteen again when the hell hound bounded out of darkness. The poor creature was jerked short on his chain. Hannah realised Mira knew exactly where to stop.

The front door opened and a dark figure growled, "Yeah?"

"Mira."

The man whistled and the dog retreated.

Mira whispered, "Keep ya mouth shut! Okay?"

They trembled at the door. The dark figure said, "What you want, Mira?"

"Me mate needs a laptop for College, don't yi, Han?"

Hannah mumbled agreement.

"Thought mebbes you had one?"

The man vanished. They stared into the darkness of the hallway.

Mira whispered, "If they has one, it's twenty quid. Don't show nothink more. Okay?"

Hannah nodded, shuffling the precious money in her pocket.

The Time Walkers

A door opened, lighting the hall briefly. The man returned to the front door. He held out a laptop.

"Twenty quid."

Hannah started to say, "Does it work?"

Mira smothered the words, saying, "Aw, thanks, Kev! Magic! Pay the man, Han!"

annah gave the man twenty pounds and took the laptop. He didn't look at the money, but stuffed it into his pocket. As soon as she held the laptop, Hannah knew it was her own.

"Thank you, thank you very much. That's brilliant!"

The man grunted and Mira turned away.

Hannah said, "You wouldn't have a paraffin stove, would yi? Me being pregnant I'm feeling the cold."

In one arctic moment, Hannah saw the fear in Mira's face. For a hundred years the man on the doorstep didn't speak. Hannah prepared to run for her life. Then the man turned away.

Mira whispered, "Why the hell did you do that?"

"It's my laptop!"

"Of course, it is! That's how it works on Springfield."

"Sorry!"

"We could be in forra slap. Don't run, There's no point. Top tip. Don't fight back! Gerrit over with."

Mira stated these words as if commenting on the weather, which made them even more chilling. The distant door opened. Hannah fought the urge to scream. The man lumbered towards them. Behind him came a teenager.

"Paraffin stove."

The teenager shoved a black bin bag at Hannah who grabbed it. The perfume of paraffin filled the air.

"Thank you."

She offered a wavering twenty pounds.

"Forty quid. This is a special. Got paraffin and everythink."

Hannah stood aghast. *Twenty quid, Don't show nothink more.*

Then she realised Mira was handing over twenty quid.

"I'll stand for it! But don't go asking no more for the baby, okay?"

"Thanks, Mira."

The man said, "Don't come round here again!"

He spoke directly to Hannah. The door closed on her terrified face.

As they walked, Mira said, "You pregnant?"

"No way!"

"Twenty quid, please!"

Hannah returned the twenty quid.

"You won't call me Han again, will you?"

"Not if you don't call me Mirabelle!"

Hannah drew a deep breath of relief.

"God, that was terrifying!"

"Wha'd'y'expect? You accused them of thieving. The laptop could be anybody's, but there's only one paraffin stove on Springfield. Everybody's on gas or electric."

"But they are thieves!"

"No, they're not! They're general dealers. They buy what the toerags bring in. It's called capitalism."

Christopher was sleeping soundly with arms wrapped about his saddle bags. The fire was dead so they put the paraffin stove back in place. Mira and Hannah drank tea and ate beans on toast in simple contentment. Such is life on Springfield.

That night Hannah dreamt again of Christopher dying unheeded by trampling boots. She cried out again in her agony, "Is this how it ends? Dying in the mud?"

She woke trembling and lay awake forever as sleep escaped her.

* * * *

Joan's Mother shook her gently. As Joan awoke, her Mother said, "Not much of a homecoming, is it?"

"No."

"We weren't expecting you."

Joan was silent.

"From Cherise, I gather you're taking the lump for somebody else's stupidity."

"She was my friend."

"Friendship stretches both ways. I don't want to interfere, but you might like to reconsider."

"Mebbes you'd like to reconsider this man and his daughter taking over our house."

Her Mother was silent.

"You're betraying my father. That's what you're doing! And me. How'd y'think I feel? That girl's nicked my room, my life! Where's all my stuff? Dumped? Or in a cardboard box in the roof? Dad's photos been dumped, have they? Everything cleared away. What a nuisance I got suspended!"

"You don't understand."

"I understand too well."

"Your father's been gone six years."

"Six years? What's six years? No time at all! And he hasn't been gone. He died fighting our enemies. And this man? What's his name? What does he do?"

"Gerald Pilgrim. Jerry. He's a banker. Works in the City."

"Oh, well, that's safe enough! Nobody's likely to shoot him. They might want to. But they won't."

She paused and cried, "I'm ashamed of you, Mum. Dad would never behave as you've done."

Joan sat against the bedhead, a child defiant, hurt beyond cure, bleeding from hidden wounds. Her Mother sat on the bed, bearing a pain without end, striving to staunch wounds, old and new.

Her Mother recited, "You don't understand how lonely I am. You just don't understand. You're a child."

"I can spell betrayal."

At the door, her Mother said, "Jerry and I have to go to dinner with friends. We weren't expecting you. When you're ready Cherise will order any pizza you like. Maybe we'll do better tomorrow."

"If I'm still here."

Her Mother froze.

"Wha'd y'mean by that?"

Joan shrugged.

"Nothing."

"Please don't do anything stupid."

"Like you did?"

Joan heard the car draw away. There was silence in the house. She focussed on the Riflemen at the ford, but nothing happened. Just when she needed to be with them it seemed she was shut out. Rejected for the second time that day.

* * * *

Laura bustled through Wavell Wing and walked straight into a prefect she didn't know.

"What're you doing here, MaCallaman?"

"Minding my own business. What're you doing?"

The prefect studied her watch.

"Shouldn't you be heading for your dorm?"

"Have to deliver an urgent family message to Melanie Mackenzie."

"Number twenty seven. Turn."

Laura interrupted with, "I know. Sharing with Natalie de Marmalade, the juiciest fruit on the tree!"

"Watch your manners, kid!"

"Yes, sir! Can I go now, sir?"

Laura knocked sharply on the door numbered twenty-seven.

"Go away!"

Laura kicked the door loudly. Natalie opened the door.

"What d'you want?"

"I need to speak to Melanie."

She tried to enter, but was repelled. She heard Natalie say, "There's some kid wants to speak to you."

Melanie appeared in the doorway.

"Does she not let you answer the door in case you run away?"

"Very funny, Laura! I'm busy. What d'y'want?"

"Came to tell you, you've been voted prize pig of the year."

Melanie shut the door against Natalie.

"Which coming from a nasty sticky kid who never washes, that's a joke. Wha'd'y'want?"

"Joan's been suspended because of you."

"Because of me? Why?"

"Your ciggie fell out of her bag right in front of Ma Savage."

"My ciggie?"
"So, she's been suspended."
"But why?"
"'Cause she wouldn't say it was your ciggie."
"When was this?"
"Today."
"I didn't know."
"Well, you know now, pig! If they don't let her come back, I will hate you forever."
Laura struggled with her tears.
"Forever, pig! And I mean that!"
The prefect watching Laura hurrying through the Wing saw her tearful face.
"That must be some message to make that little ruffian blub."

* * * *

Joan cleared her head as best she could and focussed her mind on the little encampment in the dead ground above the river. She didn't know whether it was morning, noon or night, but she knew the boy and his eight Riflemen would be awaiting the drums and bugles, the flags and pennants of the French cavalry. This formidable force would be drawn up on the farther ground, regiment by regiment. Twelve thousand glittering troopers on fine horses, preparing to cross the river in ranks of four.

An overwhelming torrent of men and horses would fall upon and slaughter the rearguard of the British Army retreating to Lisbon and evacuation. Unhindered by infantry and artillery, it was a brilliant coup de guerre. One young officer and eight Riflemen stood in their way.

Try as she might, Joan could not reach them. Whatever power had carried her back in time, it functioned no longer.

The bedroom door opened and Cherise entered.

"Didn't know what pizza you liked. So, you have a choice."

She laid three pizza boxes on the bed, dropped two cola cans, drew up a stray chair and began to eat. Joan didn't move.

"There's double anchovies on all three. I suppose they're all the same really. I just lust for anchovies. Have you ever had anchovy porridge? Anchovy and bacon sandwich? Raspberry anchovy doughnut? I could go on and on."

"Please don't!"

Joan's stomach was empty and was crying out for pizza. The rotten fish aroma of anchovies was driving her taste buds berserk. She casually flicked open a pizza box.

"Are these just for us?"

"We can order more."

"It would be rude not to eat something."

"Oh, sure! Manners maketh the maiden."

Joan began to eat pizza.

When they were sated and crushed the cans, Cherise asked,

"What's it like at school?"

"School is school."

"No boys?"

Joan shook her head.

"They bounced you for a fag?"

"They take it seriously. They don't want us to die of breast cancer."

"At Jaquemont unless you light up in class they couldn't care less."

"I think I prefer Randall's."

Cherise was silent for a moment and then said, "You're feeling pretty sick, right?"

"Wrong! I'm hilariously happy."

"My Dad's okay."

Joan had no answer.

"I really like your Mum."

"Really? I'm not her biggest fan."

"It must have been hell for her. When your Dad was killed."

"It was only six years ago."

"Six years is long enough to live in hell. Six years making it seem normal for you."

"Don't tell me I'm to blame."

Cherise packed up the cans and boxes.

"I was ten when I came home from school. Mum was coming out the front door. I asked, 'Where you going, Mum?' I watched her get into Uncle Ronnie's car. Never seen her since."

At the door, Cherise stopped to say, "Why don't you let them be happy? They've both been through hell. My Dad's a straight guy. I promise your Mum's alright with him."

Joan lay awake, head buzzing for an eternity. Her mother and Jerry Pilgrim came home at the midnight hour. She heard a confident male voice and her mother laughed. Some short time later her door opened. Her mother looked in on her seemingly sleeping daughter. She heard the male voice again and her mother answered. The door closed. Somewhat to her surprise, Joan felt pleased. They had taken time to check on her. The man had asked after her. Her mother had replied. Joan tried again to reach the Riflemen at the ford. The way was barred.

CHAPTER TWENTY-THREE

Basking in the warmth of the paraffin stove, Christopher Marlowe said, "You paid ransom to regain my stove?"

Hannah nodded.

"How much?"

"Forty pounds."

Kit whistled in disbelief.

"Forty pounds? Great steaming puddens, woman! Forty pounds? To thieves? Tell me where and I will deal with these scoundrels! Where's my sword? Fetch me my sword. girl!"

"The police took it when they searched the house in Canterbury? Remember? After you threatened to kill that ice cream man for waking you up? You frightened him so much he drove into the lamp post? Remember that happy day?"

"I was born in Canterbury."

"Well, they weren't too pleased to have you back."

Hannah remembered buying five poundsworth of ice cream they couldn't afford to encourage the man not to press charges. Christopher had gallantly attempted to eat such a quantity, but failed. They had no fridge and drank what remained that evening. He had further protested a gentleman must be armed and from a doubtful sports shop they bought a formidable catapult and bag of ball bearings. Hannah considered this something of a victory. Christopher wanted to buy an airgun.

They ate sixteen pigeons, seven squirrels, broke four windows and buried somebody's cat by moonlight before Hannah rebelled.

"It's like having a cat bringing mice home!"

The catapult and ammunition were now confined to Christopher's bedside cabinet. Any ruffian charging up the stairs would only have a ball bearing imbedded in his forehead and not find himself impaled on a rusty sword.

"My saddle bags? How much more did they squeeze out of you?"

"Nothing. They were thrown into Mira's garden. I suppose it was bogof. Buy one, get one free!"

"So how much geld do we have?"

Hannah hesitated and took a deep breath.

"I gave twenty pounds to Mira for the baby."

Christopher was as shocked as if a tiger had pounced upon him.

"Why would you buy a baby?"

"To celebrate the birth of her baby. It's customary."

"From what I have learned of your peculiar society, Mira's husband is the Government? Does not the State provide for her every need? Surely they would have given her what was customary?"

Hannah ignored Christopher's sound reasoning and pressed on.

"Forty pounds for your stove. Sixty pounds total."

"You did right to ransom it."

"Then I bought my laptop back."

Christopher looked at Hannah as if she had turned blue and grown feathers.

"My Ariel can put a girdle about the Earth in forty minutes. Your machine struggles only to reach the Amazon in ten! How much?"

"Twenty pounds."

"Leaving one hundred and twenty pounds."

"Not quite!"

"How much not quite?"

"While you slept late I paid one hundred pounds off the rent arrears. Bought six loaves and forty-eight tins of Baked Beans and Hula Hoops. Absolute bargain if you don't read the Best Before!"

"So how much do we have in coin?"

"Twelve pounds."

"Twelve pounds?"

"That's twelve pounds more than we had on Wednesday. We're warm. We won't starve. We have a roof over our heads. You have your precious saddle bags. And your stove. And I have you."

"And you have your lapdog," commented the unsentimental Christopher Marlowe, "How rich is the poor man with his backside to a fire."

Settled by the stove, stomachs full of a mixture of Hula Hoops and Baked Beans, an extravagance dictated by the inability to decide which to eat, Hannah said, "So they buried you in the churchyard of Stratford upon Avon? Wasn't that a bit of a coincidence what with Shakespeare and all that?"

"That was where Billy lived. Stratford. Nobody would notice me in Stratford."

"You're a very unnoticeable person," Hannah lied.

"That was the plan. Dissenters fled to Scotland where the welcome was a little warmer than the weather. I wouldn't want to go there. They don't speak English."

"My grandfather Cato was Scots."

"So I lived in Billy's wife's house until he decided I was getting too friendly with his good lady wife, Anne."

"You're a very friendly person," commented Hannah.

"They never got on Billy and Anne. He was too often in London trying to be the actor he never was."

"What happened after Billy put you out?"

"I lived in this hut at the bottom of her garden. Next to the dung heap. Anne would bring out my meals."

"She had a soft spot for you, did she?"

"No! I worked the garden for Anne. I painted the house. I learned to make gloves working for Billy's father. I could make you a pair of gloves if I had the leather and the tools."

"That would be nice for Christmas," Hannah suggested.

Christopher stopped and regarded Hannah's innocent sweet face.

"I'm beginning to suspect...."

Hannah interrupted to say, "Kit, I never know whether to believe you. When you talk about Billy Brakspar is that the same man we know as William Shakespeare, the greatest English playwright?"

"If you knew this Shakespeare as I know this poltroon Billy Brakspar, you would spit at the sound of his name!"

"Please, don't!"

"Have you ever seen a likeness of the creature?"

Hannah hesitantly answered, "Yes."

"The sly, false eyes of a thief? The slimy mouth of a treacherous, little rogue? Is that a face you would trust easily?"

Hannah, struggling to visualise a standard Shakespeare image, had to agree.

"You have a point. I would move my seat on the bus."

"And his nose?"

"What about his nose?"

"With that great snozzle, he could push open a door with his hands in his pockets."

"Really?"

"In the picture, he looks almost human. But Mothers used to hire him to scare their kinder to bed."

"Poor man!"

"Poor me!" Christopher said, "Trusting Billy Brakspar was my monumental error."

Hannah waited for Kit to continue, but he sat silent.

"Some people might think your nose is too big for your face, Kit. Pity we haven't a door left for you to practice on."

Her compliment was ignored. Christopher gave a great sigh and continued.

"Billy was no actor. He was useful for playing Second Devil, the Village Idiot, dead men, anything he didn't have to learn words. Oh, yes, Billy was ripe for audiences to laugh at! You only had to let him on stage to break wind and the house would be in uproar."

"I wouldn't want to be in the stalls!"

"He could play Greensleeves on his bowels most movingly!"

"You're not a nice man, Kit. You used him. Shame on you!"

"Shame on me? Wait out my story and see if you think the same!"

Hannah declared, "You used him in A Midsummer Night's Dream, didn't you!"

"He blackmailed me. I gave him Bottom. And much gratitude did I harvest."

"And he never understood you were mocking him?"

"What other would he be? Midnight mechanic trolling from cesspit to worse with his shovel and cart? Stinking so foul he has to stand outside the bothy to drink his ale?"

"Poor man!"

Christopher snorted.

"When you hear my tale you will clamour to deliver your apologies!"

"As the thief said to the policeman."

"There's something you have to understand, Hannah."

* * * *

The sun was declining beneath the gentle hills. Todd Armstrong and the girl Nell who used to be the Headmistress of Randall's School stood at the farmhouse gate looking out over the countryside.

"It's beautiful," cried Nell, "Like Heaven will be."

"Well, I'm pleased for thee, Nell. 'cause Saint Peter will surely turn me away."

Nell laughed and tugged his arm.

"Then I won't enter in neither!"

Apart from the beasts of the field, the only movement in the landscape was the carrier's horse and cart that had dropped off the pair and their bundle at the lane's end. Though Nell would've sworn she had never been here before there was something familiar about the greenly scene.

"I want to be here forever and ever," cried Nell and Todd laughed.

"We'll see what Father has to say about that."

He opened a gate that creaked like an old crow and two dogs began to bark. The girl looked nervously to the man.

"They's Tan and Lass. More bark than bite."

"You ready?" he asked of the girl and she nodded.

"Be brave!" he said and the girl answered, "For you, I can be brave as Frankie Drake!"

"No ducks here!" cried the man and they walked up the garden path to where the farmhouse door was opening.

They faced up to one another, the old weatherworn farmer and his younger mirror image. His mother sat by the fireside and Nell stood close to the door, fidgeting with the bag. The dogs sat, bright-eyed, watching, tails silent.

"We's most glad to have him home, Jacob, surely?" his mother pleaded of her husband.

"Depends what mischief he's brought home with him this coming. We never sees him without a bag of trouble."

"What trouble would that be, father?"

"Anybody coming after you? As they has on other occasions? Has you cheated some poor woman? Murdered some man in a drunken brawl?"

Nell cried out in alarm and his mother said, "God forbid!"

"So no fatted calf then, father?"

"I'd be wiser to call a magistrate!"

Todd looked to Nell and smiled at her alarm.

"Father, I has neither stolen nor murdered. We's done with London. Said our farewells. Paid our dues. I has coin I saved. You don't want us, we'll go elsewhere."

"No, no!" cried his mother, "Don't be thinking like that, Todd!"

"We's not looking for charity."

Silence sagged like the ancient ceiling beams.

"Jacob," his mother pleaded, "This is your only son! My only son! Don't turn him away!"

The old man ignored his wife and asked, "D'y'have a name, girl?"

"Nell."

"That's an honest name," the old woman said, encouragingly.

"Thee father's name?"

Nell shook her head.

"What matters her father's name?" Todd demanded.

"Can thee milk?" asked Jacob Armstrong.

"I can learn."

"I can milk," returned Todd, "And muck out. And drive and butcher. And shear sheep."

"Nor the plough neither, I guess?"

Nell shook her head.

Todd said, "I can plough, seed and harrow."

The old man studied Nell.

"Thee can sleep above the byre, girl. But take no flame up there!"

"No, she won't," cried Todd, "We's to be wed. Nell's not sleeping in the byre."

Nell stood bemused, confused, but happy.

"She sleeps in the house. And when we is wed, she'll share my bed. Like it or not, father, you're not turning your soon-to-be daughter-in-law out to the byre. And, Mother, you are looking at the mother of your grandkinder."

The old woman laughed aloud in delight.

"I'll find you a bed," decided the old woman, "And we's can start to know other."

"Thank you," said Nell.

She followed the flickering candle up the creaking stairs.

"Does his father not want Todd here?"

"Surely he does, but like a good dog he has to get his bark in first."

From downstairs they could hear two men's voices. They were not shouting at each other.

* * * *

"Miss Savage is indisposed," explained Miss Salomon.

The girl stood before her, tense and ill at ease.

"Is it so very important?"

The girl nodded. She seemed close to tears.

"I am deputising for the Headmistress until she is well enough to return to duty. Perhaps I can help you?"

"It's about Joan d'Urquart," said Melanie.

"Ah, yes. So unfortunate. I was very surprised."

"It wasn't Joan. It was me."

"I don't understand."

"Joan has always hated smoking. She would rather put earwigs up her nose."

Miss Salomon was shocked.

"Has she been putting earwigs up her nose?"

"No! It was my cigarette that dropped out of her bag."

"I see," said Miss Salomon, "Your cigarette."

"She shouldn't be punished. I should be."

Miss Salomon was silent. Melanie regarded her hopefully.

"Why did she do that?"

Melanie shook her head.

"Why did she not speak up?"
"We were best friends."
"Were best friends?"
"We had a falling out. I was stupid."
"Unfortunate!" Miss Salomon commented, "For she is more of a friend than you know. Perhaps one might say the same of you?"

Miss Salomon sat silent behind the desk. Melanie waited impatiently.

"Then we must put this right," decided Miss Salomon.

* * * *

Sergeant Springer's statement: We dug the fire pits deeper, deep enough for a man to stand. Deep enough to shield the loader. An inch or so of water rising in the bottom cause of the river. Four pits set among the shore willows, supporting each other. Four reserve pits above the camp to fall back to if needed. Doubtful if any man would reach them alive. We have four rifles to each pit. Two Riflemen to each pit; best marksman to shoot and his mate to load. Ammunition shared between the pits. This leaves the officer free to control movement and fire.

We had breakfast; scoffing everything we had which cheered the lads. I prefer to have an empty stomach. I noticed the officer ate very little. We saved the mouthfuls of what was left of the Captain's liquor for any wounded. We cleared the camp and hid the baggage and cart. The campground to the shore is wired so we stepped cautious and was in our pits before dawn to listen to the innocent chorus of the birds. I wondered how many of us would hear the birds tomorrow.

First we heard Monsewer's bands. Then we felt the faint tremor of the earth before we saw them on the higher ground beyond the river. There must have been ten thousand cavalry by regiment. They acted like it was a victory parade. The bands played. The regiments formed up for inspection. We guessed the Marshal was in the inspection party that trotted through the ranks. Every regiment cheered as the Marshal's flag and pennants passed through. The excited horses were noisy. Monsewer obviously believed no one would oppose the crossing. There was a long silence while the Marshal speechified to men and horses how they was going to win this wonderful victory, that the British Army was in disarray, that they would ride down the rearguard.

We couldn't hear a word, but I could feel the unease of the men, talking from pit to pit. The officer must have felt it too cause he went to every pit, calming the men, telling them again what the wire would do. I had no doubt the men would stand. Who's to run and leave his mates? Not Riflemen.

At last they finished all their lolly-gagging. Led by their regimental band, the first regiment, in column of fours approached the hidden roadway. We had left the first twenty paces clear of wire so that the cavalry would've broken into a canter before they hit the barbed ware. The band pulled to the flank to play them forward. Clear as a twig breaking, I heard the click of our locks as we leaned on the pit brow and sighted on the ford. I heard the bugles blow and the first regiment of Dragoons, in column of four, broke from a trot into a canter, intending to splash across the ford in great style, shouting, laughing and hallooing as they rode. I sighted on the royal blue tunic of the laughing young officer in the front rank straining to be the first to plunge into the ford and strike for the farther shore. C'est magnifique, mais c'est ne pas la guerre!

CHAPTER TWENTY-FOUR

Joan heard her mother call and hurried down the stairs. At first sight her heart jumped. For a moment the dark shape resembled her father, but then he became someone else. Her mother and Cherise in school uniform were standing in the hall.

Her mother said, "Jerry, this is my daughter, Joan."

He was tall, red-haired, smiling. Joan approached him cautiously. He didn't attempt to hug her. But held out a hand that she accepted and shook; a strong dry hand.

"Hello, Joan! Didn't get to meet you last night. And today, I have to go labour in the salt mines."

He wore an expensive suit and held a brief case. There was nothing about him not to like.

"There is going to be time, isn't there, to give you the chance to like or dislike me?"

Cherise cried, "Dad! Don't say that!"

Joan said, "We'll find out."

"Good!" he replied and smiled, "We'll find out, you and I!"

He turned to Joan's mother and said, "Do I kiss you in front of your daughter? Or would that create an awkward moment?"

Joan's mother laughed, embarrassed. For the first time Joan smiled.

"I'm not watching," decided Cherise, "It's too early!"

Jerry Pilgrim kissed Joan's mother and Cherise.

"See you later, motivators!" he recited and vanished.

They stood in silence in the hallway. Even with the three of them present it seemed empty to Joan.

"Jerry works in the City," said Joan's mother.

"Cherise told me."

"Well, now that our caveman has gone for the brontosaurus, shall we have breakfast?"

Cherise went ahead. Joan walked with her mother. Tentatively, they found each other's hand.

"I'm not expecting you to rush at him," said her mother.

Joan replied, "He's not as bad as I expected. But he's not my Dad."

* * * *

"There is something you must understand, Hannah," said Christopher Marlowe.

"Would it be liar, liar, hair's on fire?"

He ignored this feeble witticism to say, "A writer cannot help writing. However you oppress the scribe, he cannot forebear from writing. If he is in hiding, you only has to wait. He will disclose himself. Sooner or later he will write and publish some piece. Then you may take and torture him at your pleasure."

"Not at my pleasure, thank you!"

"I was not content with Anne's garden and making gloves. I began again to write. As he was always in and out of London, I foolishly gave the pieces to Billy. To sell to the playhouses."

"And did he?"

"Very successfully. Although I wasn't always aware."

"But what name did?"

Christopher interrupted to say, "Gentlemen do not put their names to play pieces. Playhouses have a dubious reputation. There is much whispering that my plays were written by the Earl of Oxford. His Lordship did nothing to dispel this mischievous gossip."

"And the money? There must have been money."

"Billy wasn't too greedy. I imagine I was receiving a quarter of what I earned. But it was my good friend Edward Alleyn who fused the petard."

"Fused the what?"

"Blew the gaff. Billy was putting his name to my plays."

"He pretended to have written them?"

"When I fronted him, he didn't deny it. He mocked me and threatened to expose me to my enemies."

Hannah said, "I was never a great fan, but I have taken a sudden dislike to this William Shakespeare. You're right! He has an evil, untrustworthy face! As near to a weasel as a man might get!"

"Then it was I made my second most grievous error."

"I'm not sure I want to know."

The cosy little sitting room, wrapped in twilight, warmed by the magic stove, seemed to Hannah to grow cold.

"I became angry. I beat the exalted playwright to within an inch of his life. That fragile thread the laundress snips at will."

Hannah's heart stopped.

"I should've killed him. But Edward stopped me when I was pulling out his tongue. If only I had taken his tongue! When next he could hobble and whisper, the scabby dog betrayed me to my enemies, Sir John Puckering, Richard Baines and the Archbishop. I was fortunate to escape Stratford hanging under a cart."

Hannah was struggling with the image of Christopher pulling out another man's tongue. Christopher noted her lack of sympathy.

"Have you any notion how unpleasant it is to travel hanging beneath a dung cart? There is a constant leakage of the least mellifluous fluids."

"Would you really have pulled out his tongue?"

* * * *

Joan and her mother were washing the breakfast dishes together in the kitchen. Before Cherise vanished to fill her satchel for school, she asked, "What's wrong with the dish washer?"

Joan's mother said, "I just feel like washing dishes today."

Joan knew what she meant without saying a word. They washed and dried together in a silence broken by Cherise's plaintive cries.

"Where's my P.E. kit?"

"I left my maths text on the sideboard, but it's not there now."

"Anyone seen my pencil box?"

"Did you charge my phone?"

Joan's mother answered every cry of despair patiently.

"Is she really so disorganised?" Joan asked.

"She's telling you she lives here."

Joan remembered what Cherise had said about coming home to find her mother leaving the house to run off with Uncle Ronnie.

There was a ring at the front door bell. Pamela, drying her hands on a tea towel, followed by Joan, went to answer the door. There were flying feet on the stairs as the door was opened. A girl in school uniform stood on the step.

She said politely, "Good morning, Missis Pilgrim."

Joan's mother's reply, "Good morning, Susannah," was interrupted by Cherise erupting down the stairs, complete with shoulder bag, satchel and Waitrose carrier bag.

"Let's go, Joe!" she urged and pulled her friend down the steps towards the waiting car.

"Don't I get a kiss?" Joan's mother complained.

"Didn't want to embarrass you in front of you know who!" was shouted from the path.

Joan's mother waved vaguely at whomever was in the car as it pulled out into the traffic.

"Does she always do this?" Joan asked.

"She's in a hurry to tell Susannah all about you. It'll be all round the school by five to nine."

They walked back to the kitchen where her mother started coffee.

"Do you like coffee?"

Joan shook her head.

"Help yourself to a cola."

Joan opened the giant American refrigerator.

"That girl called you Missis Pilgrim?"

"It's easier."

"But will you be?"

"Some time, perhaps. We need to be sure."

"I never want to be anything other than Vere d'Urquart."

"And you never will be."

She sipped her coffee.

"When she goes to school, Cherise kisses you?"

"Yes. Didn't I do that for you?"

Joan nodded.

"Would you have been uncomfortable if Cherise had kissed me?"

Joan shook her head.

"I've tried to hate her, but I can't."
"What about Jerry?"
"Don't know him."

They had found and shared some pool of comfortable silence, sipping coffee and cola, when the front door bell rang. Joan burped loudly and her mother said, "Now, who is this?"

Joan said brightly, "Let's open the door and find out. Is it too early for Father Christmas?"

It wasn't Father Christmas. On the step stood Melanie and beside her Miss Meadows. Joan's heart sang like a pit canary in sunlight and the two friends hugged one another. They needed not a word. Miss Meadows provided the epilogue to this unhappy episode.

"Good morning, Missis d'Urquart, your daughter, Joan, was sent home in error. I am Miss Meadows, a teacher at Randall's, here to redeem the situation and return Joan to school. I have her friend, Melanie Mackenzie, with me who will apologise to Joan. I apologise without reservation to you and to Joan on behalf of Randall's School. Hopefully, you will accept our sincere apology and allow your daughter to return to school."

Joan's mother said, "Apology accepted. To be honest, I think my daughter came home at just the right moment. Isn't that the way the best misfortunes turn out? All's well that ends well?"

Joan and her mother exchanged glances that Miss Meadows was a million miles away from understanding.

Joan said, "Come and help me stuff my gear in my bag, Mel!"

"Would you like a cup of coffee, Miss Meadows?"

* * * *

Joan and Melanie talked quietly in the back seats of the Shogun as it purred along the motorway.

"They were just boring. They didn't do things because they wanted to do them, but because they felt they should. We went to exhibitions where there wasn't anything you'd want to live with. And they spouted nonsense about the pictures. The worst were the art installations. Did you know our room would win the Turner prize any year?"

"Then we'll recreate it."

"What's been happening in the real world? What about Marlowe?"

"We need you to get to Marlowe."

"What about your soldiers?"

"I found the answer to the cavalry. Barbed wire. But they could all be dead by now. Or they could've stopped the French at the ford."

Miss Meadows slowed the car and spoke loudly to the girls.

"I'm turning off here, girls. Taking advantage of our being out of school to show you something unique."

From the roundabout below the motorway, Miss Meadows chose a minor road.

"Before we enter the Somerset Levels there is a unique feature known as the Red Wrekin. The colour comes from it being the ancient remnant of a volcano. Eight hundred feet high. Renowned for the views over five counties. We've been making very good time. We'll take ourselves on a short field trip."

Shortly the Wrekin came into view, remarkable in anotherwise sea-level landscape. Joan and Melanie stopped being bored.

"Ancient peoples used the small plateau of the defunct volcano for worship, but I doubt any human eye has seen the Wrekin as an active volcano. It was once a fortification, a settlement surrounded by water, an island in the marshes."

At the field entrance, Miss Meadows showed a pass. She called back to the girls, "One of the advantages of being a Member of the Royal Geographic."

They drove across the field on what once may have been a causeway and the Shogun began to climb. The Red Wrekin now held the girls' attention as the roadway spiralled around the volcano crust. There was a powerful ambience about the mound that grew as they reached a small plateau. Miss Meadows parked the Shogun facing West. The girls and the teacher climbed out.

"Stay away from the edge," the teacher advised, "I suspect it's quite crumbly."

There was a small gift shop, but the girls were entranced by the view. Streaming dark clouds raced across the late afternoon sky. Below they could see the wind stirring the face of the barley. Ripples shivered across the crop. The girls found the experience unexpectedly moving. They glimpsed why the ancient people would have stood in awe and wonder.

"Mebbe Ma Meadows isn't so bad," Joan suggested.

"Don't judge the monkey by its deposits," Melanie offered and Joan laughed.

Miss Meadows joined them to recite the counties they could see, but Joan and Melanie were entranced by the sombre majesty of sky and landscape. A skein of geese passed overhead, calling one to another.

Miss Meadows said, "I imagine the geese use the Wrekin for navigation."

She looked at her watch and said, "We must move on, girls. I hope you haven't been bored?"

"No, miss, no!" they chorused, "Thank you for bringing us here! Totally amazing!"

She saw them into the back seat and watched them secure seat belts.

"Clunk click every trip!" she smiled and closed the passengers' door.

She climbed into the driver's seat, readied the automatic gear box and then said, "Bother! I'll only be a moment."

She exited the Shogun as if to go to the Visitors' Centre, released the hand brake and slammed the driver's door. The Shogun began to move forward even as she stood back and waved the bewildered girls goodbye. The Shogun ran over the edge of the parking area and plunged down the side of the Wrekin. The heavy car gathered speed until it turned over and clumsily Catherine-wheeled down seven hundred feet. When it struck the boulders at the bottom the Shogun burst into flames that rapidly devoured the carriage. Miss Meadows from the height of the Wrekin screamed and screamed.

* * * *

The Ensign's statement. I remember most clearly the band playing and the bugles calling. The Regiment of Cavalry that had won the right to be the first across the secret ford came from trot to canter as if on display to splash into the water. They were reaching a gallop when they struck the barbed wire. The speed and the weight of the horses carried them farther than one might have expected. With such great effort, the leading horses were beyond mid-ford before they realised they were in trouble.

The officers took far too long to understand they were in mortal peril. The following troop was already into the ford and tumbling into the first. As they died, the troopers didn't understand how their mounts were trapped and that nothing could be done to extricate them. The faces of the troopers who dismounted into the water to find themselves trapped by more wire and unable to help their mounts ranged from anger to fear to panic. It was the most terrible sight to see such fine men and horses brought down.

I gave the signal and we began to kill them. It wasn't warfare. It was slaughter. Perhaps they thought from the volume of fire that a whole company of Riflemen were engaged in their execution. Firing upon these unfortunate men and horses only encouraged their officers to bring forward the next units to force the crossing. Horses were climbing over men and horses. Horses in pain and panic were kicking out, throwing their riders, biting their unfortunate neighbours. Panic roared like wildfire when the troopers realised they could not turn the horses and retire.

We continued firing as if we were some mechanical contrivance, shooting bewildered, frightened men and wild-eyed horses. In desperation, cavalry troops were sent into the deep water either side of the ford to attempt the crossing. But horses cannot swim when their legs are trapped in barbed wire. Heavily encumbered cavalrymen, even if they can swim, drown easily when their boots are trapped in barbed wire. One moment I remember most clearly was when the band playing their comrades to disaster stopped in midchord. Every regimental band, one after the other, stopped playing. I knew then they were defeated.

The rifles were burning our hands but we continued to execute these poor men and horses until no man or horse remained alive in the great net of barbed wire we had fashioned. I will never forget what I have seen. Nor will the men. I can only pray that barbed wire does not enter into warfare. Barbed wire will be the end of the

Cavalry and the foot will be slaughtered regardless. Barbed wire must be banned from warfare. Its use is inhumane.

I gave the order to cease firing. Deafened as we were, I was surprised anyone heard me. But I cannot believe there was ever a moment when soldiers were more pleased to cease fire.

While we sat or lay exhausted, we watched and listened to the French cavalry withdraw. They rode away in column of four in silence with no band playing. A group of mounted officers with Command flag and pennants rode down to the shore to survey the hundreds of dead men and horses in the water. I presume the Marshal was among them. My men looked to me, but I shook my head. I had no stomach for further killing.

My Corporal asked me, "Where are they going, sir?"

"To the bridge at Sorino they're repairing. But they're too late. Wellington has the Army safe behind the fortifications of Torres Vedra. We'll destroy the French there."

We cleared the camp and taking turns with the cart, began the march to rejoin the Army. On the march I noted the squad had taken to wearing a strip of barbed wire in their shakos.

CHAPTER TWENTY-FIVE

The night had grown old and Hannah more fearful as Christopher continued his tale.

"Once it was known I was alive, I was hunted like a dog. Relentlessly. It seemed to be a crime simply not to have died. I was not only a heretic, but also a shameless trickster! You can have no idea what cruelty one religionist will inflict upon another."

"I think I do," suggested Hannah, but Christopher wasn't listening.

"The death of the old Queen and the accession of James made no difference. Catholic Catesby stirred the pot by trying to blow up the ginger Scotsman. If I had been apprehended, I would have been hung, drawn and quartered. Or if mercy were shown, burnt at the stake. Nowhere was safe. Not England, Scotland, Netherlands, France. It was only a matter of time before I was taken. Then Edward, a faithful friend throughout, took me to a witch."

Rain beat sharply at the window and something moved in the chimney. Only the blue flame of the peerless stove was steadfast. Hannah shivered in its warm glow.

"You said witch?" queried Hannah, "What could...."

"On a flat disc world orbited by the sun, any enquiring mind may be accused of witchcraft."

"Who was this enquiring mind?"

"She was known as Old Sarah of Colchester, sold love spells to the credulous, ditchwater remedies to cure every ailment, pulled out teeth and was a time walker."

"Ah!" cried Hannah, "Sanity prevails!"

"She had walked in time, but she was truly the energy that would empower others. Her son, who was crippled at birth, travelled the world. He told wondrous tales to those who would listen. Of sea monsters, of a wall that ran forever, of mountains of ice, of kingdoms where every skin was black."

"Did she help you?" Hannah asked, struggling to overcome scepticism.

"For an expensive fee. So, I escaped into Time and seeming safety. Yet every venture ended the same. In Munich, I met four English kinder, with pretensions to be musicians. I was in idleness, so I wrote songs for them. Foolish trifles. Love songs. Just childish nonsense."

"Would I know any of them?"

Christopher pondered a moment, nose twitching, as he struggled to remember. Slowly, he recalled a hesitant list.

"Love me do. Please, please me. A Taste of Honey. Do you Want to Know a Secret? Others I hope to forget. Child's play compared with the subtleties of true song writing."

"And what happened?"

"Surprisingly, they became very popular."

"Surprising, indeed!"

"They were honest enough lads. Sadly infantile. But musicians, they were not. The more popular the band became, the more I feared exposure. I bade them farewell. So it was with every venture I entered. Success followed by flight."

"Do you remember their names, the name of this band?"

"No, they all looked the same. I believe they changed the name of the band."

Hannah found her disbelief melting too slowly.

"I can never decide how much truth you are telling me, Kit."

* * * *

Miss Salomon sat behind the desk, stunned by shock. Someone tapped at the office door. "Come in!"

Mr. Morrison, senior teacher, entered and asked, "You sent for me, Miss Salomon?"

"Yes, please sit down."

Mr. Morrison sat and looked expectantly to his colleague.

"I don't know any other way to say it, John."

"We've known each other a long time, Rachel."

"I've just been telephoned by Miss Meadows. There's been a terrible accident."

Miss Salomon was close to tears.

"Melanie Mackenzie and Joan d'Urquart are dead. Died in this accident."

"Oh, my God! How? What happened?"

"Something about the Red Wrekin. Miss Meadows was more concerned with gaining my approval to pay for a taxi to return her to school."

The telephone rang. Miss Salomon snatched it from the stand.

"Randall's School. Miss Salomon speaking."

"My name is Sergeant Humphries and I am attending the accident at the Red Wrekin."

"I understand two of our girls died in the accident."

"That's not correct, Headmistress. I have two girls here who say they jumped from the falling car."

Miss Salomon's heart stopped. To John Morrison she cried, "They're alive, John!"

He raised his eyes to Heaven in silent gratitude. In a voice she fought to control, Rachel Salomon asked, "Is it possible to speak to the girls?"

"They're standing here. Girls, your Headmistress!"

Miss Salomon beckoned her colleague forward who leaned across the desk to hear a familiar voice.

"It's us, miss. Joan d'Urquart. And Melanie Mackenzie."

John Morrison shouted silently.

"It wasn't our fault, miss. We didn't do anything to the car."

Miss Salomon ignored Joan to ask, "Are you alright? Are you hurt?"

"No, no! We're fine."

The girl hesitated.

"We jumped from the car when it fell."

It was true enough not to be a lie. Only the jumping was somewhat unorthodox.

"Thank Heaven, you're safe! Please give the phone back to the Sergeant."

Miss Salomon began to cry quietly and John Morrison took the telephone from her hand. "Miss Salomon is overcome as one might expect. I am John Morrison, senior teacher. I cannot thank you enough, sergeant. A miracle! Please thank the men who found them."

"They weren't far away, sir. No doubt concussed, confused. They said they were walking back to school. They had a long walk before them."

"Would it be possible for you to hire...?"

"W.P.C. Watson will deliver the girls to the school`, sir. Compliments of the Somerset Constabulary."

"Thank you, sergeant. You're very kind."

"Just one or two oddities, sir? If I may?"

"Please do!"

"The car fell some eight hundred feet from the Wrekin. According to eye witnesses, it somersaulted repeatedly before finally bursting into flames."

John Morrison shuddered.

"Yet the girls say they opened the doors and jumped out." "Yes?"

"The car is burnt out, but it appears from first examination that the doors were locked. The glass is gone, but the windows were closed."

"How strange!"

"Although the safety belts are gone the buckles are secure. Any chance either one of the girls is called Houdini?"

John Morrison replaced the telephone. Miss Salomon smiled at him. "It's a miracle they're alive, John. But then, they're Randall girls, aren't they? Walking back to school!"

John Morrison smiled at this simple faith.

"There's more to this miracle than first appears. Why was Miss Meadows not in the car is a question that demands an answer. May I suggest something, Rachel?"

Miss Salomon nodded, "Of course."

"I suggest the girls are confined to the San overnight for observation. No visitors. Joan d'Urquart will telephone her mother to assure her they arrived safely back at school. And Miss Meadows is not apprised immediately of the girls' survival."

* * * *

Christopher Marlowe said, "The callow youth I found in England would as easily have played a maid in any playhouse, but he could sing. He was more easily persuaded into a style that would've been recognisable to a singer of my time."

"Do you remember his name?"

"He had only one name. Or so, he insisted."

"Which was?"

"Donovan. The most successful song I wrote for him was."

Hannah sang, "*Jennifer Juniper lives upon the hill.*"

Christopher joined in, "*Jennifer Juniper, sitting very still. Is she sleeping? I don't think so. Is she breathing? Yes, very low. Whatcha doing, Jennifer, my love?*"

They ended laughing together.

"You see? Very simple. Quite unmistakably my work."

"I did long to be called Jennifer. But in the prison called Care they won't let you change your name. Otherwise they would've had a houseful of Jennifers."

"Unfortunately, Donovan was very successful. I found myself to be in the limelight again. I told him I was leaving. He wanted me to stay. I weakened and stayed too long. At an evening performance, two men came seeking me. With the departing audience, I departed too."

* * * *

Miss Meadows stood before the desk. She was trembling and unable to control her movements. She had related what had happened at the Wrekin. Mr. Morrison led the questioning.

"Why did you get out of the car once the girls were secured and you were in the driver's seat?"

"The girls had enjoyed the Wrekin so much I decided to buy them a postcard at the Visitors' Centre. I got out and the car ran away from me. I am not familiar with that type of car."

"Then why did you volunteer to return Joan d'Urquart to school, taking her best friend with you?"

"I wanted to help put right an injustice."

Mr. Morrison was not impressed by this answer. He started to say, "If you had applied the hand brake..."

Miss Salomon interrupted to say, "We're all in shock. Say nothing to anyone. Is that understood? Not a word. You may go, Miss Meadows."

When the door closed behind the teacher, Miss Salomon said, "I have never before met anyone so cold. So lacking in human feeling. I hope you're wrong, John."

* * * *

Hannah listened soberly as Christopher continued.

"I put myself in Bedlam, but...."

An astonished Hannah interrupted.

"A psychiatric hospital?"

"The warders called it the loony bin. But it was no better. They wanted to have a Christmas entertainment so I wrote them the songs. And most of the story. Another error of judgement! It was very successful. The inmates were natural actors and fine singers. Perhaps all actors and singers are loonies?"

"I wish you wouldn't say loonies! If you have to, say lunatics!"

"Fat men in suits came from London. They told me it was a breakthrough in treating loonies."

"Lunatics!"

"So, they were going to take the piece to a London playhouse. I would've been happy perhaps, but they wouldn't let the loonies go to perform in London. However much I protested."

"But it was their musical play!"

"I lost my temper and hit the fattest man. They locked me up in what they called the Coal Hole. I was in darkness for, I believe, two weeks. In that time they stole the piece from the poor loonies. Their work escaped, but they did not. I escaped because they lost interest in me. I went out in the dirty laundry."

"Did it have a name?"

"It was called The Orchard. A splendid country house. But it was a house of infinite sorrow."

"I mean the musical play!"

"I called it Little Shop of Horrors. It was a satire on the Bedlam we lived in."

* * * *

"We didn't do anything, miss!" Melanie insisted.

"No one is suggesting you did wrong," Miss Salomon agreed.

Joan offered, "Miss Meadows wanted to show us the Wrekin."

"When we got back in the car," Melanie explained, "it ran over the edge of the cliff."

Joan repeated, "We didn't touch anything, miss. We were in the back seat."

"We're sorry about the car. Can it be mended?"

Mr. Morrison asked, "How did you get out of the car?"

Joan looked to Melanie who said, "We jumped out, sir."

"How?"

Joan explained, "We opened the doors and jumped out."

"You couldn't open the doors. The police say the doors were locked."

Melanie said, "We jumped out, sir. So, they must be wrong."

"You had time to open your safety belts, unlock the doors and jump out while the Shogun was turning over and over rolling downhill? Without so much as a scratch?"

In chorus, they recited, "Yes, sir!"

"The safety belts are still buckled. The child locks are still in place. How did you escape from the car?"

Melanie said brightly, "It must've been a miracle. From God?"

Mr. Morrison shook his head at the girls, but said nothing. Miss Salomon said, "Would you be happy to bunk together again?"

"Yes, miss!"

"Joan, you must phone home to assure your mother you are safely back at school. You, Melanie, must never smoke another cigarette. Have I your sworn word?"

"Yes, miss!"

"Very well, you may go."

Joan hesitated to ask, "I hope Miss Meadows isn't in any trouble?"

"No, no, she isn't."

The Sanatorium door closed.

Mr. Morrison said, "There's something odd about this whole business. Is it possible they were never in the car?"

"I'm just grateful, John, we've come through this unfortunate incident. The children are safe. Miss Meadows' behaviour is another matter."

* * * *

"I decided to return home and found I could not. Either the witch's power was exhausted. Or they had found her. For better or worse, I am shipwrecked here."

Hannah pleaded, "It's not that bad here, is it?"

When he didn't answer, she affirmed, "I'm glad you're here."

"But there is light in the darkness. The child at that school bears the remedy."

"I like it here with you," pleaded Hannah, "Are we not happy? I look after you. You keep me safe."

Christopher turned to his precious stove.

"We must save some paraffin for tomorrow."

Hannah, rising, said, "Bags me fuggie the gardez loo!"

"There's no soap!"

From the stairs, Hannah called, "Wrong again! I borrowed a bar from the posh washroom at the pub."

From the bathroom without a door, she heard Christopher go to and open the front door.

"Are you going out?"

"No more than a moment."

Intrigued, Hannah stopped to listen further. She heard him stumble round to the back of the house. An alarm was triggered in her head. Drying her hands, she stepped out on to the landing as Christopher came in the front door.

"Is there somebody out there?"

He wriggled the bolt home and answered, "No."

"Is something wrong?"
"No. All's well. As the Watch would call."
"You just walked around the house at midnight to scare me?"
"I removed our magic machine from the front of the house."
"Why?"
"Out of common vision."
He switched off the lower light and walked upstairs.
"Why would you do that? It's been alright there."
"By the pricking of my thumbs, something wicked this way comes."
"Oh, total brill! Just the thought to go to bed with!"
Hannah lay uneasily in her bed. When he said goodnight, passing her doorless doorway, she sniped, "I didn't hear the seat go down."
He retraced his steps and flushed the toilet pointlessly. Hannah relented.
"Goodnight, Kit!"
"Goodnight, sweet princess, and flights of angels sing thee to thy rest."

* * * *

Randolph had become accustomed to evening visits from Laura. As she came out onto the roof terrace she would hear him scrabbling at his cage door to be let loose to lollop round the terrace faster and faster. An earlier fear of Laura's that Randolph would attempt to jump on to the waist-high terrace wall had faded. He was either running a marathon or contentedly sitting on Laura's lap, eating whatever she brought. Laura had become a keen member of the school's Vegetable Garden Club. She was feeding Randolph a choice head of Cos lettuce when she heard the door from the biology lab open.

She looked up to smile, anticipating the entry of the cleaner who often stopped to talk when her work was done. Miss Meadows stepped out onto the roof terrace. Laura scrambled to her feet, clutching Randolph.

"Well, well, what do we have here?"

"I'm sorry, miss. I know it's wrong, but I only come to see Randolph."

Miss Meadows approached.

"My dear, how good of you to be here! I hoped you might be. I have disposed of your friends. Now it's your turn."

Although Laura didn't understand what Miss Meadows was saying, she knew what the teacher intended. Every cell of her brain insisted she was wrong, but one maverick cell knew better. Miss Meadows was going to pick her up and throw her off the roof. *Teachers don't kill children*, counselled her brain. *Well, this one means to*, advised the maverick.

Laura let Randolph slip from her arms.

"Oops! I'll catch him in a minute, miss"

"We'll catch him together, my dear!"

Miss Meadows was surprisingly agile. Laura was intent on both keeping out of the teacher's reach and catching Randolph. Miss Meadows won the race. She caught the Giant Flemish by the back leg and hoisted him, wriggling and squealing, to torment Laura.

"Shall I drop him into the quad?"

"Please, please, don't hurt him, miss!"

Laura pleaded as she edged closer to the teacher. The rabbit twisted and turned, struggling to free himself.

"Well, then, my dear, you must put your precious charge away."

She twisted and shook the rabbit. Randolph screamed again.

Laura surrendered, moving to snatch the rabbit and run for it. She could see in Miss Meadows' eyes the teacher knew exactly what she intended. The teacher smiled. Randolph bit Miss Meadows on the thigh. She screamed, dropped the rabbit and Laura ran in to rescue Randolph. The teacher grabbed Laura by the arm and tripped over the rabbit. With a supreme effort, Laura pulled her arm away and launched Miss Meadows over the terrace wall. As she realised what was happening, the teacher gave a wail of terror. As she scrabbled for a handhold on the terrace wall, Laura saw such terror in her eyes she would never ever forget.

"Help me, help me, please!"

Laura stepped away. Miss Meadows fell screaming to the quadrangle. The child heard the sickening thud as the body hit the flagstones. There was silence.

Laura gathered up Randolph, popped him into his hutch, adding her choice vegetable selection. Then she left the roof terrace, passed through the silent laboratory and down the flights of stairs without meeting anyone. She went to her dormitory, escaping a chiding from the prefect for unpunctuality by minutes and went to bed. Somewhat to her surprise, she slept soundly.

CHAPTER TWENTY-SIX

The silence was broken only by birdsong. Joan and Melanie stood amid calf-high grasses. Melanie was the twelfth time walker. The Riflemen's camp had vanished as if it had never been.

Melanie commented, "Very rustic, but there ain't nobody here but us chickens."

"They were here. I promise you."

"That's soldiers for you. Here today and gone the same afternoon."

As they moved across the campground, the voice of the river spoke to them.

"It is the right place. They were here. I recognise the rock. We sat on that rock."

"Not together, I trust. My mother said to me, 'Whatever you do, don't marry a soldier.' Every photo in our house is one soldier or another. Still, sitting on a rock together doesn't count as being engaged."

"You're not taking this seriously, are you, Mel?"

"To be honest, Jo, it's difficult to take anything seriously after our Biology teacher clunk-clicked us into our seats and pushed the car over a cliff. Did you notice she even waved us goodbye?"

"As we go down to the ford, step carefully. Barbed wire!"

"They didn't have barbed wire in eighteen ten."

Melanie stepped over the first ankle high tangle of barbed wire. A bulb switched on in her head.

"You gave them barbed wire! You stole it from the farm!"

"I don't feel the least guilty. Something very important for the Army. For our country happened here. One young officer and eight Riflemen stopped the French cavalry."

Picking their way through the barbed wire to the shore they stared out across the river.

"Oh, look!" cried Melanie.

On the ford were three skeletonised deer; a stag and two hinds. It was evident they had struggled desperately to escape the wire, ignorant of the truth that the more they struggled the more entrapped they became.

"That's what happened to the French cavalry," Joan explained.

Some distance from the shore something glinted dully under water. Joan began to wade very carefully towards it.

Melanie called, "I wish you wouldn't do this!"

With the same infinite care, Joan returned. She was pouring out green water from a mud-sodden French cavalry shako. The royal blue was soured, the gold badge and chinstrap sadly tarnished. The once defiant red and white plume had no memory of glory. It stank of decay. On a sudden impulse Joan threw the shako back into the river.

"So much for the fields of glory," Melanie decided.

They sat to enjoy the afternoon sun. The crickets played percussion and the birds filled the air with sweetest melody.

Joan said, "It's strange how quickly Nature repairs our follies. This is a place where hundreds of men died. Look at it now."

Melanie said, "Why did Ma Meadows do what she did?"

"Because we've been time travelling. More importantly, because you're the energy source that frees us from our own time."

"I don't believe you."

"At home I was stuck in the Now. Soon as you turn up..."

She left it unfinished.

"Christopher Marlowe brought the... Let's call it infection. He is looking for someone like you who has the energy to send him back where he belongs. There are people from somewhere hunting him. When they catch him, they'll kill him, as they believe they have killed us. But don't ask me why."

"You figured out all this?"

"Elementary, my dear Mel."

"Then Ma Meadows will go after Laura!"

"The Cactus Kid won't be so easy to catch as us two morons. Laura told me Ma Meadows is a murderer. I didn't believe her. We idiots smiled and said, thank you, miss, as she tipped us over a cliff. When she waved, you waved back, Mel! Don't deny it!"

"I don't know why I waved," Melanie confessed, "I suppose I was being polite."

Looking out over the river, Joan said, "I didn't even ask his name."

* * * *

"Remorse, do you think, John?" Miss Salomon suggested.

The atmosphere in the office was bleak.

"She wouldn't understand remorse. Meadows was an evil woman. She intended to murder our girls," commented Mr. Morrison, "God knows why! Remorse? I'm glad she jumped off the roof!"

Miss Salomon shuddered.

"She would have been arrested as soon as the police questioned her."

"I wish the Head was here. I'm not sure I'm doing…"

A knock on the office door interrupted her passage of thought.

"Come in!"

Miss Skilling to announce, "The ambulance has gone. The school is undisturbed. Mister Simpson has cleaned the flagstones."

"I must be sure to thank him. He is an absolute treasure. I would imagine any other porter would shy at dealing with a corpse in these circumstances.

* * * *

The darkened ward was silent but for the quiet voice and footsteps of the nurse going from bed to bed. She didn't see Nell who came to join her. The nurse checked Miss Savage's pillow, marked her chart and moved on. Nell sat down on the bedside chair.

To the sleeping form, she said, "We knew this was going to happen sooner or later. Our poor old heart!"

Miss Savage lay silent, too close to the eternal sleep to respond. Nell continued, her quiet voice unheard by the nurse passing the bed.

"When John died in that ghastly accident, we knew there was no one could take his place. Perhaps we should've tried a little harder? Instead, we've given a lifetime of service to other people's children. And no one will ever remember, but the children..."

She paused to stroke stray, grey hair from Miss Savage's brow.

"We were prepared to grow old alone. But in some weird way we've been given a second chance. Time has reversed itself. I'm going to be a farmer's wife in the seventeenth century. A miracle? I shall bear his children without twenty-first century medical aid. I'll be at his side, come sun, rain, snow, plague, famine, Civil War, come whatever. An untutored man, but a good man. When he could've left me to die, he didn't. I shall stand with him."

Nell rose and kissed Miss Savage's brow.

"I won't be coming back."

The nurse didn't notice Nell leaving nor the sound of her bare feet on the plastic compound flooring.

* * * *

"Please, please, make more of that burnt bread?"

Hannah suggested, "Make it yourself!"

"I wish I could! But the imp who lives within that box affrights me. Every priest should have such a box."

Rising from the chair, Hannah said, "I know I shouldn't ask, but why?"

"Stick his parishioners' fingers in there to give a foretaste of Hell! That would loose their purse strings."

"Here! I'll make some more."

Hannah surrendered her plate to Christopher who took the toast eagerly. From the kitchen, she called, "You don't understand electricity, do you?"

The revving of an engine took Christopher, plate in hand, to the window.

"Across the road. The boy has him a motorcycle. And sidecar. Very shiny. Very noisy."

Across the road, a glittering motorcycle and sidecar were the envy of the neighbours. No one would have imagined there were so many

The Time Walkers

idle young men and women on the estate. They appeared as if by magic to admire, worship and envy. The proud owner with his excited girl friend and baby settled onto bike and sidecar.

The young man revved the engine repeatedly to the approval of the onlookers. Suddenly, he roared away down Springfield Park Avenue with his girlfriend hanging on perilously to the screaming baby. And as suddenly, wrenched the bike around, almost spilling his passengers onto the tarmac. Only childbearing hips glued the girl to the sidecar to save her and the child. Gunning for the admiring crowd at an alarming speed, he stood on the brakes and the three of them, Daddy, Mammy and Baby, almost flew head over heels from the machine. The crowd applauded rapturously.

"A very riband in the cap of youth! Yet needful too for youth becomes the light and careless livery it wears!"

"Brill! The light and careless livery that he wears is gona put that foolish girl and her baby in the hospital or the morgue."

Hannah appeared from the kitchen with her plate stacked with toast.

"There's only the crusts left. Then we raid Mister Stanley's bin."

Christopher took two slices. Hannah sat down to eat her breakfast. The racket continued outside in the road.

Hannah opened her laptop to view the news. She drew breath at the damage to the casing.

"Why would they try to prise it open?"

Christopher shrugged.

"You bought it back."

As Hannah refused to part with any more toast, Christopher went to view the carnival from the window.

"He's teaching the kinder to drive the bike," Christopher cried, "God's blood, but the kitten drives it better than its Daddy!"

There was silence from Hannah and he turned to find her staring at the laptop with an open mouth dribbling crumbs.

Alarmed, he cried, "I warned you, did I not? These vile machines are the province of the Devil! Put the damned thing down and step away! Do you know any appropriate prayers to deal with demons?"

Hannah waved a distracted arm at him. Christopher maintained a discreet distance,

"Are you stricken dumb? Blind? Do you still control your bowels?"

Hannah read aloud from the screen.

"Astonishing discovery! Elizabethan playwright Christopher Marlowe's grave discovered in Trinity Church graveyard, Stratford upon Avon."

"But I told you that! Now you see, I was telling you the truth!"

Hannah cried, "Listen to this, Kit! This amazing discovery validates documents recently come to light regarding the playwright. The papers, including the playwright's burial certificate, will be auctioned at Sotheby's. A spokesman for the auction house said it was the most exciting find of the decade. A reserve value has been placed on the documents of one hundred and twenty..."

Christopher interrupted to say, "And we got two hundred! Excellent!"

"One hundred and twenty thousand! Thousands, Kit! One hundred and twenty thousand pounds!"

Christopher stared at her uncomprehendingly.

"I don't believe you."

"At the auction, the winning bid has to exceed one hundred and twenty thousand pounds"

"This is terrible!"

"Terrible? This is wonderful! This is the answer to our problem!"

"It is the problem! We'll be exposed to my enemies and murdered. Same old story. Everything I do opens a lantern on me. We must leave immediately."

Christopher strode to the window to turn an anxious eye on the world.

"We're not going anywhere before we've talked to John Lambert about money. Our money!"

"We're not safe here."

"We've never been safe! But so long as our rude mechanicals are playing Kamikaze on that bike no one will come near us."

Christopher invited Hannah to the window.

"Come see! Five, six, seven of them mounting the bike!"

The engine roared, the spectators applauded and the overloaded bike kangarooed and then accelerated down the road.

Hannah came to the window to see the motorcycle return shedding everyone, but the driver to wild cheering and laughter. There was immediate, scrambling competition for places from both young men and girls for the next run.

"You don't see anything wrong with this, do you, Kit? Good, robust sixteenth century entertainment? Which one of them is Peter Quince?"

"They're building a pyramid!" Christopher cried, "Six, seven, eight, nine! What sport!"

"Where's that poor baby?"

"In Daddy's lap."

"Please tell me you're joking!"

"All is in order! Mammy's riding on the handlebars."

CHAPTER TWENTY-SEVEN

Joan, Melanie and Laura tumbled into the computer room. The prefect regarded them with the suspicion.

"Why are you three always in a desperate hurry?"

"Because we're keen?" Joan suggested.

"The keenest girls walk in, sign the book and go quietly to a carrel. With you, it's like a wrestling match."

"There's only one chair at the carrel," Melanie suggested.

"There's no shortage of chairs."

"The one that gets there first gets the mouse," explained Laura.

"Who's signing the book?"

"Laura!" chorused Joan and Melanie,

"That's not fair!"

"Whoever signs the book gets the mouse."

"Brill!" cried Laura, "I don't care what everybody says about you, McNulty, but your X Factor top prefect in my book!"

The prefect was left feeling confused. Laura signed the book and added xxx in gratitude.

"Scroll down," Melanie commanded, "Whoa, stop!"

Joan began to read from the screen.

"In two years, Wellington had created a fortified line across the peninsula from sea to sea; the lines of Torres Vedra. Rivers were diverted, swamps created, hills reshaped."

"We know all this," Laura complained. Joan ignored her.

"Every strongpoint supported another. Ranging for cannon was measured and marked. Clever traps were set that would lead assailants into killing grounds. The most astonishing factor was that building the lines of Torres Vedra was accomplished in secrecy."

"We want to know what happened."

"She's telling you!"

"The French were given the impression of the British Army in disarray and were drawn onto the killing fields where they suffered grievous defeat. One heroic action that delayed the French was…"

"You never even knew his name!"

"Holding an overwhelming enemy at an hitherto unknown ford by a Cavalry troop led by the gallant Captain Vernon Brooke Randall."

"But he didn't!" cried Melanie.

Laura complained, "That's all lies!"

The prefect rose like a heron from the reeds to regard our heroes. Joan mimed apology.

Melanie said, "The first casualty of war is truth. Quote whoever."

Laura protested, "But not like this!"

In muted tones, Joan said, "I know this man. He is a despicable coward. He hates the Ensign. Somehow he's managed to steal the glory from the true heroes, the Ensign and his Riflemen.

Laura said, "There's a link to the school!"

"Click the link."

"The public was so desperate for a hero in the black days of defeat in the Peninsula that Captain Randall was immediately promoted to Major General."

"Absolutely sick-making!" Melanie cried, "I really do want to be sick!"

Joan said, "Hold the sick bag! There's more! The public was not satisfied by this promotion, but demanded that the Saviour of the Army, as the Press featured him, should be rewarded as Marlborough was."

"Who's Marlborough?" asked Laura.

"Another war. But Marlborough was a real hero. As a reward a grateful nation built Blenheim Palace for him!"

Joan said, "Remember at this time, Napoleon was triumphant in Europe. It looked as if the Army was about to be kicked out of Portugal. Or slaughtered at Lisbon. Wellington did a good propaganda job deceiving the French. He also terrified John Bull."

Laura read from the screen, "It was decided that the costs of a school for girls of Military parentage should be raised by public subscription. The Major General joked it would take his daughters off his back and give him peace at home. He also volunteered personally to interview female members of staff."

Melanie said, "I've never met him, but I know he is the grossest creature you'd never want to meet."

"And he invented our school?" asked Laura.

"Not really. We just got stuck with his name."

They sat in silence.

Melanie said, "There's a footnote."

"You can't have one foot," said Laura, "You mean feetnote."

Melanie ignored her and read the footnote. "A squad of Riflemen whose duty it was to oppose any French crossing, but who fled from their duty were court-martialled. All nine were sentenced to flogging and ten years' hard labour. The officer was also stripped of rank and paraded in disgrace before the Regiment."

Joan fled from the computer room to hide her tears and wept aloud as she ran; a terrible wailing of despair. A prefect called, "Don't run!" Joan didn't hear her. The prefect closed her mouth on, "Don't cry so!"

Melanie and Laura shut down the computer and left in a stony silence. The computer room prefect was disturbed. It seemed the girls had suffered a sudden bereavement of a loved one. She checked the computer. They had been exploring the Peninsular War. There was no breaking news of any dead celebrity.

* * * *

There was silence in Springfield Park Avenue; what passed for silence in that ill-favoured neighbourhood. Somewhere the barking of a dog, the crying of a baby waking from a nightmare of motorcycle wheelies, the passing of a police car, muddled male voices staggering home from the Swan aka the Dirty Duck disturbed the ether. The motorcycle and sidecar in the garden of number one hundred and seventeen shone in the moonlight, engine slowly cooling. In the darkness behind one hundred and eighteen slept That Thing, cursed by Hannah, but the pride of a playwright's heart. Peace reigned too in the sitting room of number one hundred and eighteen where Hannah and Christopher ate Baked Beans and Hula Hoops from the can, basking in the glow of the paraffin stove.

Christopher belched and scraped out the empty Hula Hoops can.

"I assume belching was approved of in Elizabethan society?"

"Justly so, my dear Hannah! It was a sign of gustatory enjoyment! One's host would've been disappointed if his guests had not shown their appreciation audibly."

Christopher belched again because Hula Hoops were his second favourite treat; the first being Baked Beans. There were four items he greatly approved of in twenty-first century England: Baked Beans, Hula Hoops, motorcycles and his paraffin stove. Christopher, licking the fork, eyed Hannah's can of beans greedily.

"Do you need any assistance, my dear peasflower?"

Hannah drew her legs up onto the chair.

"Come any nearer and you're a dead man, Kitopher!"

She threatened him with the spoon.

"Everybody believes Billy Brakspar wrote your plays. You need to assert your rights as the author."

"In what manner would I so assert?"

"The first Folio of your plays is/was published in 1623. You need to…"

Christopher sat up straight.

"How do you know this?"

"It's all on my laptop."

"Show me!"

Hannah rose reluctantly and put her bean can on the mantelpiece.

"I know exactly how many beans I have. Touch not!"

She returned with her laptop.

"You told me gentlemen did not, do not put their names to theatrical pieces. Billy, we know, is/was near illiterate."

Christopher interrupted, "He went to Grammar School by virtue of his father, a glover. I spent seven years at Cambridge. Translated Ovid from the Latin. Gained two degrees and was awarded my Doctor of Philosophy."

"You're preaching to the choir, Vicar. The publishing of your plays under your name would be indisputable proof of your authorship."

"Where did you, a simple wench, learn to speechify thus?"

"It's all in the magic box, sire."

Hannah turned the laptop screen to him. Christopher flinched and crossed himself.

"May Almighty God preserve us from the evil that walks by day and crawls by night! Amen!"

Hannah watched Christopher read from the screen, his lips moving as he read. He nodded and crossed himself again.

"Enough!"

Hannah closed the laptop and retrieved her can of beans. Christopher sat silent for some time.

"I must go and put my name to my work whatever the risk."

He didn't say we. He said I.

"Then we must go together. Whatever the risk."

"We must go to the school. Find this child. Persuade her to let me go back to put things right."

He didn't say us. He said me.

"D'y'want to finish off these beans?"

"You're sure?"

"I've lost my appetite."

Hannah went upstairs to bed. Listening to Kit downstairs, happily strumming his guitar and singing one of the songs he wrote for the Beatles, Hannah wept quietly. He wants to go home. When he finds out how, will he leave me here alone?

When Christopher came upstairs, wandering from bathroom to his bedroom, he forgot to say goodnight as he passed her darkened doorway. Hannah knew this meant he was deep in thought, four hundred years away. He returned to the bathroom to flush the toilet, muttering to himself. As he passed her doorless door, she called to him.

"Goodnight, Kit!"

He seemed startled he was not alone.

"Goodnight, Hannah!"

But he did not add *and flights of angels sing thee to thy rest.*

* * * *

"Where would the court martial be held?" Melanie queried, sitting cross-legged on her bed.

"Horse Guards," said Laura.

"They're Riflemen."

"Horse Guards is a building in Whitehall. It was the Army Headquarters back then. It's a museum now. My Dad was going to take me. He was going to take me to loads of places, but he never did."

Laura sat silent as an old wound reopened.

Melanie said encouragingly to Joan, "Horse Guards. That's where it will be. This isn't regimental level. This is top brass."

Joan cried, "I wish I'd never heard of time travel. I hate myself for getting mixed up in it. It's all gone wrong because of that."

"This is not like you, Jo, to give up," Laura complained.

Joan said, "I don't know what to do. Because there's nothing I can do."

"You know what to do. You have to stop it. They're innocent."

"What could I do? Tell the court I'm a schoolgirl from twenty-first century England. I know what really happened. Please don't flog these men because I couldn't bear it!"

Laura answered, "Anything's better than self pity."

She looked suddenly amazed she could be so direct.

"I know what my father said. If it gets to a court martial, it's assumed the man's guilty."

Laura pleaded, "But you could be there. He would see you. That would mean a lot to him."

She hesitated, but pressed on.

"And to you. To see him for the last time."

"I don't want to be there when they're found guilty."

Melanie said, "Your father was a Rifleman. Would he stop fighting for his men?"

Laura said thoughtfully, "I know you think I'm not very bright."

She waited, but was not contradicted.

"But I think there's one question somebody should ask Major General Scumbag Brooke Randall."

CHAPTER TWENTY-EIGHT

Robert Simpson, Rifleman, 3rd Regiment and porter at Randall's School, was totally surprised when, marching only an hour or so from victory, the squad had been ambushed and arrested by the Captain of Cavalry without explanation. Surrounded by jostling horses and pricked by spiteful swords there was little chance of resistance. They had been deprived of rifles and bayonets. The Ensign had surrendered his sword.

To his further astonishment, the Ensign and his Riflemen were charged with dereliction of duty, namely abandoning their post in the face of the enemy. This charge, in the worst case, was punishable by death. Bob Simpson wisely bit his tongue and stifled his protest. They were held in hot sunlight, plagued by flies until the Captain, his Ensign and trooper visited the ford and returned. The Captain was in high good humour. He jumped down from his horse and saluted the Ensign with a flourish of his sword.

"Well, sir, I must salute you! I don't know how you did it, boy, but you've done a damn fine job! Most courageous action I have ever heard of!"

"Thank you, sir!" said the Ensign, starting to rise. The cavalry sword pushed him down again.

"Unfortunately, you have abandoned your post! Shown the yellow flag! Shamed your regiment! Run away like the American rebels! And the credit for stopping and killing Monsewer will pass to other hands! As we pass you by, digging ditches under guard, you will hear not only the jingle of our bridles, but also the jingling of medals on our chests. Am I right, lads?"

The troopers enthusiastically agreed that their Captain was indeed correct. They could feel the weight of the medals and the scent of the girls who would flock to greet such heroes. Rifleman Flanagan rose to protest and the flat of a blade knocked him down again.

The Captain addressed the Riflemen, "We cannot have cowards and deserters taste the fruits of victory! Riflemen? I spit upon you! You were never soldiers! At the first bang you run away!"

To the Ensign, the Captain smiled, "I did warn you, boy, that when I found the opportunity I would destroy you. Now, up on your feet, you lily-livered gutter filth! Let's go seek my Lord Wellington! I'm sure he'll have a warm welcome for you!"

* * * *

Melanie complained, "I sometimes feel very tired. Twice I've dozed off in class. Whatever this 'power' I've been stuck with maybe the battery is failing? Perhaps there won't be too many more trips into the bright blue yonder?"

"I'd vote for that," Laura agreed.

Joan excused herself, saying, "I would only start blubbing. I don't want to do that to him."

"Randall girls don't blub. They stand by those they love," Melanie commanded and put a hand on Joan's brow.

Joan vanished and Laura jumped a foot in the air.

"Wow!"

"D'y'think I've done the right thing?"

"She loves this soldier boy."

"Unfortunately, yes."

"What if she's trapped in the nineteenth century?"

* * * *

Joan recognised she was standing on the drill square of Horse Guards which quadrangle was very much a contrast to the darkness of the store barn. A rainbow of uniforms was revolving about her, but no one took notice. She knew she wasn't being seen.

No one, officer or private soldier, took a short cut across the sacred square. She was alone. She walked towards the stairs that led up to the front door of the imposing building. At the door she waited until someone entered and followed after him, dragging her burden. Across the hallway, there was a small group of officers outside a splendid door topped by carved instruments of war. When someone came out, she took the chance and stepped inside.

It was the court martial. Opposite to her, behind a polished table sat three polished senior officers, gold and brass competing with the burnished glitter of their bald heads. As she advanced farther into the room, she saw the Ensign and his Riflemen to the right, standing like sheep in a wooden pen facing the tribunal. They were stripped of any indication of rank or regiment. The Ensign recognised her immediately and almost smiled. But to her surprise, one of the Riflemen started in recognition. The man could see her, seemed to recognise her.

She saw to the right, the despicable Major General Brooke Randall, in all his finery, lounging in a chair, laughing and talking with three fellow officers. There was a rapping on the table and the President of the court martial declared, "If we are to conclude this sad matter today, gentlemen, we must press on."

Joan went to stand beside the Ensign.

"Major General Randall, continue, please!"

The elegant figure rose, striking a dramatic pose that must've been distasteful to any officer in court.

He recited, "We apprehended the deserters fleeing from their post of duty and gave them into the charge of my Ensign. Despite his protests that he would be left out of the action. I then led my troop to the river crossing where we were in time to give Monsewer a stiff drubbing that forced him to withdraw."

He anticipated applause but no one laid hand to hand. The Major General sat down, said something to a toady and shared a smile. The Riflemen shifted their feet and grunted. The Ensign looked along the line. His men were steady enough, standing at ease, clasping a thumb behind each straight back.

Joan said, risking no one could see or hear her, "There's one question you must ask the Captain."

She whispered into his ear. The Ensign addressed the President, "Sir, may I ask the Major General a question, sir?"

"Is it relevant to the matter in hand?"

"Yes, sir."

"Very well!"

"Major General, sir, would you please tell this court martial how you defeated the French Cavalry?"

The Major General shared laughter with his cronies as he rose. The President chided him, saying, "This is not a matter of amusement, sir."

"I stand corrected, sir, but if this officer doesn't know yet how the Cavalry deal with the enemy...."

He left the sentence unfinished.

Emboldened, the Ensign asked, "I apologise for my ignorance, sir, but I would very much like to learn how you defeated the French Cavalry."

The Major General grew purple in the face and roared, "With the blade, sir! With the blade! As we have done countless times before!"

His cronies applauded and the hero posed heroically. The assembly was silent.

"My scouts reconnoitred the arrival of the French Cavalry in force. They estimated…"

The President interrupted to say, "You asked permission to ask the Major General a question."

Crestfallen, the Ensign answered, "Yes, sir. I apologise."

"Apology accepted. Please carry on, sir!"

A flustered Ensign cried, "Carry on, sir? But…"

"I am interested in the Major General's answers."

Taking a deep breath the Ensign continued.

"We estimated the French Cavalry at ten thousand. You, sir, told me my Riflemen wouldn't last two minutes when the French Cavalry crossed the ford. I would be grateful to learn how a troop of twenty-four cavalrymen defeated ten thousand."

In the ensuing silence, Joan crossed to the side door as an aide entered. She looked outside and returned to the Ensign's side. She whispered in his ear. The whisper was passed down the line.

"Well, sir?" asked the President.

"By the only way it's ever been done, sir. By the sword and the valour of the men behind the blades. They knew not how many there were of us. We met every charge blow for blow. When we had killed enough they withdrew leaving the field to the victor."

His cronies applauded. The court was silent.

The President asked, "Well, Ensign, how did you and your eight gallant Riflemen defeat thousands of very capable Frenchmen?"

"We didn't, sir."

The atmosphere in the courtroom was electric. The Major General looked triumphant.

"You didn't? Is this the first honest statement made in this court today?"

"We had help, sir."

"From whom, sir? If you suggest supernatural interference, I will terminate this court martial immediately. And not in your favour!"

"If you will indulge me a moment, sir?"

At a nod from the Ensign, two Riflemen went to the side door and returned with a roll of barbed wire. Borrowing two chairs to stand instead of stakes, they began to unroll the savage wire across the court. The President and his associates stood up.

"What on earth is this, sir? An explanation, please! I have been lenient as your age and severity of the charge permits, but!"

The Riflemen crossed and re-crossed the court laying out a wicked maze of barbed wire.

"This is barbed wire, sir. We knitted the wire under water from stake to stake. We turned the underwater roadway into a death trap from which no one could escape, man or horse. The horses became entangled and the troopers could not withdraw their mounts. If they dismounted into the water, they became entangled. In the deep water on either side of the ford, the horses drowned because their hooves and legs became entangled. When the troopers left their horses, they too became fatally entangled. We shot every trooper and every horse. No one fired a shot at us."

The silence was awesome. Even the Major General was silent, mouth gaping. The Riflemen began to roll up the barbed wire. The President watched them work.

"You can lay it as easily as this, sir?"

"Yes, sir. Two soldiers could lay it in the path of approaching cavalry very quickly."

The president said, "Unfortunately, you have destroyed the Cavalry, sir."

"Isn't that what we mean to do in war, sir?"

"But not like this! This is disgusting! Barbaric! Where did you get this wire?"

"From a nearby farm."

"We must never allow this devilish contraption to enter warfare."

The court agreed.

He turned to his colleagues and they spoke for some minutes before the President turned to the court.

"This court martial is now completed. The Ensign is to be brevetted as Captain. His Riflemen will be restored to their ranks and privileges."

Not a Rifleman moved.

"Major General Brooke Randall will be removed from the Army List immediately. He will be allowed to retire on grounds of ill health. Pension and privileges denied. He has dishonoured himself before this court martial. He will present himself to Horse Guards tomorrow morning at eight a.m."

The Riflemen fought to restrain their joy.

"On the matter of the public subscription for the building of the school, that will be undisturbed. The public deserve their heroes and the children deserve a good school. When one of our officers fails in his duty, it reflects badly on us all, but must not disturb the innocent. Mr. Brooke Randall will give an undertaking never to approach the school or to publish in any fashion, material best left undisturbed. That is all."

As his Riflemen turned to him, the Ensign said to Joan, "I must talk to you. I'll meet you at the Whitehall Gate."

He slipped from her embrace into the grip pf the triumphant Riflemen who hustled their officer away, hoisted into the air on their shoulders.

* * * *

Joan stood outside the Whitehall Gate watching the passing throng. It seemed odd there was no Cenotaph. Two ragged men passed her and then looked back. With a sudden alarm, she realised they could see her. They returned, blocking her against the wall.

"Well, my sweet blossom," the big man asked, "What is you doing here? Was you waiting for us?"

He was pockmarked and lacking teeth. His breath stank. Joan strove to appear confident.

"I'm waiting for a friend. He'll be here in a moment."

The second man fingered her blazer.

"You has a style of ya own. Very stylish, my duck!"

"My friend's a soldier," Joan asserted, struggling to control her fear, "You won't like him!"

"But we likes you," Rotten Teeth agreed, "And we's going to a very tasty gaff. You can come along with us, sweetheart. There's those as will be delighted to see you!"

He laid a hand upon her sleeve and Joan struggled to free herself. Then both men released her and fell down. Joan realised a Rifleman had banged their heads together with the most furious force.

"I know you!" Joan cried, "You're Mister Simpson!"

"And you shouldn't be here, miss!"

"But I'm waiting for...."

"My mates are not gona let him go today, miss. Not after what he did for them. Sorry!"

They were standing in the Great Quadrangle of Randall's.

Joan's greatest regret seared her heart.

"I am never going to see him again. And I never even knew his name."

"His name is Harold Peter Vere d'Urquart. Known to his mates as Harry. Known to me as Sir."

A bewildered Joan cried, "But I'm Joan Vere d'Urquart!"

"Then I reckon you're his Great Great Great Granddaughter, miss."

* * * *

The noise that disturbed Hannah was metallic. She thought immediately of That Thing, the bane of her life. Somebody was stealing or damaging that grisly machine. Her reaction was to wish them good fortune and slip back into sleep. Then she heard urgent voices from the street and reluctantly crawled out of bed, wrapping the duvet about her shoulders. She struggled to the front landing window to stare blearily into the street. She realised Christopher was already at his bedroom window.

"What's going on, Kit?"

"Someone's at the bike across the road."

"Is it the Noise Abatement Society?"

She heard his window open and knew what he was doing. She heard him fit a ball bearing to his catapult and draw back.

"Don't, Kit! You'll blind somebody!"

She heard the scream. The motorcycle tipped over. A light appeared upstairs in the house opposite, illuminating one man lying on the pavement, clutching his left leg and two men bending over him. Hannah heard Christopher's catapult fire again. One of the men bending over his fallen comrade screamed, jumped in the air and clutched his backside. A voice threatened from the upstairs' window. The men struggled to lift the man from the ground and made off running and limping towards the bypass. Across the road, lights came on downstairs. Two young men came out to set the motorcycle upright and shout obscenities into the darkness. When they went back into the house, Christopher quietly closed his window. Hannah heard the springs protest as he got back into bed. She stood at his bedroom doorway.

"What was that all about?"

"They came to check out where we live."

"But they got the wrong house."

"The motorbike was outside."

"There are other motorbikes on Springfield."

"This one has a sidecar."

Hannah was silent.

"They'll be back. And in number."

"Why did you interfere?"

"In my time, the houses are wooden. A popular method of murder is to fire the house. If they had found the right motorbike we would've slept on as the house burned. By the same measure, I could not let them fire a house where a baby slept."

Hannah returned to her bedroom.

"Hopefully, I have broken the leg of the Confessor to the Archbishop of Canterbury."

He laughed. Hannah snuggled under her duvet.

"Tell me you're joking. No Archbishop is going to be mixed up in crazy business like this!"

"You are mistaken. Archbishop Whitgift sends the deluded to do his dirty work... A foolish, wicked old man. These supposed servants of God! They won't give up! Their righteous anger carries them through time to tear a man into four pieces! To have the heretic repent his sin even as he burns, tied to the stake! Such is the message of God they carry! If you won't believe the nonsense we preach, we will teach you with a branding iron!"

Hannah was silent. Tentatively, she questioned.

"You sound very angry, Kit. Don't you believe in God?"

"Not their God."

A police car passed the house and carried on towards the bypass.

"A time for confession then," said Christopher.

"Yes?"

"In my saddle bags, I have all my plays. With all my scribbles. What else would I save?"

I don't think I'll confess when once you slept I took a peep.

"Goodnight, Kit!"

"Goodnight, sweet princess. May flights of angels sing thee to thy rest."

CHAPTER TWENTY-NINE

"Laura was right," Melanie confessed, "Scumbag Brooke Randall couldn't explain."

"He was too arrogant. He thought no one would question an officer and a gentleman."

"He was neither," Laura declared.

"And so we attend a school dedicated to a cruel, wicked rogue and renowned liar."

Laura thought this exceptionally funny and nearly fell off her chair, choking on chuckles. The computer room prefect rose above a nearby carrel and coughed sternly.

They had feared to wake up to find the name of the school changed or themselves at home without a school. Nothing appeared to have changed.

"Randall girls," recited Melanie, "never believe anything the Government tells them and only rarely anything an adult says. Whitewash is not expensive."

It was so much Miss Savage, all three laughed.

"I will always love him," Joan confessed.

Melanie said gently, "He was a brave, handsome boy. He deserved to be loved."

"He must have loved someone, married her and had screaming brats," Laura offered practically, "Or you wouldn't be here."

Three imaginations shied away from the image of an aged Great Great Great Grandfather d'Urquart, dozing in a chair.

"Which creates a paradox," Melanie declared.

"We had one but it died," said Laura, "We wanted to get two and breed them, but Mum said no."

Melanie threatened, "Have you ever had a Chinese burn?"

"No. Does it hurt?"

"Very, very much," Melanie assured Laura.

Joan said, "Can we get back to creating paradoxes, please?"

"Let's say you defied convention," Melanie suggested, "stayed in the nineteenth century, married Harry and raised a family."

Joan said wistfully, "We would've called our first boy Harry!"

"Then you wouldn't be here in the twenty-first century. The line of descent would be different. Therefore, you wouldn't be there to marry him in the nineteenth century because you wouldn't exist in the twenty-first. Does that make your head spin?"

"Too hard," Laura complained, "Scroll down. Let's see if anything has changed."

Laura was breathing nervously down their necks. The computer room was busy and Laura lost out at Musical Chairs. With a slightly shaky hand, Joan scrolled down the history of the Peninsular War. All three held their breath. All was as it had always been. Wellington's brilliant stratagem had worked and the French were broken on the lines of Torres Vedra.

There was no mention of any court martial. No Ensign and his Riflemen were sentenced to flogging and hard labour. They expelled a grateful sigh. Joan began to cry quietly. Melanie chided her.

"Randall girls do not create paradoxes. Randall girls buck up and wipe their noses before we are thrown out of the computer room."

Joan blew her nose.

"That's better! Now we must find Christopher Marlowe."

* * * *

Hannah stopped chewing toast and stared at the laptop.

"Listen to this, Kit!"

"If it's about one creature swallowing another, I would not wish to know."

"'Record sale at Christie's. Four documents concerning the Elizabethan playwright, Christopher Marlowe, fetched a record price at auction yesterday. After brisk bidding by telephone, the documents fetched the astonishing total of two hundred and thirty thousand pounds. The buyer wishes to remain anonymous.'"

Hannah could think of nothing to say. Christopher said, "Didn't you make an agreement with that man at the pub to share any profits?"

Hannah nodded dumbly. She found tongue enough to say, "John Lambert."

"The man who keeps gadzooking me?"

"There'll be commission to pay," Hannah calculated, "But our share must be something like a hundred thousand pounds."

"Then, shall we go and collect our money?"

Christopher sang all the way to the Falstaff Arms. Hannah wondered how she could make Christopher understand they would receive a slip of paper and not sacks of coins. There were only a handful of cars outside the Falstaff. Christopher refused to stay with the motorcycle. There was no Security on the doors at this time of morning. They entered to the hum of hoovers and cleaners speaking Spanish.

"Leave this to me," Hannah decided.

They approached the young woman busy with paperwork at the reception desk. She looked up and smiled.

"Good morning! Can I help you?"

"We'd like to speak to Mister Lambert, please?"

The young woman shook her head.

"Mister Lambert no longer works here."

Hannah sensed the first breath of anxiety.

"He's gone? Where's he gone?"

The young woman was not feeling particularly patient. Her workload had abruptly altered overnight.

"What business is it of yours?"

"Please?"

"London? He was in London yesterday."

"I don't understand."

"Well, as I understand it, Mister Lambert won't be coming back to the Falstaff. If it's about a job, you'll have to wait until they appoint another manager."

Hannah felt suddenly sick.

"Thank you," she said and drew Christopher away from the desk.

"I'll explain outside."

They stood in the cool morning air. A flight of pigeons passed overhead. On the road a man ran for a bus as it was leaving. The bus stopped to let him aboard. In the pale blue cloudless sky, Hannah counted three contrails. The dream was only a dream after all. When one wakes, the dream ends. She noted these details as she fought, sick at heart, to find words for Christopher.

"There is no money, Kit."

"But it said on your magic machine?"

"We've been robbed."

"By who?"

"John Lambert."

"How?"

"There's nothing written down. I trusted him. My fault. All my fault."

"But he'll come back from London today, surely! He's given up his position because of the money, but he'll be back to share with us."

We could've had a house with doors upstairs.

"He knows where we live. Then we go home and wait."

"Then we'll wait forever. He's stolen our money, Kit. I should've known when he didn't tell us about the auction. But then, I'm stupid. So stupid!"

"But we made him rich!"

"Yes, we did. How generous of us! I'm so sorry, Kit!"

Christopher walked away to the motorcycle. Hannah followed sorrowfully behind him.

"Do you blame me?"

"I truly do. For being so foolish as to consort with me."

* * * *

Mary Savage was dying. She was not afraid. She was aware she was leaving, but felt no regret. John stood at her bedside. John, the strong and dependable, whom she had loved for a lifetime, so many decades beyond the accident in the fjord that had robbed him of this life. So strange it had seemed, to be planning the wedding with her friends and to be called to the telephone where an officer she didn't know explained there had been a problem with one of the boats. So surreal to return to those friends and apologise that John won't be with us. A problem with one of the boats. There followed so many solitary years of service to other people's children.

She could hear voices and the nurse's feet on the ward. She wanted to say goodbye, but John picked her up off the bed. The last spark shone and died.

In the big bedroom at Armstrong's farm, Nell woke to a bright frosty morning. Beside her the bed was empty. Todd would have risen at half-light to join his father bring in the cattle for milking. Nell was privileged this morning as the previous evening she and Todd had announced her first pregnancy. She rose and dressed quickly to join his mother in the kitchen. It was the first bright morning of the new century, the first day of January in the year of Our Lord, sixteen hundred.

* * * *

Christopher rode the motorcycle through the open gateway round to the rear of one hundred and eighteen Springfield Park Road. Across the road young men at the motorcycle cheered. Christopher and Hannah entered through the kitchen door to find a surprise awaiting them. Two teenaged girls in neat black blazers and skirts were in the sitting room. Hannah recognised Joan. Christopher recognised the uniform.

"There are no doors upstairs!" Melanie complained.

"Open plan," said Hannah, "Very stylish."

"So, Council houses don't have doors upstairs?"

"How did you find us?" asked Christopher.

"We googled you," Joan explained.

As his mouth opened, Hannah said, "Don't ask!"

Christopher said to Melanie, "You're the girl who manipulated time. At our unfortunate demonstration at your school."

"I didn't ask for it!"

Hannah said, "I'm sorry. He didn't mean to do any harm."

"Well, I think I'm losing it. If you want to go home, I don't think there's much puff left in me."

Joan asked, "Do you have anything to prove who you are?"

For answer, Christopher opened his saddle bags. He laid out on the table manuscripts with familiar titles. Below the titles were the words... A Comedy, A Tragedy, A History by Christopher Marlowe Esquire.

An outburst of angry voices brought them to the window. Five or six men in be-ribboned bonnets, crested doublets, patterned hose and silver-mounted cavalier heels were fighting with the young men at the motorcycle.

"Is it a carnival?" cried Joan.

"Believe it or not," Hannah said, "the Archbishop of Canterbury's Ecclesiastical Guard has come to kill Kit. Only they've got the wrong bike."

As the girls watched astonished, two older men and two young women rushed out of the house to join the fight. The men had baseball bats and the women heavy pans that they swung with gusto. Perhaps even Bisto? From next door, Mr. Stanley and his gargantuan sons ran out to join in the sport. His sons swung iron bars freely while their father favoured a heavy hammer.

Four young men armed with cricket bats hurried to the wicked, unwilling to miss the fun. *Hurry, hurry, it'll be over by Christmas and you'll miss the Victory Parade!*

"Springfield Cricket Club," Hannah explained.

They knew how to use their bats effectively. Within minutes the English summer sound of willow upon leather bonnet resounded along Springfield Park Avenue. *Play up, play up and play the game!*

As Springfield was reinforced so did more of the Archbishop's Guard appear until what would have passed for a sizeable medieval battle raged on Springfield Park Avenue with more and more Springfielders joining in. It surprised later historians that the inhabitants of the estate were so well armed and strategically adept. The principal weapon was the baseball bat although no baseball game has ever been recorded as being played on the estate. A favourite among younger Springfieldians was the simple glass bottle that could be thrown in quantity or used as a club.

A heavy chain was a popular choice. Once an opponent had been brought down even the youngest children could join in the sport and kick the unfortunate fallen in cranium or codpiece. No one cried, "Let loose the dogs of war!" but the local pit bulls, roused from their gentle slumber, were gnawing many a tasty kneecap. As reinforcements for the Archbishop's forces appeared at Sunnyrise corner, the Springfield artillery opened a devastating barrage.

From the security of ravaged gardens, women and older children fired catapults and hurled bricks and water bombs of bleach at unsuspecting men in be-ribboned bonnets, crested doublets, patterned hose and silver-mounted cavalier heels. A battery of petrol bombs caught flimsy garments alight but caused more damage to the roadstead where the tarmac burnt freely. The battle raged until Christopher could bear it no longer and snatching up the redundant poker rushed out to join in despite Hannah's protests.

She cried to the girls, "Stay here! Do not come out!"

She rushed to join Christopher, picking up a brick that had chocked the motorcycle's wheel. Christopher, in his element, wielded his poker with devastating effect on the enemy's backs, breasts, heads and hands. Every enemy who fell felt the punishment of Hannah's brick until both obtained a cudgel and set about to work off their frustrations. Every blow struck was intended for treacherous John Lambert. It was exhilarating, enjoyable exercise. Christopher began to shout, "Springfield! Springfield!"

The cry was taken up until the whole Springfield line was chanting, "Springfield! Springfield!" Reinforcements for the Archbishop's forces faltered and failed. Their line was overwhelmed by the exuberant forces of Springfield who, like Christopher and Hannah, were enjoying working off the frustrations, humiliations and disappointments forced upon them by local and national government. Never in the field of inhuman conflict was so much concussion inflicted for so little. Archbishop Whitgift stood only four feet eleven inches on his high heels and was beaten to the floor, to be trampled over by heavy boots.

"If this is life on a Council Estate!" cried Melanie, "I'd jolly well like to give it a try!"

Like all good things, the battle came to an end, fizzling out as the enemy cut and ran. The victors stood breathless, united, exhilarated, enjoying possession of their own territory. The dogs rejoiced, panting and barking madly. The children played with the burning tarmac building bonfires of broken fences. Women brought out beer for the men while keeping the eggnog and turpentine sherry in the kitchen for their mates. Mr. Stanley solemnly shook hands with Christopher. Hannah struggled to escape his sons' salivary kisses. To this day the Battle of Springfield is known locally as the Battle of the Nancies. The Archbishop's Ecclesiastical Guard was recruited from the town of Nancy in France.

CHAPTER THIRTY

The overwhelming scent of the print house was warm paper and sour ink. The most constant sound, the tapping of mallets the printers used to knock the page blocks into shape. It seemed the whole house was working like fury to create Christopher Marlowe's First Folio. To prepare, print, complete and publish a volume of some three hundred pages would take a year. The first print run would assemble eight hundred copies to be bound individually to the customer's taste.

The cry, "Master Marlowe, sir!" went up from the other end of the print house to be echoed across the building. Christopher, Hannah, Edward Alleyn and other friends of the great man unknown to Joan and Melanie walked through the busy assembly to where the publishers, Isaac Jaggard and William Blount awaited.

"The title page, sir," announced Isaac Jaggard, "We's about to pull off."

The brace was spun and the press lifted to reveal a virgin sheet of paper that an apprentice began to peel from the inked press. No one dared breathe. All hearts paused as the apprentice turned the sheet over for their appraisal.

There was a fair likeness of Christopher Marlowe, the strong face, long midnight hair, the lively intelligent eyes, the mouth about to smile. Melanie's heart turned somersaults.

"Oh, that's sweet!"

Hannah commented, "The snozzle's spot on. Y'could lift a drawbridge with that."

Melanie scowled to hear her hero besnozzled.

Set out in the traditional manner the frontispiece announced Mr. Christopher Marlowe's Comedies, Histories and Tragedies, Published according to the true original copies. LONDON. Printed by Isaac and William Jaggard and Edward Blount. 1623

The party, including the printers applauded. Christopher stood silent, basking in the moment of achievement. Hannah, adoring, flung herself into his arms. Melanie was jealous. Joan took her arm to dance a jig of delight.

"It's done, Mel!" cried Joan, "It's done and cannot be undone!"

Christopher signed the first dozen title pages. The last he handed to Melanie who blushed and seemed ready to cry.

"I won't forget what you've done for me, sweet maid. And I know what it has cost you."

Melanie found nothing to say, but clutched the precious paper. Christopher kissed her on the cheek and Melanie's feet lifted off the floor.

They said goodbye to Messrs. Jaggard and Blount on the doorstep of the print house. Happy and contented Christopher, Edward, friends, Hannah and the girls stepped out into the busy noisy street. It was the first time Melanie had met the outrageous smell of a seventeenth century London thoroughfare. Then it happened too quickly for comprehension.

Five, six men came out of the crowd and blades flashed in the sunlight. Edward Alleyn cried out and fell back bleeding. Friends scattered or reached for weapons. Melanie and Joan clung to the wall. Hannah stood frozen. It happened as it happened so often in her dream. Two men hacked at Christopher who strove to muffle their blows with his cloak. He cried out as the blade reached him and fell on his back in the mud, unheeded by trampling boots. Hannah fell to her knees beside him. Blood was pouring from his neck. He smiled at her weakly. Tearing at her dress, she knew she couldn't stop the outgush of blood. Christopher Marlowe had only moments to live. Devastated Hannah cried out her agony, "Is this how it ends? Dying in the mud?"

Joan saw how she was answered. One man bent to slash at Hannah's throat and everywhere was spouting blood. To Joan's horror, Melanie threw herself on top of Hannah and Christopher. The thug grinned and reached to kill her.

* * * *

The Time Walkers

They were all four, standing unsteadily, on Clifton Suspension Bridge over the Avon Gorge, Bristol.

Joan, astonished, cried, "What're we doing here, Mel?"

Melanie apologised, "Sorry. All I could think of!"

The bridge vanished. They stood on the promenade deck of the Blackpool Tower.

"Whoops! Sorry!" cried Melanie.

Joan said, "Leave this to me!"

They stood in the sitting room of one hundred and eighteen. There was no blood. Without a word, Christopher bolted upstairs. Hannah flopped into the chair, struggling for breath.

Joan said, "If you hadn't acted when you did, Mel, it would've been too late. That was really, really brave!"

In the doorless house they could hear Christopher vomiting in the bathroom.

"Poor Kit! In his moment of triumph."

Melanie felt suddenly sick and sat down on a chair.

Joan said, "Time to go," and they were gone.

* * * *

Melanie, exhausted, fell asleep as she lay down on her bed. Joan spoke to her, but the voice was silent and the mind absent.

When the dinner bell rang, Melanie didn't stir and Joan didn't trouble her.

To the duty prefect, Joan said, "Melanie Mackenzie not feeling very bright. Please to be excused."

"Very well," said the prefect, "But if she's not better in the morning, you must report her to Matron."

"Thank you, I will."

Before dinner was served, Miss Salomon announced the peaceful passing of the Headmistress, Miss Savage. A memorial service would be held at an appropriate time. The emotional response was muted. Miss Savage, a somewhat distant figure, was respected rather than loved. Miss Salomon announced that until the proper procedures were carried out she would be acting as Headmistress.

There were no cries of horror. Miss Salomon was known as a firm, but understanding teacher.

Her worst joke was to say, "Although my name is Salomon, I am not necessarily always solemn."

Melanie had explained the jest to Laura who remarked, "That's not a joke. That's just sad."

Melanie offered, "Although my name is Laura, I am not a Laura laughs."

Laura pretended not to understand this fabulous witticism.

When Joan returned to the room, Melanie was awake. Joan had brought back a chicken leg and an apple.

"Sorry. All I could get."

Joan watched her friend eat and was content she was refreshed by her sleep. Between bites at the chicken leg, she offered, "I don't think I've much puff left."

"Not with trips to Bristol and Blackpool. What about a trip to Disneyland, Paris? Better still, Florida!"

"I've decided how we'll use it," she paused and continued, "Would you like to see your father?"

Melanie put the chicken leg aside awaiting Joan's reply.

"Laura told me if she stopped her Dad going to that bomb somebody else would only have to do it. She's a very brave kid. I'm not. I'm totally selfish. If I went to see my Dad I would drag him away from that bullet and I wouldn't care who else died as long as my Dad didn't."

Laura didn't wait to knock on the door, but bounced in breathless to ask, "Did it go well?"

"Hope so, but we don't know yet."

Puzzled, Laura cried, "Eh?"

"Do you know how attractive you look with your mouth hanging open like a dead cod fish?"

* * * *

They stood in brilliant sunlight in a desolate place on a dusty road in a merciless world. There was silence apart from the odd word carried in the stifling air from the dust-clad soldiers, standing around the vehicles. No one needed to ask where they were. Melanie pointed to a soldier sitting in the open back doors of an armoured troop carrier. He was dressing in what might have appeared as a deep-sea diving suit.

Melanie said, "There's your Dad, Laura."

Laura shook her head.

"This is our last trip. We think you should speak to your Dad."

Laura stood irresolute.

"Any time now, he's going to be walking up the road,"

Joan stated, "For the rest of your life, you're going to regret you didn't take this chance."

Laura cried, "You are both utter pigs. I hate you and I shall never speak to you again so long as I live."

"So long as you speak to your Dad."

Laura walked over to where the soldier was tussling with unco-operative straps. Her shadow fell on him and he looked up. Laura said, "Hello, Daddy! I've come to see you."

Her father studied her carefully.

"It's me. Laura."

"I suppose it's not unexpected. I've been at this too long. What sort of illusion are you? Come here."

Laura approached. Her father reached out and took her hand.

"Remarkable! Warm. Solid. How did you get here?"

"It's a long story, but I've travelled through time to see you."

"That sounds very logical. Travelling through time. In fact, that's wonderful, Laura! Are you going to give me a hug?"

It was an untidy hug. But a deep pervading peace surged through Laura and she sensed within his horrid toad suit her father enjoyed the same abiding peace of a thirst satisfied, of a hunger fulfilled. He did not release her hands.

"You've certainly grown, kiddo! And you look so much like your mother! My word, I'm going to have to keep an eye on you when I come home. How is that rascal Peter?"

"He's grown too, Daddy. You wouldn't recognise him. He goes to school now. And you'd laugh! Mum went to his school sports. And she decided to win the sack race to show who was top Mum."

"That sounds like Jess! Did she? Win?"

"She won and then she didn't!"

"She put her foot through the bottom of the sack?"

"Worse than that, Daddy! She says she read the rules and the rules said contestants had to have both feet in the sack at the start and must cross the finishing line with both feet in the sack!"

"Don't tell me! Don't tell me!"

"Mum had two feet in the sack. The race started. She took her feet out. Ran up the track. And put her feet back in the sack to hop across the line! There was an awful row!"

Her father began to laugh. Laura began to laugh. They clung together and laughed. It was the most astonishing sound in that waiting room of Hell. Soldiers turned to look at their officer. Father and daughter laughed together, a wonderful defiant laugh.

"Oh, my word, Laura! That's just like your Mother! Did they arrest her? Lock her up? Expel Peter?"

"No! Peter begged them to expel him, but they wouldn't. But Mum's not allowed to take part in Sports Day ever again! They were really very stuffy about it. They asked her if she had anything to say. So, she blew them a raspberry!"

Her father laughed again and hugged his daughter.

"Oh, I'm sure you're going to grow up just like your Mother! You are, aren't you?"

"I'm trying, Daddy!"

One of the soldiers shouted something and her father stood up.

"Have to go and do a little chore, darling! I'll be back in a few minutes! Just you wait here! I want to hear more about you and your terrible Mother."

Laura nodded dumbly. Her father kissed her brow. He looked at her and said, "Wow! This is my daughter?"

"Yes, Daddy! This is me!"

"How did I get to be so lucky!"

She watched her father walk away, carrying his ugly helmet. He turned and waved at her. Laura waved back. The two soldiers walked together into the dusty distance beyond the vehicles. Laura ran weeping to Joan and Melanie.

"I didn't tell him anything! I never told him I love him! I never even told him I love him!"

"I think you did, Laura. We saw him laughing."

CHAPTER THIRTY-ONE

They were back in the familiar bedroom with the dust of Afghanistan in their shoes, clothes, hair and hearts. No one said a word. Laura lay down on Melanie's bed and fell asleep. The tear tracks dried in the dust on her cheeks. Melanie and Joan spent a long time to display the title page of the First Folio of Christopher Marlowe's Plays, Tragedies, Comedies and Histories.

Looking at Laura deeply asleep, Joan whispered to Melanie, "R.A.S.C. Run Away Someone's Coming? Like stink they do!"

* * * *

Returning from labouring in the fields, Todd and Nell Armstrong paused to look back over the pasture to the far woodland. A chorus of sheep and an occasional cock pheasant charmed the air.

"Would you exchange this for Deptford, Nell?"

The girl laughed. Her body ached. They had worked from first light to twilight.

"Not if I were buried in coin," she answered.

As Todd opened the gate to allow Nell, Lass and Tan to enter, he was unaware another couple, Harry and Angie Armstrong and another Lass and Tan trod in their footsteps.

* * * *

The letter was short, but much to the point in what it didn't say.

Dear Melanie,

Yes, it's me. Cherise. Nobody told me to. But I was thinking of you and I thought, what've I got to lose? Hope you're staying out of trouble. Looking forward to seeing you at Christmas. Shows how desperate I am, right? Your Mum and my Dad are planning to take us to a pantomime. Would you believe it? They think we're five years old. I'm painting the spare room. My Dad bought the pinkest paint you ever saw. So, I went and changed it for black. He won't even notice. So, you can have your bedroom back. I've cleaned it out and put back all the stuff your Mum said you liked so if you don't like it you can blame me. I've written this in biro because if I used the laptop, you never know what They look at. Writing by hand is very tiring. See you Christmas? Cherise

Lying on her bed, for no reason she could think of, Melanie began to cry. Sitting at the table, working on her French, Joan asked, "What's wrong, Mel?" She started up from her chair. Melanie shook her head.
"Nothing. Nothing's wrong."
Joan took the letter from her hand and read quickly.
"So? Nobody's dead."
"You're right. Nobody's dead."
She wiped her eyes and refolded the letter. She held out her hand for the envelope, which Joan returned.
"You did notice she addressed it to Cell 666, Randall's Institute for the Irretrievably Insane?"

* * * *

Having completed his evening rounds to check the security of the school, Robert Simpson returned to the Lodge. He locked his front and back doors, drew his curtains and poured himself a modest whisky tempered by water. He switched on the standard lamp to illuminate the room and the lamp above the desk to banish the shadow. He carried the tumbler carefully and sat down at the desk. He took a sip from his glass and turned on the computer. He quickly found the file he wanted. The title came up to greet him. THE RIFLEMAN by Robert Simpson. He scrolled through, stopping here and there to read for a moment until he reached the headline, Chapter Seven. He sat for some time in the calming peace of his sitting room and then began to type.

The Time Walkers

Following the officer, we scouted along the river bank always aware of who might be behind the willows on the farther bank. I hoped whoever might be similarly viewing our progress might mistake our humble squad as merely the scout of a large battalion, accompanied by dashing cavalry. Some hopes! Yet no one fired upon us. I could hear Flanagan behind me cursing away to himself as he struggled through the willows. Then the Corporal signalled halt and we all crouched, wishing to be smaller than a water rat. Through the willows, we strained to view the river. Nothing moved. Flanagan is complaining he has cramp. Then we saw what the officer had seen. Three big deer and a little one came splashing across the river where there was no ford.

Bob Simpson stopped for a moment, read through what he had written, sipped his whisky and continued.

* * * *

Anyone who has any information as to the baffling robbery at Malstruther House this morning is advised to ring 0130 185 1234. Mr. John Lambert, the antiques dealer familiar to television viewers, was approached first by telephone by a man wishing to sell a rare early seventeenth century flintlock pistol.

When Mr. Lambert admitted him to the house the man, dressed in Elizabethan costume, demanded a large sum of money. He threatened to shoot Mr. Lambert with the antique pistol. If the pistol didn't fire, he would beat him to death with the gold and silver engraved butt. A threat he would complete even if the value of the pistol suffered. Mr. Lambert decided discretion was the better part of valour. The man was obviously unhinged.

With the thief at his elbow, he unlocked the safe and transferred its contents to a Waitrose carrier bag. Mr. Lambert joked he wouldn't have complied so easily if it had been an Aldi bag.

The thief apologised for threatening him with the pistol. Which he declared was not loaded. This he demonstrated by pointing the weapon to the floor and pulling the trigger. Unfortunately, he was wrong and Mr. Lambert was shot in the foot. The thief made his excuses and left. If anyone spots a man dressed in historical costume, carrying a Waitrose bag and antique pistol, do not approach him. Telephone 999.

* * * *

The slide projector was in position. On the lectern was a spare bulb. Laura had placed the screen to Melanie's satisfaction. Everything was in order. Joan, Melanie and Laura took seats in the front row. It was the first Sunday lecture of the season and Miss Salomon had promised the school a pleasant surprise. When the acting Headmistress entered, the students rose. Miss Salomon waved the school to sit and went to the back row.

"Cancel the prison break, Chuck," Melanie whispered, "No way with the Governor in the back row."

Mr. Morrison came into the hall.

"Dead man walking! The searchlights'll be playing on the walls tonight."

Mr. Morrison announced, "Girls! As promised, we're starting the season with a popular choice."

The familiar figure of the retired Merchant Navy Captain stepped forward. The audience nearly screamed in horror, but good manners restrained them. They screamed silently.

"Thank you, girls, thank you for inviting me to return to your wonderful school. I haven't forgotten the reception you gave me on the last occasion. Well, I have kept my promise. I have now, four hundred and fifty slides of knots to show you."

If the poor man had expected an enthusiastic reception he was disappointed. Except for one younger girl who gave a terrified squeal, Randall's maintained a dignified composure. Randall girls face four hundred and fifty black and white slides of knots with the steadiness they would face a herd of charging buffalo.

"We must've done something really bad for God to punish us like this," sighed Laura.

* * * *

The rabbit on the verge listened to the silence of the world. A silver moon lit the tarmac highway. Though the stink of petroleum fumes lingered, the traffic had vanished as the darkness deepened. From a distant sleeping village, the notes of midnight chimed. No scent or sound of fox tickled nose nor ears. The rabbit tensed, preparing to scuttle across the alien tarmac to the farther safety of the bracken. Yet a whisper of human discord troubled its ears. A distant glimmer of light appeared. The clatter of an engine broke the pool of silence. Drawing ever nearer, louder and louder the mechanical contraption approached. The rabbit relaxed. Experience taught such beasts would pass without threat. From the rattle of the ageing engine the rabbit could distinguish two human voices entwined in melody. Faster than a falling tree, the old motorcycle and sidecar swept past its solitary witness.

They sang together, man and girl, song lost in the passing draughts. The girl clung close to the man, arms wrapped about him. Not because she was afraid of falling, but because she loved him. As rapidly as it had approached, the machine passed and sped on, bearing two loving hearts to where they knew not, but feared not. The motorcycle and sidecar vanished into the distance, leaving the world to silence where a rabbit lolloped across the moonlit road to vanish into the bracken.

All yet seems well; and if it end so meet,
The bitter past, more welcome is the sweet.

ALL'S WELL THAT ENDS WELL
by
CHRISTOPHER MARLOWE.

FEET NOTE

No one noticed William Shakespeare had been displaced. All texts the girls checked presented the author as Christopher Marlowe. He was buried in Holy Trinity Churchyard, Stratford upon Avon and lived in Anne Hathaway's house. Tourism and the theatre were undisturbed. Pictures, busts, engravings, postcards showed a true romantic hero. A vast improvement on the shifty, smug glover's son. But who would have denied the rightness of it?

William Shakespeare, son of a glover, attended Grammar School, but enjoyed no further education. He had no access to theatre in his early years, never travelled abroad, his daughters were illiterate and his will made no mention of plays, manuscripts or playhouse. Yet everything else was meticulously recorded even to his second bed, knives, spoons and chamber pot.

Christopher Marlowe was born in Canterbury, had early access to theatre, was an exceptional scholar at Grammar School and went on to Cambridge University where he gained two degrees, Bachelor and Master of Arts. He was recruited by Walsingham, Elizabeth's spymaster, carried out dangerous missions to uncover Catholic conspiracies, travelled widely in Europe and mixed with the most distinguished in the land.

He was the first playwright to create serious drama in blank verse. He won overwhelming acclaim for his masterpieces, Tamburlaine, Doctor Faustus, Edward II, The Jew of Malta, The Massacre of Paris. Faced with charges of heresy and in danger of his life in 1593, Christopher Marlowe vanished, but continued to write under the pen name of William Shakespeare.

Alex Ferguson
31.08.2018

Lightning Source UK Ltd.
Milton Keynes UK
UKHW021837040619
343846UK00010B/843/P